Custodians

The Prophecy

DAN ALEXANDER

To the emergency services and all their families.
This one is for you.

CONTENTS

ACKNOWLEDGMENTS

This book wouldn't be possible without the help of my
friends and family, who have all been there by my side
throughout this journey.
Thank you to all my beta-readers, for engulfing yourselves
in Marco's story before the wider world had chance to.
To Cheryl, for your intricate eye for detail and helping to
polish the final incarnation.
To the wonderful teachers throughout the years that
coveted my creativity and let my individuality blossom.
And my final thanks go to Drew.
Thank you for believing in me.

PROLOGUE

The tranquil sea breeze blew through the night sky of the Island of St Mary, as the brilliant moon danced upon the ripples of the tide. The waves of the ocean broke against the cliff rocks, the peace never being clear in this small corner of Cornish paradise. There were a handful of homes scattered throughout this southern point of England, with each residence displaying its own individuality.

One stood out from the others, at the far edge of a cliff - nothing but the very depths of the sea beyond. Appearing to be derelict, the mansion loomed above the rest, with colourful stained-glass windows being the only thing breathing a smidgen of life into it.

The grounds covered acres of land, with a single, white gravel pathway cutting through the middle, leading up to the entrance, with shadows casting from barren branches lining the edges. A dusting of rust covered the iron gates, which bordered the estate.

The mansion's reclusive inhabitant lay in her bed, her long, white hair draped across her pillows. A pair of curtains lifted towards the ceiling, from a surprising gust seeping through a discreet crack in the window.

The moonlight crept through the exposed glass, highlighting her gaunt features - her knuckles turning white from tightly gripping an amulet perfectly positioned at the centre of her neck. The jewellery stood out from anything else in her home, exposing her lack of taste for modern décor and unwillingness to upkeep the residence. A single jewel encrusted in its centre, shone through the gaps between her fingers in a glimmer of colours. She was at peace; in a home she spent a significant part of her longevity.

Her lungs expelled air as she let out an involuntary gasp, shaking off her disorientation as it took several moments for the mind-fog to clear. Sensing something wasn't right, she pulled the bed sheets from over her and struggled to her feet. The wind took hold of her long nightdress, rippling like a ghost, exposing her petite and skeletal figure.

In her younger years, she would have soared across the wooden floorboards without so much of a whisper of her being heard, yet tonight, her steady steps creaked with every movement, tightening the already forming knot in her stomach.

As she sluggishly moved around the tall corridors of the upper floor, the moonlight followed the woman, reminding her of a wartime search light, highlighting the numerous cobwebs from decades of neglect.

She glanced to each side of the hallway, taking a moment

to admire the hand painted oil portraits of her many ancestors; each of them sat in a regal pose.

The lady stopped still in her tracks, her impeccable hearing picking up a whispering of a voice from the lower floor. As the chatter continued, she followed the sound the murmurings like a beacon, which took her down the grand staircase.

As she reached the bottom, she squinted her eyes at a beautiful golden candelabra covered in a thin layer of dust, sat upon an end table. Living alone, she was a renowned hermit - not favourable to any guests, let alone trespassers.

She fought through the combination of her failing sight and dark surroundings, using her remaining heightened senses to take hold of the candleholder in her frail hands. She tightly gripped the base of it, taking a moment to appreciate every ridge and curvature.

The woman came to a halt, as the hair on the back of her neck stood on end, sensing a sizeable presence behind her. Attempting to twist herself around to investigate, she dropped to her knees, a sharp pain striking the back of her head - quickly realising she'd been hit with something blunt.

Her eyes fought to return to focus as she recovered from her momentary black-out, her attention now on the flamboyant artexed ceiling. A large, towering figure crouched over her – the lack of light masking its facial features. She lay helpless as the figure drove its hand towards her neck, aiming for her pendant.

As their grip drew nearer, the atmosphere turned electric, a warmth emanating from the piece of jewellery laid on her chest, as it began to glow a fiery red. The glare emphasised the chiselled features of the stranger; the old woman instantly recognising them as their eyes met.

The two hollow ovals in place of the figure's eyes didn't faze her, as they emanated an emerald glow. Not only were they familiar to her, but she also intuitively knew their intentions.

"You will fail!" she croaked, fighting with every ounce of her breath. "They will come for you!"

The demonic visitor let out a sinister laugh, before using brute strength to push his talon through an invisible barrier created by the amulet, grimacing as it repelled.

Her magical necklace expelled a large, cascading blast of energy, disintegrating the unworldly being into a mere pile of dust upon its touch. As the shockwave ruptured throughout the decaying building, each window shattered upon impact, scattering fragments of glass across outside like confetti.

The explosion turned the manor into kindling, setting alight the entirety of its contents. The woman watched in horror as her beloved home erupted in flames, sweat dripping profusely from her brow as the heat around her intensified.

She extended her hand out in desperation, squinting her eyes at the dancing fire, willing for it to perish. However, despite her abundance of will power, it continued to ferociously devour her home.

Giving into defeat, her arm fell to the floor in exhaustion as she let out a gut-wrenching moan.

"Seek the Custodians." She strained to whisper to herself, as the amulet illuminated. Rather than being a harsh, destructive force, the light tickled the surface of the necklace and manifested into a sphere of vibrant colours, before vanishing through the ceiling into the night sky.

Knowing full well her life was going to come to an imminent and horrifying end, she clutched her chest, closed her eyes, and muttered a few words of Latin to herself.

Once she spoke the final phrase, her arms dropped by her side, and she lay lifeless as she did in her bed only moments before.

However, this time, she was gone.

Her name was *Agatha*.

ONE

I grudgingly flickered my eyes open as my work phone danced around on my bedside cabinet. My cat like reflexes kicked in as I managed to grab it before it took a dive to its death on the wooden floor. The screen lit up my face, accenting the heavy bags under my eyes, barely allowing my pupils to adjust to the sudden change in light. I rubbed away the pockets of sleep dust from my eyelids and groaned as I looked down at the time on my alarm clock.

Four twenty in the morning.

I resisted the urge to let out a large sigh as I saw my colleague Louisa's name flashing up in the centre of the screen. It took all my willpower not to press 'decline,' especially as I felt like I'd been dragged backwards through a row of hedges. However, I went against my urges and unenthusiastically pressed 'Accept.'

"Lou. Please tell me this is important. Do you know what time it is?" I whispered at her, slightly annoyed. I gave my eyes a quick massage with my free hand, hoping to relieve the fatigue. I let out an extensive yawn, before kicking my leg out from under the duvet as a bout of unexpected cramp struck up the centre of my calf like a bolt of lightning.

"Sorry to wake you boss." Louisa apologised, my frustration quickly dissipating at her soft and soothing tone. *"But I think this one is worthy of an early wake up call."*

"Go on," I winced, rubbing the back of my leg to ease the tensed muscle.

"House fire. Believed to be deliberate. Fire Crews unfortunately have found one deceased inside."

"Blimey." I raised my brow. Although horrific, this type of incident was business-as-usual in our line of work. A yawn crept up upon me, as I desperately tried to fight the impulse to fall back asleep. "I take it we've got a crime scene on?"

"First thing uniform did." she assured me.

Being the Detective Inspector of a Major Crimes Team certainly had its moments. The responsibility of the rank meant I regularly received these types of calls at unsociable hours.

Louisa Sellen, one of my Detective Sergeants, joined my Team only three months ago. Her reputation during her short career was certainly distinctive; she was enthusiastic and dedicated to the service and highly thought of among the senior staff.

I was fortunate enough to have sat on the panel during her interview, and she immediately impressed me. She exuberated confidence, but not to the point where she appeared arrogant, and perfectly reeled off some first-class examples of why she should have been given the role, eventually scoring the highest marks out of ten candidates.

Her passion and drive made her stand out from the remainder of my Sergeants, who were all hardworking, but lacked Louisa's spark. You could say she was my favourite; although if asked under oath, I would deny it.

"So where has this happened?" I asked her, my detective brain already devising a plan for the next few hours.

"Brace yourself." Louisa prepared me. *"The Scilly Isles."*

I widened my eyes in shock and took a couple of seconds to process what she'd told me. "Did you just say the Scilly Isles?"

"I did. St Mary's Island to be exact."

"Right. Okay." I paused for a moment, flooded with confusion at the fact a serious crime occurred on the most isolated area of my jurisdiction; an area where the crime rates were non-existent.

"I'm guessing you're wanting to come down to this one in person?" she asked, reading my mind.

"How did you know?" I playfully laughed, as I jumped up to my feet. "I'll be there as soon as I can. Have you called up for CSI?"

"You don't have any faith in me, do you boss?!" she sarcastically scolded me. *"They're already on their way. See you when you get here."*

What would have usually been a fifteen-minute journey to Newquay Airport, took me no longer than ten, thanks to the lack of traffic at such an unworldly hour. As I parked up outside one of the many rows of hangers, a small passenger jet flew over me; the fierce, powerful engines shaking the car as if it were subject to an earthquake.

I looked up at the entrance to a hanger of interest to me, clocking the discreet 'Cornwall Police Air Support Unit' sign fixed to the side – if you didn't know where to look it would have easily been missed.

I entered the secure hanger with my credentials granting me access, and searched the corridors, trying to find the crew. I eventually veered into a refreshment room and recognised one of the two men on duty.

Sergeant Stuart Chamberlain was one of the Police Air Support operators and a good friend of mine; we served as Custody Sergeants together at Truro Station when I first transferred from London. A man in his late fifties, with salt and pepper hair, he was only a about two years away from retirement.

"Morning Stu." I greeted him with a lively smile, being unusually jaunty for this of the morning.

"Rambo!" His eyes lit up when he recognised me, calling me by a nickname I'd not heard since my days at Police training school.

'Rambo' was given to me by my classmates at Hendon, as I always went rogue in the officer safety scenarios. Earning my Black belt at sixteen, the self-defence drills taught by the trainers seemed incredibly soft and low key.

I'd told Stu this story during one long and dreary night shift in the cells, and he took it upon himself to revive the name. I didn't mind though – in fact, I secretly enjoyed the teasing.

"What brings you here, mate? How's Inspector life treating you?" he asked.

"Busy mate." I sighed. "I would love to stay and catch up, but there's a job on the Isles I need to get to. I was hoping you could give me a lift over."

"Of course, we've been going back and forth all night with your lot, anyway." He said, devouring a bacon sandwich drenched in ketchup, which dripped onto his navy overalls. "Just finishing this off then John will take us over." Stu's head gestured towards the helicopter pilot as he used a napkin to clean himself up.

I looked over at John, sat across the room, sprawled out on a worn leather sofa. He was glued to the large, widescreen television mounted to the wall, which played an episode of Family Guy, although he barely reacted to any of the humour.

He was closer to me than Stu in age, and dressed in an olive-green flight suit, with an RAF emblem neatly sewed on his left breast.

"Morning John." I smiled over at him.

John glanced over at me and gave a nod of acknowledgement with a slight grumble, but nothing I could interpret as anything intelligible.

"Ignore him Rambo," Stu rolled his eyes, his cheeks swollen like a hamster. "He's not one for working nights."

About half an hour passed whilst RAF John went out to complete his pre-flight checks and delivered me a very unenthusiastic flight safety briefing, which he read word for word in a monotone voice, from a laminated card.

CUSTODIANS: THE PROPHECY

I made my way onto the tarmac, where a navy-blue helicopter, with fragments of yellow paint across the tail and doors, stood with its propellers bouncing up and down in the coastal breeze.

Stu provided me with a bulky headset, about three times too big for my head, and directed me into the vacant, single seat rear of the helicopter.

Once Stu and John placed themselves comfortably in the front, the roaring of the propellers began to echo throughout the cockpit as the craft lifted off from the ground and hovered. I watched in awe as blades of grass on a patch of greenery nearby were blown horizontal from the turbulent wind.

My stomach churned as the helicopter gained higher altitude, and eventually whisked off toward the Scilly Isles.

The view was magnificent, even if I did get startled by a sudden glare of orange sun reflecting on the agitated waves of the Atlantic Ocean.

The Cornish islands came into view, after about thirty-five minutes of us being airborne. I took a quick glimpse of RAF John, who began pulling back on the controls, making a decent towards the Island of St Mary's.

As we bridged the gap the closer, we got to the island, I noticed a stream of smoke rising into the air coming into view. It appeared to originate from a large wooden house sat on the top of a cliff.

The sea of blue flashing lights signalled a series of Emergency Service personnel present at the scene. I made a mental note of them as they became clearer; Air

Ambulance, Fire, Coastguard and Police - all hustling around the large manor estate like a colony of ants.

RAF John landed the helicopter as close to the edge of the scene as he could. Stu opened the door for me, and I alighted the chopper, shaking the hand of my old friend in gratitude.

Once I'd thanked John, and removed my headset, I made my way towards the scene.

As soon as I arrived at the cordon line, I immediately scanned around for Louisa. It didn't take long to notice her – a twenty-something year old with long blonde hair tied into a dishevelled ponytail; wearing leopard print, fashionable glasses, and a mismatching light suit jacket, with the sleeves rolled up. Being the height of summer, the temperatures peaked in the late twenties – even at this early hour.

"Boss!" she yelled from across the scene, holding her hand up as our eyes met.

I smiled back at her and gestured in return, acknowledging her presence, simultaneously glaring up at my watch and making a mental note of the time.

Six forty-five.

The cordon line was defined by a fluttering stream of Police tape, guarded by a young male officer, barely out of training school, clutching hold of a rolled-up scene log. His hat was ten times too big for him and his florescent jacket sparkled like new.

I watched on as Louisa walked ardently towards me.

"You made it in good time." She smirked.

"I said I would be here as soon as I could," I reminded

her, the corner of my mouth mirroring hers. "Right, do you want to catch me up?" I asked, flashing my warrant card at the scene guard, who wrote my information and greeted me with a 'Sir.'

The title made me cringe. It made me sound twenty years older – I'd rather people called me by my first name.

The novice officer lifted the tape, for me to perform a very awkward limbo.

I reached into my bag perched on the edge of my shoulder, which co-ordinated with my smart-casual outfit, and I pulled out a large notebook. I selected my lucky pen from inside my inner breast pocket; a small engraved, silver click top Biro my partner Grayson gave to me as a gift when we first moved from the 'Big smoke' about six years ago. The 'click' it made always satisfied me, I didn't really know why.

Louisa brought me up to speed in a matter of minutes, informing me one of the nearby residents were awoken by an explosion at around three in the morning, and noticed the house ablaze.

They called 999, however, by the time help arrived, there was little, if anything, to save. Fire crews discovered a severely charred, unidentifiable body inside the house.

Louisa checked Census and Electoral Roll records and concluded it to be the body of an Agatha Lockwood, the sole occupant of the house. She had been described as an eccentric recluse by the small, tight-knit community.

I thanked my DS, appreciative of her comprehensive update, before tasking her with further enquiries, which she delegated to detectives – some of whom I didn't recognise.

I'd concluded they'd been drafted in from all areas of Cornwall.

As she wandered off, I stood for a moment, mesmerised at the smouldering remains of the building, as numerous jets of water streamed in differing angles, some producing a shimmering rainbow as the droplets hit the glow of the fully risen sun.

A lone firefighter, not tied up with subduing the fire, looked over in my direction and purposefully walked over.

He took off his helmet to reveal an extremely good looking, dark-haired man with black charcoal marks dotted around his face.

I became slightly infatuated by his chiselled features.

Even with the large amount of protective fire padding that made up his uniform, I could tell he was extremely broad; however, I couldn't quite decide whether there lay a significant amount of muscle underneath.

"Sorry, can I ask that you stand back?" he shouted in a thick, Cornish accent. He motioned his helmet free arm towards the Police tape, directing me to stand the other side, giving me the impression he expected me to follow suit.

I reached into the back pocket of my beige chinos and pulled out my identification. I looked down at my horrendous, sunburnt mugshot - never again would I have a work photo taken the day after I came back from holiday. I flashed the card towards the burly firefighter. "Detective Inspector Marco Ramirez," I formally introduced myself. "Cornwall Police Major Investigations Team."

"Ah sorry, my fault." He apologised, clearing his throat from a bit of smoke he'd inhaled. "I don't recognise you.

You're not local, are you?"

"No, I'm not. This is my jurisdiction, but I'm based in Newquay, so as you can imagine, I don't get over this way much." I replied. "This is quite unusual for this neck of the woods."

"You're telling me!" The firefighter chirped, before going silent for a handful of seconds. He took off his glove and reached out a sweaty hand towards me. "I'm Jason, but my friends call me Jayce." he smiled.

I took the man's strong hand, which clutched mine in a brutal grip, giving me the impression his broad appearance *was* due to being muscularly gifted.

"Good to meet you, Jason." I smiled back at him.

"Jayce, please." he insisted.

As our palms interlocked, a small jolt of static electricity sparked between our palms, both of us pulling away in unison, as a slight burning sensation encompassed my hand.

"Must be from my gloves," Jayce theorised, as he rubbed his hand like a dog cowering at an injured paw. "The heat gets so intense I forget how much static it must build up."

I brushed my hand up and down the side of my trousers, to try and cast aside the residual burning pain. "Don't worry, I've experienced worse." I laughed to myself. "Is your boss about, Jayce?"

"Yeah, he's over there." He pointed in a diagonal direction towards an older man dressed in a matching firefighter's uniform, the only difference being his colour of headwear; white rather than the industry standard yellow. He also wore a red and white chequered tabard, with the words 'Fire Commander' prominently displayed on his back.

"Thanks mate, it was nice to meet you." I nodded as I parted ways with Jayce. I annoyed myself for acting like a smitten teenager at his outlandish looks - but I'm sure Grayson wouldn't have blamed me if he'd seen him.

As I approached Jayce's commander, I noticed he accompanied a tall, slim woman dressed in an all-in-one red jumpsuit, her long, dark hair, tied up into a messy bun.

As I walked closer to the pair, the woman turned around, her face a picture of natural beauty. Her chiselled cheekbones contrasted her dark eyes which sparkled as they caught the shine from the emergency vehicle lighting. Her skin, though pale, was smooth as silk.

I smiled at the woman and her acquaintance, introducing myself as I approached.

In contrast to her deceptive warm exterior, she gave me a freezing reception, only nodding at my presence, giving me the impression, she thought I was beneath her.

This surprising welcome from her threw me off, so I focused my attention to the fire commander, who introduced himself to me as 'Dave.'

He, like Jayce, originated of Cornish blood and possessed an overly broad local twang when he spoke. He didn't hesitate in providing me with all the intricate details about the fire response and advised me he would hand over the scene within the next half-an-hour. He then turned to the rude, stuck-up woman in red stood stiffly next to him.

"This is Doctor Yi Chang. Air Ambulance." Dave gestured to her.

Despite her icy welcome towards me, I offered my hand

out to her, which she hesitantly accepted. As our palms touched, another jolt of static immediately manifested. We both withdrew our hands back in surprise.

"Sorry. No idea where that came from." I said, laughing slightly, desperately trying to relieve the tension between us.

She rolled her eyes, obviously unimpressed by my poor attempt to lighten the mood. "I'm sure you'll live." She said, with an extremely patronising tone.

Well, that was rude! I thought to myself, as I shook my head in disbelief; I didn't know why she'd taken an instant disliking to me. *Was it because I was a Police Officer?* Even with all my years' experience as a detective, there were some mysteries even I wouldn't be able to solve.

I spent the next hour building a picture of the unfortunate occupant. Her name continued to permeate through my mind's eye - Agatha Lockwood. *Who was she? Why was she a loner and a recluse?* There were no Police records of her, so we had little information to go on.

"G'day" A voice from behind me disturbed me from my trail of thought.

I spun on my heel to see a medium height man no older than twenty-five, stood at the edge of the cordon. His messy, golden hair, which tickled the tip of his ears stood out in contrast to the glow of his bronzed skin. Dressed in bright shorts, a hooded top, and flip-flops, I was curious as to why this young man had approached me.

"Morning" I said, giving him half a smile. "How can I help?"

"Is everything OK, mate?" The brightly clothed man

asked. "I heard something's gone on in Crabby Aggie's house?" Judging by his accent, I quickly placed him from Australasia, which wasn't uncommon for this region during the summer months.

"Crabby Aggie?" I asked, intrigued as to why he'd referred to her in such a colourful manner.

"That's just what I've heard them call her here. I've never met her." He crossed his arms and began stroking the small patch of beard on the end of his chin. "Apparently she was proper cranky and used to spout all this shit off about dark ones and the end coming."

I started to get a better understanding of who she was, albeit a slightly unusual character.

"That's interesting," I raised one of my eyebrows whilst scribbling down a summary of his conversation in my notebook with my chicken scratch handwriting. I looked up at him and met his gaze, his eyes a striking blue. "Sorry I didn't catch your name?"

"M'name's Brandon mate. Brandon Turner." he introduced himself, holding out his fist in front of me. "I'm a lifeguard here on the island."

I hesitantly placed my pen in the hand holding my notebook and formed a fist, 'bumping' it together with Brandon's. As our skin touched, a sharp shock of static hit both of us; powerful enough to propel us away from each other like opposing magnets, practically knocking us off our feet. The cascade caused me to drop my notepad and pen in a nebulous puddle, created by the streams of jets from the firefighters. *Not my favourite bloody pen!*

"What the fuck?!" Brandon expleted, holding his hand

up to his face, intricately examining it in disbelief, whilst I scrambled to rescue my paperwork and sentimental pen from the murky water.

"I think there's probably a lot of static in the air from the fire," I said, quickly trying to make sense of a situation I couldn't entirely explain. "It was great to meet you Brandon, but I must get on. We'll call you if we need anything else."

"… yeah. Of course, bud." Brandon replied, a bewildered expression still clear on his face.

I shot him a friendly smile and swiftly made an exit, heading back over to where Dave and Yi were standing, both still engrossed in deep conversation.

"Are you okay for us to have a look inside yet?" I politely interrupted, quite eager to get a start on the investigation of the scene. I was impatient at times and wanted everything done yesterday - a trait of mine, often loathed by my team, but celebrated by my superiors.

Dave looked at me with a bemused expression, giving my request some thought.

"Going against my better judgement, I'll give you five minutes inside. Make sure you wear a hard hat and be extremely careful. That building is bound to come down at any minute."

"Of course. I really appreciate this." I was respectful of Dave's conditions of his decision, as he only thought of my safety.

I looked over at the scorched remains of the house; it was without a doubt seconds away from collapsing, hence my eagerness to get a scope of the scene as soon as I could.

After consulting with the Crime Scene Investigator, who arrived from the mainland, I suited up in a not so flattering white forensic jumpsuit; a pair of latex gloves and a disposable facemask and I was ready to take on a nuclear fallout.

Louisa also kitted up in matching attire, ready for us to conduct a preliminary walk through of the house. I always wondered the need to dress this way at arsons, especially with the fact gallons of water had been used to extinguish the flames and eliminated most of the forensics.

I suppose it was more of a public perception routine, to bestow the public with confidence the Police were actually doing something.

As we walked over towards the seared building, I clocked the news cameras and press photographers who had manifested at the edge of the cordon, the flashes of their cameras lighting up like strobe lighting. I would have bet three years of my salary on the top story of the Cornish Gazette.

We entered through what used to be the front door, which was now a gaping, charred void. The smell of burnt wood overwhelmed my sense of smell, penetrating through my mask.

The house was unrecognisable; the fire had ripped through it like a tornado, destroying everything in sight. As we stealthy ventured deeper into the building, we came across a burnt carcass of a human. There were no remnants of any clothing, no hair, only charred flesh, and bone. To any general member of public, this would be a gruesome sight, but scenes like this were common for the likes of us.

"This must be Agatha," I whispered, as I knelt beside the smoking remains. "Sorry this happened to you." I said to her as I gingerly brushed her forehead with the back of my hand.

From early on in my career, I'd always been taught to treat the deceased with respect - after all they were still someone's loved one.

Whilst inspecting Agatha's body, I noticed something around her neck, covered in a thick layer of soot. Intrigued, I rubbed vigorously at the black coating of dust, revealing a pristine, gold amulet, untouched by the flames. I closely examined the array of Latin words engraved in a circular pattern which surrounded a central groove, where a jewel or diamond once encrusted.

I read aloud the inscription in the best Latin accent I could muster.

"Cum protector perit in custodes erit excitare."

Not understanding a single word of the ancient language, I had no clue what it meant. However, the fact this survived a severe fire, manifested a variety of questions in my overactive brain, and I wanted to return it to the station for further forensic analysis.

I tried to undo the clasp of the necklace with care, ensuring I kept the disturbance of Agatha's remains to a minimum. Louisa held open an evidence bag as I took hold of the pendant. As my hand grasped it, an ample gust of surprising wind circled around me like a hurricane, with an assortment of leaves and twigs weaving within. The amulet glowed a vibrant green, as the gust intensified, the earth starting to shake violently beneath us.

"Are you seeing this?" I asked Louisa, beginning to question my perception of reality.

"Yep," she muffled, barely being able to hear her from underneath her mask.

Before either of us could suggest any explanation for these peculiar happenings, the necklace returned to its original state, and the harsh winds died down to serenity.

I sprung to my feet and looked over at Louisa, both standing in absolute silence. Not wanting to over-analyse what we'd seen, I placed the pendant in the bag, which Louisa quickly sealed up.

Soon after, a powerful 'thud' hit the hard hat I wore. An object bounced off and fell on the floor in front of my feet. A long, scorched piece of black lumber lay on the ground, swiftly joined by a loud creaking noise from above.

"I think we need to go." I suggested to my colleague, a sudden bout of clairvoyance heightening my senses. We sprinted towards the remnants of the entrance, without any haste.

We made it out in time, before the building caved in on itself, a firefighter yelling at the top of her voice, warning for people to stay back. An avalanche of dust clouds shrouded the remnants of the mansion and advanced towards the ring of firefighters working on the site. Everyone rushed to safety until the dust cloud decimated.

Louisa and I fled out of harm's way, narrowly escaping the subsiding building. We headed back to the CSI tent and changed back into more comfortable apparel, handing over the exhibited pendant to one of my detectives, Aoife McGuillian, a speak-no-nonsense Irish lady in her early fifties.

I had a bit of a soft spot for her. Even from looking at her, you knew she had a kind, bubbly, and caring personality - my team regarding her as a 'work mum.'

She sat at a white, plastic garden table and what looked to be an extremely uncomfortable chair, whilst she documented the find from us in her evidence log.

"You were lucky there governor!" she nodded towards the now smouldering ruins. "I thought you were a goner for a minute." She nervously chuckled.

"You're telling me," Louisa huffed, trying to get her breath back.

The two of us were joined at the tent by Dave and Yi, who both rushed over to check on our welfare.

"I told you to be careful!" Dave scolded us, wide-eyed. He was furious, but at the same time I could sense a sprinkle of concern in his tone.

"Are you okay?" Yi asked, the resonance of her voice still capable of freezing over the entire River Thames.

"We're fine," I smiled. "Thanks for asking. Luckily, we both have no problem passing our fitness test every year." I let out a timid titter, still trying to crack through her stone-cold exterior, however, she didn't react in the slightest.

"Well then, you won't be needing me." she said, callously, before turning her back on us and marching off into the distance.

I involuntarily rolled my eyes as I turned towards Louisa. From her expression, I could tell she wasn't impressed by my new friend either.

"Bitch." she muttered under her breath, once Yi passed

out of earshot.

My stomach startled me, as it replicated the most rambunctious growl. I'd not eaten anything all morning.

"How about we head back to the mainland and grab something to eat?" I suggested to my Sergeant.

"This, Boss, has been your best suggestion all day!"

TWO

It took us over an hour to return to Newquay on mainland Cornwall, with the help of my friend Stu and RAF John – whose last name I still didn't know.

I offered to take Louisa out to a nice ocean view café for our breakfast, one I often visited on my days off, situated above Towan Bay. Despite the influx of summer tourists, I became lucky enough to find a prominent parking spot close by.

I ordered a full English fry up, whilst Louisa selected a healthier choice of Avocado on toast. Being a fitness lover, this wasn't my usual choice of cuisine, but I'd earned it - a session in the gym later would easily counteract my sneaky indulgence.

We both shared an appreciation for a decent cup of coffee; I requested a cinnamon latté, whilst she sipped at a piping hot Americano, both poured into opulent glasses.

"So, Boss," Louisa smiled. "How are the wedding plans

coming on?

I rapidly chomped on the mouthful of hash brown and baked beans I inhaled, before eventually answering her question.

"Very slowly." I replied, my disappointment apparent. "Grayson's had a big Crown Court case for the last three weeks and you know how busy I've been."

"But it's May next year? You've only got eight months," she annoyingly reminded me. "And it's not a long time when you think about it."

"Yes, I realise that; but it will be fine. Even if we have to pull out all the stops a month before, then so be it." I took a swig of coffee to wash down the final mouthful. "We have a date and a venue – that's all that matters."

"Fair point." Louisa nodded, taking a gentle sip from her steaming beverage. "So will you be stepping in when Carole retires next year?"

"I hadn't even thought about it to be honest," I said, neatly placing my knife and fork on my plate, and relieved she'd decided to change the topic. "I've not long been promoted to Inspector, so I don't want to get too ahead of myself."

"Boss," Louisa looked at me from above her glasses, clasping her mug tightly with her hands. "You're the best in the unit. Everyone knows that. All the Sergeants love working for you, present company included."

I smiled at her comment, wondering for a moment if she attempted to suck up to me, or if her comment genuinely aired sincerity. I knew her well enough to realise it was the latter.

"I'm not just saying that!" she laughed, slightly. "I genuinely do enjoy working for you. I mean I wouldn't want to get on your wrong side but you're nothing like old cranky pants Waldring."

Timothy Waldring was a fellow Detective Inspector who worked in the Major Investigations Team, or 'M.I.T' as we were affectionately known, albeit he covered the north of the county.

Whenever I ventured away from the office, he would cover for my area, and vice versa. None of my team particularly enjoyed working for him; he was a grumpy, white-haired, stocky man in his early sixties who bore a negative outlook on the world. His social skills were also a lot to be desired.

He and Carole often clashed, I imagined this was due to his jealousy of her for being promoted over him. I, however, forced myself into an alliance with the man, especially as I sometimes needed his back.

"Lou!" I chuckled, raising an eyebrow at her comment, almost covering her with a mouthful of my coffee. I appreciated my Sergeant felt she could be open and honest with me, but I needed to remain impartial. "Be nice."

"Oh, I always am!" she defended herself, sitting sharply upright on her seat. "It's just…."

A whimpering, feeble scream from outside, cut Louisa off. As we were sat at the back of the café, overlooking the beach, we both couldn't quite see out onto the main street. As the screaming continued, both Louisa and I swiftly made our way to the front, to try and get a better view of the source of the commotion from outside.

I spotted a slender figure dressed all in black, with a balaclava covering their face, trying to grab a handbag from a woman in her late eighties. Neither one of them were dressed for the summer weather, as she sported a long lime green coat, which contrasted with her silver permed hair.

My law enforcement instincts kicked in, as I immediately ran out onto the street, shouting at Louisa to call for backup.

"Stop! Police!" I shouted towards the disguised figure as I closed in on them.

Once the masked figure realised I was in pursuit; they gave one final tug at the handbag and loosened it from the terrified woman's grip. They swiftly ran away from the scene, heading out of the town centre.

I continued to keep to their speed, determined not to let them get away. They used their free hand to remove their balaclava whilst still running at an Olympic pace. The figure revealed themselves to be a gaunt man with a series of tattoos on his face and neck, dripping with sweat.

"Stay where you are!" I yelled. I'd been fortunate enough to compete in the London Marathon the previous year, so I tapped into my training and stamina to keep up with him. He continued to run, slaloming around pedestrians in his path.

"Stop!" I scolded, thrusting my arm out in front of me, not expecting what was about to occur.

The ground started to shake, violently, stopping me in my tracks. The pavement started to crack, filtering out towards the running robber. Weeds, branches, and vines began to magically sprout from the orifices, stalking the path of the man, who still ran, despite the unexpected earthquake.

The foliage became attracted to him; entwining his ankles, which caused him to fall to the ground.

I stood frozen in shock, not gauging at what happened.

What the hell was that? I looked down at my hand, as a tingling sensation tickled my palm. When I looked over at the man I was chasing after, I cupped my hands over my mouth in horror and closed my eyes, as I realised the robber had been encased in a cocoon of branches.

Did I do that?

I struggled to remain upright, as the ground shook under my feet once more; the vines loosening around the man and retreated into the pavement, a small number of feint cracks being the only reminder they ever existed.

The suspect continued to lie on the floor, trembling in fear at what he experienced.

I stood in a brief trance, contemplating what had happened, before snapping myself back to reality. I ran over to the criminal, who laid face down on the floor and grabbed hold of the man's arms and placed them behind his back. I pulled out a pair of folded handcuffs I always kept in my back trouser pocket, for situations such as these.

"You're nicked for Robbery," I said, before reading the suspect his rights, slapping the cuffs on his wrists.

"What the fuck did you just do?!" The man on the floor yelled at me, his face still painted with absolute terror, as he struggled to comprehend the situation.

I couldn't even fathom what happened, but I tried to rationalise it all in my mind. I decided to keep this to myself until I could find out what actually occurred; maybe it was an hallucination from being overworked. Google would be my friend for the coming hours.

"I don't know what you're talking about. You tripped up." I replied to the man I'd arrested, hoping he would buy my explanation.

"Boss!" I heard a familiar voice bellow from behind me. I was relieved to turn around and see Louisa running into view, her face painted with exhaustion and a phone held to her ear.

"We're on the junction of Beach Road and Beachfield Avenue, suspect has been detained by DI Ramirez." She finished her conversation with the call handler before aiding me with getting the rogue to his feet. Louisa took one look at his face and instantly recognised him.

"Ah, Gandalf!" she sarcastically smiled at the man. "I thought last time we saw each other you said you wouldn't do this anymore?"

"Ah come on PC Sellen!" he shouted, instantly recognising my Sergeant from her days as a neighbourhood officer. "I needed to score; you know what I mean?"

"Doesn't mean you need to pray on elderly ladies though, does it?" she said, angry he tried to justify his actions with his drug habit. "And it's DS Sellen now." She corrected him.

The man Louisa nicknamed 'Gandalf' was in fact Joseph Tyrant, a renowned Thief, Burglar and Robber in the local area. He used to wander the street with unkempt long silver hair and a beard, hence the self-proclaimed nickname.

"I knew you'd get promoted." He said to Louisa, a slight gruff to his voice. "You're one of the good ones. Not like your mate here." he gestured his head towards me.

"I think you'll find he's also one of the good ones."

I smiled slightly at her positive character reference of me.

"Nah. He's dirty mate. A bent copper. Did something to me didn't he!"

"Right, that's enough!" I scolded him, pushing him up against a wall. He actively resisted my grip, so I had an excuse to use a bit more force to restrain him, when in fact my main intention was to prevent him from running his mouth of about the peculiar happenings.

It only took a matter of minutes for a duo of response officers to arrive in their squad car and help us both with securing Tyrant and recovering the handbag he dropped mid pursuit.

As they drove him off to Newquay Police station; I returned to the café and apologised to the manager for our eat-and-run, explaining the reason behind our sudden departure. I tried to pay for our breakfast, but they immediately refused, telling me it was on the house. Acts of kindness towards Police were exceedingly rare; so, I struggled to accept it. I couldn't walk away without paying anything, so I placed a ten-pound note I had lurking in my wallet in their tip jar.

As I walked out, I nodded at the local CID detective who sat with the elderly victim, taking a report from her; still visibly shaken by her ordeal.

I walked over to the woman and placed my hand gingerly on her arm.

"Hello, my love," I crouched down to her level and gave

her a warm smile. "The man's been arrested, and we've managed to get your handbag back."

The woman's eyes lit up with joy and I spotted a slight tear run down her cheek.

"Oh, thank you dear!" she smiled with jubilation. "You've made an old woman very happy."

"Glad to be of help. My officer will make sure you get home safely." I said, looking towards the detective, who nodded back in agreement.

Louisa headed back to the Police Station in a patrol car, whilst I decided to walk and leave my car in town – it wasn't any further than fifteen minutes on foot and I needed the time to gather my thoughts.

On the way, I kept looking down at my hand and wiggling my fingers, trying to make sense of what happened on Beach Road.

Was that me?

I shrugged it off again and put it down to over-exertion.

I walked up into the rear car park of the Police Station and transferred my warrant card from my leather wallet into a lanyard, before placing it around my neck. I swiped myself through a set of secure doors, making my way up to my team's office, located on the third floor.

As I entered, there was a hustle and bustle of detectives, chattering on phone calls, pinning up photographs on various display boards and typing away at computer terminals. Louisa was already parked at her desk, I assumed she'd started on her duty statement documenting the Robbery.

I walked into my office on the perimeter and sat at my desk. I logged onto my computer, which seemed to take an eternity to load. I opened my e-mails and sighed at the sea of spam and unnecessary round robins, which took me at least five minutes to work through. I had to make sure I read them all, or risked missing something important.

I then came across an unusual e-mail; with 'Custodes tellus' in the subject bar.

Intrigued, I opened it, but it was blank. What confused me even more was the vacant sender's address. I shrugged it off as spam and deleted it, but it came as a surprise when it re-appeared in my inbox, unread.

I spent the next few seconds trying to delete the e-mail, but it continued to regenerate back into my inbox as if always being there. Although I was comfortable with using technology, I didn't understand what was happening.

"Is anyone else having issues with their e-mail?" I peered from my doorway to ask my team; a shake of silent heads was all I got in response.

I wheeled myself back to my desk and reached over to pick up the phone to dial IT Support, when the blank message section began to write itself.

Vauxhall Underground Station, London. 2.30pm. Tomorrow. Tell no one.

I looked through the gap in my office blinds out to the office, trying to identify a culprit who would have the technical knowledge to pull off a practical joke like this. I then recalled 'custode' was one of the words written on the amulet I seized earlier.

I opened up Google on my desktop computer and typed

'custode tellus' into the search bar.

'Custode tellus – Latin meaning 'Protector of the Earth''

A wave of nausea overwhelmed me. I connected this unexpected e-mail to the strange happenings on Beach Road and the amulet I'd discovered. I even went as far to suspect the sender of this e-mail may have been involved in the arson itself. I contemplated whether to get rid of the message and put it to the back of my mind, but I needed answers.

I now had the task of attempting to get the next day off, so I could travel down to London, and hopefully unravel the series of mysteries I had begun to acquire.

I approached the office of my boss, Detective Chief Inspector Carole Rose, conveniently located next to mine. Carole wasn't only my boss but also my friend; she had a no-nonsense approach to those who slacked off and didn't pull their weight, but her heart and compassion was her legacy amongst her officers.

Carole's office door always remained open, unless she had an important meeting or a difficult day. Luckily for me, it was propped open. I hovered by the doorway and saw Carole typing away at her desk.

A short woman in her fifties with light blonde hair down to her shoulder and dazzling blue eyes, she wore her usual shade of bright red lipstick, which made her look ten years younger than she actually was. Her eccentric patterned nails and her love for Bulgarian Merlot stood her out from the rest of her senior colleagues.

"Guv, have you got a minute?" I said, knocking gently on the door simultaneously.

"Hello darlin'!" she smiled at me, her broad east London accent shining through. "What can I do for my favourite DI?"

I instantly smiled at Carole's infectious and joyful personality. I could always rely on her to lend an ear and help lift my mood if I ever needed it.

I had to quickly devise an excuse of why I needed to take a trip to London at such short notice. I did contemplate telling her the truth, as she was a very open-minded person, but I don't think even she would've believed me.

"Sorry, this is last minute, but Grayson's asked me to go to London with him tomorrow for a work thing. Would I be able to take it off as leave?" I hated lying to her.

"Is everything okay?" Carole could tell something wasn't right; I could feel her gaze cutting right through me, analysing every inch of the expression on my face.

"Yeah, we're fine. It's just an important work thing and I'd totally forgotten about it. He's been so good to me, it's only fair I can go if I can." I tried to sound more convincing, knowing full well she'd become suspicious.

"I can catch up with anything on Friday." I assured her.

I knew Carole still didn't one hundred percent believe in my request but went along with it anyway. I'd never really done or said anything in the eight years we'd known each other, for her not to trust me.

"As long as both of you are alright. I've bought a bloody dress and everything for your wedding, so you'd better not change you minds!" she chuckled.

I got the impression everyone, apart from us grooms-to-be, were excited about our upcoming nuptials. I made a mental note to approach the subject with Grayson once he'd got through his big case.

"Oh, don't worry. It's still on." I smirked. "So, I take it as a, yes?"

"Of course, my sweetheart." She smiled at me and winked. Not typical behaviour you would expect from a Chief Inspector, but it's what made her unique.

"Whilst you're here." She clasped her hands together on her desk as her tone turned serious. "How did you get on with the arson job over in Scilly? Do we think it's a potential murder?"

"I would treat it that way," I began, hoping she didn't request any intricate details. "Early fire investigation and initial Crime Scene reports suggests it was deliberate."

"Okay darlin.' If you can update me ASAP, the Chief Super wants a full brief later this afternoon." She rolled her eyes before picking up her jewel encrusted pen, which matched most of the stationery in her office, and wrote something down in her diary. "He's not bothered; he just wants the Chief Constable off his back as he's already getting phone calls."

"Already?" I sighed; Agatha's body hadn't even made it to the morgue and the big bosses were already demanding answers, even if my team didn't yet have them. "I'll get on it straight away. Thanks, Guv."

For the rest of the day, I couldn't concentrate. I kept thinking back to Agatha and her amulet and the strange events with Joseph Tyrant. I couldn't make sense of any of it. Louisa had been the only witness to the ordeal with the necklace, but she was keeping quiet about it all, I assumed it being down to her reluctance to jeopardise her career.

Louisa left about eleven o'clock that morning as she had been on shift for a good twelve hours before, leaving me to make sure Carole had all the information she needed to brief the Chief Super.

When Debbie, my late shift Sergeant came on duty, I was pleased to see her. She'd just returned from holiday in Tenerife, evident by her bronzed glow.

I enquired about her time away, politely refusing a viewing of her hundred strong holiday snaps.

I eventually updated her on the morning's situation, tasking her and her team with outstanding enquiries.

Carole then discreetly sent me home, usually unthinkable of a Senior Investigating Officer during a critical incident investigation.

I took a leisurely stroll into town to pick up my car, not before stopping off for a quick drive-thru coffee, then home. I couldn't really recall the drive back; my mind vacant and unable to concentrate. I stood at the front entrance to the communal doors of my apartment, taking a deep breath to compose myself, clutching hold of my beverage.

I finally gathered the momentum to open the doors and force myself inside.

I always enjoyed coming back home, especially as Grayson always made sure a fresh smelling scent filled the hallway to add a homely touch. It was empty, with Grayson not being expected home for hours.

I kicked off my shoes, turned off my work phone and

ran myself a nice bath.

When Grayson eventually come home from work about seven o'clock in the evening, we enjoyed a home cooked meal of Lasagne which I'd prepared, and sat down together in the living area, watching television whilst we ate.

We recently discovered a new LGBT+ Netflix series called Heartstopper. With both of us being touched by its sweet love story, we became slightly addicted, watching it for the fifth time.

"This is my favourite one." Grayson smiled. We watched as the two main characters, Nick and Charlie, kissed during a house party after weeks of slowly falling for one another.

"Mine too," I agreed with him.

Both of us grew up in the archaic era of the anti-gay Section 28, so unfortunately, neither of us had the freedom or prominent role models to discover our sexuality, as young people did today.

It brought a smile to my face knowing the next generation wouldn't have to go through half as much as what me and Grayson did.

He looked over at me, gently swirling round his glass of white wine.

"How was your day?" he asked.

I'd dreaded this question all day. Grayson, like Carole, always sensed when I wasn't telling the entire truth. I paused for a minute, trying to form in my head the fabricated story I would tell.

"It was interesting," I said, taking a sip of a beer I clutched in my hand. "There's a lot of unanswered questions about the arson, but I think there may be a lead in London.

I'm going there tomorrow."

Grayson finished his mouthful of wine and held his goldfish bowl sized glass on his crossed over knee. "London? What leads have you found?"

I tilted my head and raised my eyebrow, giving him a disapproving look. "C'mon Gray, you know I can't go into too much detail."

Grayson held his hand up.

"I know, I'm sorry. You know I like to ask questions. Blame the barrister in me."

"How did the Timpson case go today?" I asked, quickly trying to change the subject, and avoiding any further questioning from him.

"Adjourned, frustratingly." Grayson rubbed his eyes, the fatigue he endured very apparent. "I reckon this will continue longer than we thought."

"Ah, that is frustrating! You're so close to the end!" I jeered, knowing too well how hard he worked on this case; it caused us both many a sleepless night.

"Well," he sighed. "I want a decent outcome for this one. This is the first time in a long while where I actually want to take someone down. The evidence is overwhelming, but the defence barrister takes no prisoners."

I looked over at him with empathy and finished the last swig of my beer, looking down the barrel of the glass to make sure I'd not missed a drop. I hoisted myself up from the sofa and made my way over to where Grayson sat, planting a quick kiss on his forehead as I passed him.

"Not as much as you do, though." I whispered in his ear. "Anyway, I'm off to bed – I've got a long day tomorrow.

Night."

Grayson smiled up at me, content.

"I won't be long. Night.."

THREE

The drive up to London the next day wasn't invigorating in the slightest. However, I preferred to drive over the hassle of changing at three different train stations, to spend a mere few hours in the capital.

It didn't make it any better I'd such a terrible night's sleep. I'd been awake for most of it, lying on my back and staring at the ceiling, reviewing my mind's playback of the day.

It took me slightly over four hours, with a collection service stops, coffee breaks and repeat of my favourite 'Steps' album in between, to drive to Boston Manor. A Piccadilly Line tube station line off the M4, it had parking which wasn't extortionately priced. I manoeuvred into a narrow space, struggling to fit between two poorly parked cars.

I bought a ticket from the machine and made my way onto to the platform. I looked at the matrix board; I didn't have a long wait for the next train to the city.

The Underground network had a reduced service, so I packed myself into the carriage like a sardine, squeezing in between two commuters; a blessing I only needed one change.

I sighed with relief when the Victoria Line train I caught at Green Park was scarce of people. I placed myself near the door so I could make a swift exit, on the off chance I became trapped again.

The journey to Vauxhall took forever. I passed the time looking around the carriage, making note of the eccentric personalities who surrounded me. I glanced over at a group of foreign students all huddled together speaking in their native tongue, tightly clutching hold of their oversized suitcases. A luggage tag with the letters 'LHR' sealed around one of the handles proposed they'd not long arrived in the country.

This was in contrast to the commuters; a suave, sophisticated businessman sat opposite me, dressed in a three-piece tailored suit, clutching a copy of the complimentary newspaper in his hand. Waves of nostalgia flooded me, reminding me of my childhood and my time spent working in England's capital city.

"The next station is Vauxhall" the automated female announcer echoed throughout the carriage. "Change here for national rail services."

I commenced my usual routine of checking my pockets for my wallet, keys, and phone; sometimes unnecessary, but reassured me to know I'd not lost anything in transit. The warmth emanated from fellow travellers queuing behind me as the train approached the station.

I looked at my watch – I'd still fifteen minutes to go, before I hopefully found out answers to the variety of questions I'd drawn up.

The train jolted without warning, and came to a sudden stop, almost knocking me off balance.

I looked around at my fellow passengers, expecting a similar reaction, but I gasped when I came to the realisation, they were all still like statues, frozen in time.

"What the-?" I muttered.

I waved my hand in front of a young, cleanly shaven man, dressed in a tweed suit, to my left-hand side, enthralled in pages of a novel he grasped single-handedly. He didn't even flinch.

"Welcome to MI6." A masculine voice announced with a deep, bellowing tone, replacing that of the silky and sultry feminine vocals.

The doors in front of me opened into the darkness of the underground tunnel, a family of rats scuttled alongside the carriage as I looked to the tracks. The power cables weaving along the walls, keeping the sub-terrain railway network in action, were quickly replaced by a set of metallic doors, which unsealed into a sterile corridor.

My sight adjusted to the bright lights running down either side of the ceiling. A small platform extended up to the open doorway of the train, inviting me to alight and follow its path.

I hesitantly stepped in, looking around in amazement at the secret corridor which appeared.

I took a lengthy walk towards the end of the passage and

came to another set of reflective doors. I placed my hand on the steel surface, cold to the touch, leaving an imprint of my palm when I pulled away.

Seconds later, the doors opened to reveal a tall woman. Her long dark ringlets of hair presented neatly in a ponytail, and she sported a bright coloured blouse and a pencil skirt, with pointed heels which gave her the appearance of being a foot taller than her actual height. She was the epitome of beauty; her eyes emanated by her dark skin and her lips met perfectly with the dimples either side of her cheeks.

"Good afternoon, Mr Ramirez." She welcomed me, in an accent which would have easily fit in amongst Eton. She held an electronic device by her side, which she brought in front of her to review.

She tapped at the screen, and a projection of my bust materialised, spinning on an imaginary podium.

"I just need to confirm your identity before we pass through."

This has got to be a dream. I shook my head vigorously with my eyes tightly sealed shut, desperately trying to wake myself up from this dream. When I came to opening them after a number of passing seconds, reality hit me as if I jumped into a pool of ice-cold water.

I *wasn't* dreaming, and this *was* real.

"Sure… okay?" I said, in a meek tone, still coming to terms with the realisation that this world wasn't a manifestation of my wild imagination.

"Year of birth?" the woman asked me, standing very upright, a hypothetical rod of steel running through her spine.

"Why do you need that?" I defensively asked. It was against my nature to divulge such personal information to a complete stranger, especially one who'd manifested out of the ether.

"Mr Ramirez, I can assure you I mean you no harm. This is purely precaution."

"Fine." I surrendered. "Nineteen-Eighty-Seven."

"Mother's Maiden name?" She asked the further question and looked at me, awaiting patiently for a response.

"Seriously?" I smirked with disbelief at the interrogation.

I paused for a moment.

All my natural instincts urged me to run, but my curiosity wished to see how this would all play out; especially if I managed to get some answers. "Cortez." I replied, after some internal deliberation.

The woman tapped my reply into her futuristic device before holding it in front of me. I peered at the device and saw an outline of a computer-generated hand glowing on the screen.

"Please place your right palm here." The woman instructed, pointing towards the slate.

I followed her request. It took seconds for the device to chime in acceptance and a emanate a green glow from beneath my palm.

"D.N.A confirmed." The tablet chirped.

"Thank you," The woman smiled. "Now that's all done, please follow me." She turned on her heel and walked down the corridor, her stilettos echoing on the steel floor as they tapped in a rhythmic beat.

"Wait, a second! Are you actually going to tell me what

the hell is going on around here?!" I scolded, my pent-up emotions erupting to the surface. I had, after all, complied with every single one of her requests without any protest; the least she could do was explain to me what was going on. "What happened to all those people on the train?!" I asked.

My extreme fatigue and frustration were getting the better of me, my face turning a vibrant shade of red. At the same time, the ground beneath me violently shook, the woman holding tightly on to the wall to steady her balance.

"I need you to calm down, Mr Ramirez." She held her hand towards me, in a bid to show me she wasn't a threat. "I am here to explain everything, but I need you to remain calm. I can assure you those members of public are fine."

Calm down? Why do I need to calm down?

Then, it dawned on me; *I* was making the ground shake.

I attempted to subdue my highly emotive state, taking deep, soothing breaths, and creating picturesque scenes in my psyche of exotic beaches me and Grayson visited over the years.

The shaking stopped.

The woman composed herself, tucking an assortment of loosened hair strands behind her ear, brushing off any creases which appeared on her suit, before heading back down the corridor.

"Thank you." She said, not even phased by the manifestation of an earthquake. "Now, please, follow me."

I did as she requested.

She guided me through a maze of mirrored corridors, and security accessed doors, which she breezed through, unlocking with the touch of her palm.

We ended up in a large open plan office, ten times larger in scale than the one I'd become accustomed to. I surveyed the room as the woman weaved me between the dozens of government employees sat at their sleek and modern desks.

They were all in possession of the same innovative technology and gesturing over a variety of virtual projections. I noticed this contrasted with the mythological artefacts displayed on podiums down the centre of the room, originating from differing cultures and time periods.

The woman led me towards a room, where an engraved plaque sat neatly mounted on the centre of the door; **'Harriet Brookman-Smith – Director, Operation Myst.'**

She opened the entrance to the room with conventional means and held her hand out toward a chair, inviting me to take a seat. I accepted, walking into the room, before taking a moment to appreciate the interior art decor design. This must have been this mysterious woman's office.

It was a complete contrast to the rest of the modern complex. As I took a seat on a large, leather-bound armchair, I scanned the various paintings and portraits decorating the wooden-clad walls of the room. They composed of a collection of women of different ages and generations posing in a similar elegant posture. The crackling of a raging fire at the far end of the room danced in the centre of a Victorian fireplace. The room felt cosy; a small pang of jealousy formed when I compared it to my own office.

The woman sat behind a large oak desk and placed down the device that she clutched in front of her, before resting her elbows on the surface, clasping her fingers together under her chin.

"Mr Ramirez." My attention was drawn to her serene tone of voice. "Marco Phillipe Constantos Ramirez. Born in Valencia, Spain. Moved to Hammersmith, London, at six months old. Attended Hammersmith School for Boys until you were eighteen, when you joined the London Metropolitan Police. Five years as a Police Constable. Eight years as a Sergeant, before transferring to Cornwall Constabulary. Promoted to Detective Inspector a year ago."

"Urm. Yeah. That's me." I stuttered, not overly concerned about the reels of information she had in her possession. I sat in a building dedicated to intelligence; not to mention that this could easily have been obtained from my personnel file.

The woman slipped her glasses back from the edge of her nose, perfectly positioning them at the top of her bridge. Her eyes softly gazed towards me, before looking at her tablet. "Your father died in a car accident did he not?"

I nodded, intrigued in which direction she planned to steer the conversation. My father's death remained a prickly subject for me, though he died during my early childhood.

"You don't believe it was an accident, do you?" she continued.

My eyes widened.

Was she reading my mind? She couldn't be. That's absurd.

"You believe it was all a cover up by those in high office, preventing anyone from really finding out what happened that day." The woman arched an eyebrow, anticipating a reaction from me.

"How do you know that?" I abruptly asked, moving to

the edge of my seat, knowing full well she couldn't have researched that from any database.

I remember the day my father died, as if only yesterday. I revisited it in my mind, thinking back to when his Inspector visited us at home to inform my mother of the news. She collapsed in a heap on the floor and broke down in tears, whilst me and my sister watched in anguish.

When my mother told us that he wouldn't be coming home, I was distraught. Up until that point, I worshipped the ground my father walked on, as far as I was concerned he was the best Dad that anyone could have.

The powers that be always claimed his life ended in a car accident, whilst pursuing a stolen vehicle. However, as far as I was aware, a Police investigation or a public Coroner's inquest never manifested.

Once I joined the Police, then subsequently promoted to Sergeant, I experienced more about investigations into deaths of serving officers. I started to question the circumstances around his death and used all my power to get to the truth; unsurprisingly palmed off by my superiors.

"Your father's death wasn't an accident." The woman took to her feet and traipsed around the outside of her desk, perching on the edge, keeping full eye contact, which felt slightly eerie.

"Sorry?" I nervously laughed, unsure whether I heard her correctly.

Harriet folded her arms tightly into her chest and glanced at her feet, before meeting my gaze. "This will all sound strange; I must warn you."

"Try me." I said, in a confident tone.

"My name is Harriet. I am the director of Operation Myst, which is a covert operations unit within MI6." She began. "Only the Director of the Secret Service, the Prime-Minister and the Queen know we exist."

Harriet took to her feet and began pacing around her office, her heels repeating the same tempo with each step.

"Operation Myst founded seventy years ago, to investigate unexplained supernatural occurrences."

A headache formed in my temples; I travelled all the way from the Southwest of the country to find answers, to find myself becoming more confused by the second.

"I'm sorry," The pounding of my head began to blur my vision. "I'm struggling to follow you."

I rubbed my temple, struggling to get her back into focus.

"What has any of this got to do with me and the death of my father?" I asked.

Harriet walked over to her fireplace, my body following in my chair. She waved her palm at the space above the mantelpiece, and a virtual image of two demonic beings appeared.

They possessed pale white skin and dark unkempt hair, with sharp yellow fangs which peered over their bottom lips. Their eyes glowed with a fierce green aura. Royal blue cloaks covered their unnaturally broad muscular figures, their fingernails like claws, with sharp bloodstained tips. They looked inhuman.

"These are Hellions." Harriet began. "Millennia ago, the Hellions escaped from their underground realm and unleashed their evil on our world."

As she swiped her hand, the image followed suit, changing to a woman, dressed in an elegant gown, with long hair draped down her back. She stood tall in front of a gathering of people in periodic clothing.

"This is Elia." Harriet continued. "She was an ancient and powerful sorcerer that guarded all of the world's elements. Sensing a threat and being too weak to fight the battle alone, she gifted a select group of human beings with the power to control an element, to help bring an end to the Hellion's wrath."

Harriet waved her hand again, to reveal a montage of a war scene, which pictured the demonic creatures engaged in battle. The still projection flickered numerous colours.

"The gifted humans won the battle and drove the Hellion's back to their realm; however, at a cost – Elia unfortunately lost her life."

A depiction of a golden amulet appeared next, identical to the one I seized from Agatha's neck.

"An amulet was forged and enriched in an unbreakable metal. The gifted ones renounced their powers into it, and a guardian chosen to protect it until the magic was needed again."

Harriet commanded the projection to play a short clip. The moving images pictured battles with the demons over differing time periods, each time waging war with a group of humans who conquered them with magical abilities.

"The Hellion's have tried to destroy our world many a time, throughout the millennia, however, they have always been defeated by a group of these supernatural humans, called 'Custodians'."

I struggled to follow this bizarre fairy tale. Everything this woman, Harriet, said was ludicrous. I adore tales of folklore and magic, but that is all they were, tales, fantasies for us to submerge ourselves when we needed some time away from the burdens of life.

"It was no accident you being on call last night when you were called to Agatha's home."

"Let me guess, you think I'm a…"

"Custodian, yes." She finished. "More specifically, the Custodian of Earth."

Harriet began to annoy me. It was clear she'd been behind all the strange experiences I'd encountered the previous day, yet she felt she could pass it off as some made-up story about supernatural beings. I wasn't having any of it. Surely, she had help in devising this outrageous, but imaginative prank.

"This is ridiculous!" I laughed, shaking my head in disbelief. "Who put you up to this? My brother-in-law? He will always go that extra mile to piss me off!"

"I told you this would sound strange." Harriet said, calmly.

"Strange?! This is more than strange. This is absurd!" I yelled. "I admit I haven't been able to explain these last twenty-four hours, but what you're saying is just plain insane."

"Mr Ramirez. I know this is difficult to accept, but I can assure you that what I am telling you is true." She paused, looking at me with a bemused expression. "Maybe I can convince you another way."

Harriet walked over to me and crouched to my level. She

took off her glasses and placed them on her desk next to me.

"I need to you to keep perfectly still." She instructed, placing two fingers on the top of my forehead. As our skin touched, a shock of paralysing energy struck through me, my muscles turning heavy, like stone.

Harriet looked deep into my eyes, probing my mind, overturning every brainwave and electrode.

I instantly ventured to another time. The images she'd shown me moments before, manifested into my cognitive reality.

I witnessed Elia, the Hellions, and the Custodians.

I fought all the battles.

I winced at the pain.

I celebrated all the victories.

I lived through it all.

I met Agatha, thriving and well.

I experienced my father's glowing smile again.

I jolted back to reality and sat in complete silence, trying to make sense of what I'd just endured.

I understood it all.

"Do you believe me now?" She asked, upstanding, aligning her glasses on the bridge of her nose once again.

"Yes." I nodded, still bewildered. "How did you do that?"

"I'm a telepath." She explained. "I come from an extensive line of them. We use our gifts for the forces of good, to guide those in need."

"Did you freeze all those people on the train?"

"Yes."

I unnaturally accepted my new destiny, thanks to Harriet's memory invasion. It remained hazy, but I tried to make sense of everything.

"How old was Agatha?" I asked, intrigued.

"She protected her amulet for six hundred years." She replied.

"Six hundred?!" I widened my eyes.

"The guardians of the amulet do not age as the rest of us do." She explained, her voice soothing and calm, sensing the chaos in my mind. "They bestow the gifts to the chosen ones, then watch over them, acting as guides and instructors until the gifts are no longer needed. They refer to themselves as 'Overseers'."

"I don't see what all this has got to do with the death of my father." I said, struggling to see the connection between Agatha Lockwood and Serefino Ramirez.

Harriet sauntered over to her desk, my eyes following her. She stood prominently next to her chair, clasping her hands together in front of her lap as she cleared her throat.

"Your father was also a Custodian." she said, bracing herself for my reaction. "He died in a Hellion battle. You believed it to be a cover-up; that's because it was."

"I knew it!" I exclaimed. "I knew it was a cover up!" I rose to my feet, my body filling with rage. The more I thought about the death of my father, the stronger the anger consumed me. My newfound gift filled the surrounding space, causing the floor to shake again.

Harriet braced herself using her desk, as she struggled to remain on balance.

"You…. have to…. understand…… Mr Ramirez….."

She watched through the window as her colleagues all scurried around falling debris, screaming as rubble fell inches away from them.

"Marco...!" Harriet shouted, trying to snap me out of my fury.

Reacting to her yell, I realised the destructive damage I was inflicting, and shut my eyes. I took a long deep breath and immersed myself back to the serene images, which temporarily subsided my earthquake conjuring abilities.

"Marco, please understand it to be necessary. Custodians must remain secret for their own protection. If the world knew of their existence, then the Hellion's would easily track them down and win." Harriet clarified. "Agatha was your father's Overseer. She tried to do everything in her power to save him."

"Why is all this happening again now? I take it these demon things are back?" I asked, not a hundred percent sure I wanted to know the answer.

"I am sure the Hellions killed Agatha. When an Overseer knows they are facing death, they will cast a spell to attract the next chosen ones to receive their powers and take the amulet into their protection until another Overseer can be found."

My headache intensified with my brain pulsating from underneath my skull.

"What now?" I asked her.

"You need to first find the remaining Custodians." she commissioned. "Then together, join them with the amulet so they can receive their gifts. Once all four of you have received your powers, you will be unstoppable."

"I wouldn't know where to start." I shrugged my shoulders. Despite being a detective, I couldn't even begin to think how I could work this out on my own.

"Before she died, Agatha entrusted me with the names of all the Custodians who came before. According to her, the prophecy of Elia states that the eldest offspring of every Custodian will be granted the gift in time of need." Harriet explained, handing me a weathered scroll with a vibrant red ribbon tied around the middle. "This should give you all the information you need to seek out the others."

I took the scroll hesitantly, being burdened with an unfathomable responsibility. I was used to high pressure in my job, but nothing like the fate of the entire world, which ended up in my hands.

I loosened the ribbon and opened the centuries old scroll, managing it with care.

There were four columns: *'Earth,' 'Air', 'Fire'* and *'Water'* in beautiful calligraphic handwriting.

A list of names displayed under each heading, many of the surnames similar, signifying the prophecy continuing through generations. I scanned my way to the bottom, where I saw my father's name, making a note of the people to the side of him.

S. Ramirez   S. Chang   T. Stevens   S. Turner

M. Ramirez

"Chang?" I whispered to myself. I then crossed my brow, desperately trying to remember where I recognised that name. Then it hit me.

Doctor Yi Chang.

FOUR

I spent much of the evening at MI6 with Harriet, more time than I'd anticipated. She filled me in on the work of her team and where her extensive knowledge of my plight originated.

Her telepathic abilities were inherited from her mother and father, who passed away when she was a child. Agatha, a fellow telepath, and a close acquaintance to her parents, felt responsible for their demise, as they died at the hands of Hellions.

Her and her younger sister Ruby, were taken in by Agatha, who moved into a central London home owned by the Lockwood Family, who had social links to the Royals. When the two siblings came of age and started their independent lives, the old woman returned to her home in Cornwall, where she shut herself off from the world.

It turned out our parents knew each other; telepaths are destined to support Custodians in their battle to rid the world of the evil Hellions, being their eyes and ears. They supported my father in every battle he waged, but it unfortunately cost them their lives.

Her authoritative personality dwindled the more we got to know each other, referring to me as 'Marco' more often than 'Mr Ramirez.' She invited me to share a glass of wine with her at a quaint local pub nearby called 'The Rose', where we continued to discuss our history.

Harriet disclosed she too grew up in Hammersmith, albeit a neighbouring district. We continued to compare notes and discovered that we went to the same Sunday school, enduring the monotone teachings of Mrs Bartholomew. The classes were intimate, so I was surprised that I couldn't remember her.

I was pleased to unearth a different side, one I felt more personable to.

Grayson sent me the twentieth message asking me what time I would be home, so I knew I needed to head back to Cornwall. I sent him a brief text, letting him know I would get back at approximately midnight. Harriet provided me with her number to call in case I needed any assistance with the supernatural, before we exchanged pleasantries and left the pub; agreeing to touch base every couple of days.

I stepped on the carriage servicing the Piccadilly Line at Green Park station and noted the Coke bottles and sweet wrappers littered throughout; a sign of the day coming to an end, before the overnight cleaners worked their own magic. As I sat, it wasn't long before I nodded off from the therapeutic rocking of the train.

I woke upon the arrival at Boston Manor, alighting the

train and heading straight out to my car, still squeezed between the two horrendously parked vehicles. I sent one final message to Grayson before setting off towards the M4.

Twenty minutes into the journey, I glanced into my rear-view mirror and spotted a black Land Rover closing behind me at speed. I travelled at the maximum limit, so it must have been doing at least ninety miles per hour. I pulled into the nearside lane, to let them pass; they mirrored my manoeuvre and changed lanes simultaneously.

I peeked in the reflection of the stern, mindful of keeping my concentration focused on the road; luckily the lanes were scarce of traffic to cause any significant congestion.

The lights of the Land Rover expanded in my mirror, signalling it was approaching at significant speed.

Bump!

I jolted forward as it rammed into the back of my car, causing me to swerve into another lane. My pursuit training quickly surfaced as I stayed in full control, putting my foot firmly down on the accelerator, building up speed in order to escape this crazed driver. My heart raced in my chest as adrenaline pumped furiously through my veins.

I sped up and the Land Rover matched my speed, closing in on me once again.

Bump!

I launched forward again, with considerable force, my neck creasing in a sharp pain. I put it to the back of my mind whilst I concentrated on my live version of Grand Theft Auto; viewing through my wing mirror the vehicle drawing back and switching lanes.

It let out a large rev, squealing down the motorway, aligning perfectly with my driver's side. I took a quick browse at my speedometer – close to a ton.

We were both extremely lucky the roads were so deserted, as the tactics being used from both sides were dangerous.

Bang! Smash!

A sound resembling a gunshot, shattered my rear driver side window. I dodged and cowered, with one arm shielding me from shards of glass, which scattered throughout the cockpit. I prayed a traffic car would be witness to the erratic driving, but knowing my luck, and years of government austerity, this would be a miracle.

I could feel my heart pounding in my throat. I'd been through a variety of close calls in my established career, but nothing so deadly as a high-speed chase involving armed suspects – this scene could have easily been placed in the latest Vin Diesel movie.

I caught a glimpse through the open window of the offending vehicle, trying to identify any features of the occupants. Thanks to the combination of the night sky, and our lightning speeds, I could barely see an outline.

I continued to race down the motorway, approaching a set of roadworks near to the city of Reading; a row of tapered cones bringing us down to a single lane, where I managed to get ahead of my opponent.

The truck remained relentlessly on my tail with no signs of stopping its pursuit. I sharply turned my steering wheel to narrowly avoid a fatal collision with a construction worker, who dived out of my path in terror. This caused my car to spin out of control, the friction between the tarmac and tyres letting out a high-pitched screech. The momentum caused my car to flip onto the grass verge, thrashing me around inside like a rag doll and eventually landing on the roof.

I opened my eyes, to find myself still strapped in. I dangled upside down, battered and bruised, my entire body pulsating in aches and pains. I let out a large groan as I came to, not realising I'd blacked out for a minute, the engine emanating a sizzling sound.

Still slightly dazed, I rummaged around in the pitch black, unclipping my seat belt and falling in a heap on the roof. I barely noticed a bone protruding through my trousers from my leg. *This should really hurt!*

I'd had an open fracture when I was about nine years old whilst playing football, quickly recalling the excruciating pain.

This barely felt like a papercut.

Then the bone mysteriously clicked back into place, with no pain or any discomfort whatsoever. I repeatedly tapped my leg in disbelief to discover there wasn't a trace of even the slightest wound. I still tried to come to terms with my new purpose in life, so I shook this miracle off as part of my new supernatural persona.

The front driver's window of my car had smashed in the tumble, leaving a perfect exit for me to escape. I crawled through it, just able to see the trees and foliage outside from the guidance of the moonlight. I pulled myself up onto my feet, patting my back trouser pocket and pulling out a surprisingly unscathed mobile phone.

I stood for a moment. *Who was I going to call?* It was almost half ten at night and Grayson would have been tucked up in bed, fast asleep by now. Then my mind went straight to Harriet - she'd be able to help me.

As I began to search for her in my list of contacts, I heard a loud crackle, which followed with a sudden flare of intense light, sniping past the side of my head.

Terrified, I ducked for cover, fumbling my phone back in my pocket, before aimlessly sprinting away from the scene; I wasn't about to stick around to meet my assassin. The hairs stood up on the back of my neck as the heat from another beam darted across my left shoulder, leaving a potent smell of burnt leather from my jacket.

I quickly looked back in the direction of where the discharge originated from and witnessed two figures chasing me. *Were these the same ones who ran me off the road?*

I spent the next five minutes, dodging and darting a continuous stream of the death rays at an athletic pace, before stopping still in my tracks. It wasn't fatigue that brought me to a halt, but the realisation I'd no idea where I was.

I bravely performed a one-eighty to face my attackers, as they continued to target me with their mysterious weapons.

My eyes focused with help from the light generated by the full-moon, and the shapes morphed into two masculine figures, their faces lack of any emotion.

"Who are you?!" I shouted at them.

They fell silent, stopping ten metres short of me, uncomfortably staring with their beady eyes. They were tall and broad, both dressed in matching black suits with a crisp white shirt and tie.

"We're here to destroy you!" One of them hissed, the unworldly tone to their voice having an unnatural echo.

"Who the hell are you?" I strained my throat from my powerful yell.

Neither replied.

Instead, one of the duo lifted their arm up towards me, displaying their palm, which emitted an eerie glow and electrified the air around me.

The aura surrounding the hand began to intensify into a crimson red; I concluded they were not from this world.

Were these those Demons that Harriet was telling me about?

How did they find me?

I'd so many questions.

I sensed their imminent attack, usually combated by more conventional means, but deduced physical defence was going to be worthless against these opponents.

I'd only been a magically enhanced superhero for slightly over a day, but I'd always been able to harness new skills more rapidly than the average human.

I closed my eyes and thrust my arms out with my fingers spread, in the direction of my enemy, the veins in my temple pulsating with sheer concentration. The ground began to shake, which inherently became my signature move. The two men grabbed hold of one another as they fought to remain upright, whilst I maintained my balanced composure.

I attempted to recreate the web of foliage I engulfed Joseph Tyrant in, but instead, the ground cracked open and solid branches began to sprout from the crevasses around the two men, latticing to form a cage.

This is new.

The men made a desperate attempt to escape, peering their arms through gaps in the branches and shooting the deadly beams from their hands.

Yet, my earthly creation remained indestructible.

I watched in awe as they began a metamorphosis, standing with their backs arched and letting out horrific, gut-wrenching screams. They grew several inches taller, and their muscular figures bulged out to three times their size.

Their skin turned to an ash grey leather as their eyes narrowed, glowing a fierce shade of green. Their teeth grew into thin spikes, protruding over their newly extended jaws.

They looked identical to the images Harriet showed to me at MI6.

These were *Hellions*.

The transformation bestowed them with superhuman strength as they tore through my improvised magical cell with ease. I raced away, putting unprecedented pressure on my calves as I continued through an infinite field.

A homely farm cottage came in to view, with cosy lights on shining through the Tudor style windows. I'd half a mind to continue running, not wanting to put innocent lives in danger from these menaces, but I needed to get them off of my tail.

As I drew closer to the cottage, sensing the two demons closing in quickly behind me, I scanned for anything less inhabited. To my luck, the farm came with a large wooden barn, which I veered myself towards, hoping that the Hellions would follow suit.

I stopped short of the barn, counting two large doors shutting off the inside from intruders - a rust covered padlock chaining them together. I vigorously pulled at it, hoping I'd been granted the same magical might as my adversaries, but I disappointingly hadn't.

Their monstrous footsteps swept through the long grass like a countdown. I tried once more, tugging as hard as I could at the stubborn lock.

Then it hit me.

The barn was made of *wood*.

Wood was made from the *earth*.

I can *control* the *earth*.

A long shot, but I thought I'd try.

I took a giant leap back and closed my eyes, holding my palms out at arm's length. I pictured the wood in my mind's eye; it's connection to the earth; the family of trees to which it once belonged.

I willed for the doors to open.

My power discharged a slight rumble on the ground - nowhere near as harsh as previous incarnations - my palms attracting the doors like a magnet, creaking and cracking as they creeped towards me.

The doors magically opened, the padlock diving to the floor as it snapped under the intense pressure. I ventured into the black abyss of the barn, barely noticing the various stacks of hay-bails neatly arranged in the centre.

I squinted my eyes, desperately seeking out anything I could use to rid myself of my stalkers. To my luck, inside the entrance to the right of the door, were several farmers implements: shovels, rakes, pitchforks, and hoes all hanging symmetrically on the wall.

The aura of the moon supplied me enough visibility to explore my way around the barn, gingerly taking hold of a pitchfork, trying my utmost to not obtain a splinter from the jagged wooden handle.

The growling of the two creatures signalled like a war cry for me to prepare for battle, as I tucked myself in against the wall, pitchfork primed at the ready. My heart raced, and my brow sweated profusely. The growling intensified, and I could sense that they were within meters of the entrance.

They cautiously entered; each footstep laid down in a calculated move; their heavy breathing slightly elevating the temperature in the air. I stayed incognito, camouflaged behind the door, anticipating I could take the pair by surprise.

I needed to formulate this plan carefully as any wrong decision on my part would surely be fatal.

I'd never been so scared.

Now!

I sprinted towards the men, my weapon of choice poised directly at them, like a soldier entering into a battle zone.

I drove the pitchfork hard into the back of one of the demons, the squelch resonating, as it tore through the skin and into his body. They let out an agonising scream and instantly collapsed to the floor.

I swiftly dislodged the fork out of him, priming myself to strike again, a slight pang of guilt filled my stomach as I stood over the body of the helpless creature.

I'd never stabbed anyone before.

These aren't 'anyone' though are they? I reminded myself.

I recalled myself back into the fight, as the surviving being turned to face me. He grabbed hold of the tool I tightly grasped, in an attempt to force it from my grip. The being reminded me of his unnatural strength, but my determination was a force to be reckoned with.

I focused my attention on the wooden handle of my pitchfork, my influence over the elements taking control and assisting me in winning this tug of war; I was beginning to get used to my powers.

The creature screeched, taking numerous swipes at me with his talons, narrowly missing the centre of my chest. As I launched myself backwards, I saw the opportunity to pierce him in the chest with my makeshift weapon.

He dropped to the floor in a screaming heap, joining his comrade. They were severely injured and immobilised, enough for me to use my power to engulf them in an array of vines to allow enough time to escape.

With my serious lack of any sense of direction, I relied purely on instinct and the mapping system on my phone, to navigate my way back to the wreckage of my car.

My battery percentage decreased by the second, so I picked up the pace. A sea of blue flashing lights emerged from the horizon, near where I thought I'd deserted my car, so I used them as a homing beacon.

As I reached the wreckage site, it was clear the emergency services had discovered it; a marked BMW 5 series parked up stationary on the road parallel to where my car remained on its roof.

A traffic officer, identifiable by his white cap, examined

the interior with a poorly lit torch. I approached him and cleared my throat.

"Officer," I said to him, sheepishly. "This is my car."

The officer turned to me, startled, and took a minute to compose himself.

"Marco Ramirez?" he asked.

"Yeah, that's me."

"Thank God. We've got search parties looking out for you!" he exclaimed, with a large sigh of relief. "Romeo-Papa-Five-Three to control." He began talking into his radio mounted on the left side of his vest. "Stand down all units searching for potential Misper. He's returned to his vehicle."

Being referred to as a 'Misper,' Police terminology for a 'Missing Person,' wasn't one of the proudest moments of my life.

"I'm not a Misper, don't worry." I quickly corrected him, trying not to get too frustrated, as he was only doing his job. "I'd been run off the road by a maniac and I was trying to find a phone to call for help." It wasn't in my nature to fabricate the truth, but concerned me it started to come to with so much ease.

"Did you not have a mobile phone with you?" he asked, his tone oozing with suspicion.

"My battery died."

The traffic officer examined me up and down. I figured he was determining whether my explanation was plausible.

"Okay." He eventually said, giving me the benefit of the doubt. "How did you manage to escape this without a scratch?" He gestured towards the wreckage.

"No idea," I replied. I wasn't sure he'd come across the blood inside, but either way I needed to play along with this charade.

His eyebrow raised inquisitively as he continued to ask routine questions any officer would ask at the scene of a traffic collision, such as alcohol intake, medical issues and if I wore any corrective vision aids. I of all people knew the guy was doing his job, but this didn't subside my impatience. I was expectant of the brethren of demonic assassins to re-appear at any given moment.

I reluctantly disclosed to him what I did for a job, and his attitude towards me changed significantly.

"So, you're Cornwall Police?" He probed, his manner completely casual and friendly. "Where abouts?"

"I'm in the Major Investigations, a DI."

"Oh, sorry Sir."

There it was.

Sir.

I hated that bloody title.

I appreciated that it was a sign of respect, however, it seared through me like nails on a chalk board.

"Please, call me Marco." I insisted. "I don't want any special treatment. I understand you're just doing your job."

The officer smiled at me and provided me with his name, Dan. He looked slightly relieved at the fact that I was being so personable. I had a distinct impression that Thames District's Inspector's weren't as affable as me.

Dan went on to explain that my vehicle would be recovered to their local recovery agency, whilst they began their investigation into locating the offending vehicle. I peered around the vicinity of the car wreckage; the Hellion's vehicle had miraculously vanished.

He offered to arrange me a lift to the Cornwall border, but I respectfully declined.

Instead, I moved into a discreet line of bushes, away from prying ears, and called Harriet.

Thank heavens she answered.

I'd spent the first ten minutes of our conversation explaining my encounter with the Hellion brethren and how I'd scathed death and lived to tell the tale. She was most concerned at the fact that they possessed shape shifting abilities.

"This is worrying. They've never been able to pose as humans." She said, her voice daunting. *"This means they'll be even harder to track."*

"What do I do know? They obviously know about me."

"Try and stay out of sight. Limit your contact with people you don't know. Change your normal travel routes."

"That's going to be difficult with the job I do!" I reminded her.

"I know, Marco, but you must try. Also, you must find the other Custodians, quickly. Then we stand a chance of defeating them."

"I will. As soon as I get home. My car has been towed away by Thames District Police, so I'm a bit stuck at the moment."

"Leave it with me." She assured me. *"I'll get one of my agents to pick you up and sort you a replacement car."*

"Are you sure?" I asked.

"Of course. Think of me as your Agatha."

FIVE

I'd managed to get home about two o'clock that Friday morning, creeping into the bedroom and gingerly lifting up the duvet as to try not to wake up Grayson.

He stirred and muttered something under his breath, incoherent and more than likely divulged in his sleep.

I was exhausted. My body ached all over and pains manifested in areas I didn't even know existed. As I laid in bed, I convinced myself I would struggle to drift off, but as I closed my eyes, I instantly fell asleep.

I woke up a solid eight hours later, reaching over to see if Grayson had gone to work, my arm patting the empty bed on his side. Having no concept of time, I did recall him planting a kiss on my forehead, but I wasn't entirely sure if it had been a daydream or not.

Luckily, I was on a day off from work so hadn't the need to get up. I managed to haul myself out of bed and slipped on a pair of shorts and a T-Shirt with a Captain America shield proudly showcased on the chest, symbolising my fascination with all things Marvel.

As I shuffled into the kitchen area, I forcibly stretched out the knots in my upper back and let out a large, pleasuring yawn and concentrated on relieving an annoying, itchy patch of my severely unkempt hair. Grayson had already opened the blinds, so the full force of the August sun beamed ferociously through the windows.

I prepared myself a bowl of cereal and poured myself a mug of coffee, hoping the influx of caffeine would implode me with a burst of energy I severely lacked. I leaned against the kitchen counter, shovelling in copious mouthfuls of cereal, taking a moment to relive the events of the night before. It had been an intense forty-eight hours.

I walked over to the front door, cereal bowl still in hand and munched away like a hamster, checking to see if the post had been. A brown envelope lay on the doormat, with a handwritten 'M' on the front - obviously hand delivered with the absence of an address.

Suspicious, I hesitantly picked up the package with my spare hand and held it at as far away from me as I could, treating it as an explosive of some kind, running into the living area and placing it gingerly on the dining table. I stared at it for a while, crunching on my remaining mouthfuls of breakfast, before plucking up the courage to open it.

Inside, was a set of car keys, identical to the ones seized from me the previous evening, and a typed note on an official MI6 letterhead which read:-

DAN ALEXANDER

HM SECRET INTELLIGENCE SERVICE
MILITARY INTELLIGENCE SECTION 6
OPERATION MYST

M,

Please find enclosed keys to your replacement car. I've sorted out the issues from last night; Thames District have dropped the investigation. Keep this one to yourself.

Stay safe out there and hurry with your mission.

H.

CUSTODIANS: THE PROPHECY

It took me about three read-throughs to engrain the contents of the letter. I quickly threw on some slippers and raced out of my front door, keeping it on the latch and clutching tightly to the new set of car keys. I waltzed down the set of spiral stairs that led down to the resident car park and made my way over to my parking space.

I was shocked to see a shiny, black Ford Fiesta parked perfectly in the bay, with my old registration plate neatly mounted on the front grill, as if the crash never happened.

I was impressed, but also relieved at the fact that I wouldn't need to explain my involvement with another Police Force to Carole when I got back to work on Monday - especially as she thought I was with Grayson.

I wondered if Harriet used her mind warping abilities on the poor unsuspecting traffic officer. If so, it was entirely necessary, but I'd jumped to some very rash conclusions.

I made my way back into the apartment and took the quickest of showers. I changed into a pair of cargo shorts, a plain plum coloured T-Shirt and my favourite pair of converse. As per Harriet's note, I needed to get on with the quest in hand.

Venturing into the back bedroom, which we referred to as our 'office', I opened the top drawer to the oak computer desk. I hid the scroll there, knowing this was one of the places that Grayson never looked. I removed the scripture with a gentle hand, and unravelled it, the beautiful italic handwriting strikingly impressive.

I studied the three names next to my father's. Somehow, I had to locate their eldest offspring - with just a name. I'd already figured out one of them, the Custodian of Air,

Doctor Yi Chang.

Before I could do anything else, I needed to get that amulet back. It had been secured and guarded within the evidence store at work; I needed to figure out how to obtain it without alerting anyone - or jeopardising Agatha's murder investigation. This was beginning to become complex.

It was remarkable how my life had changed within the space of twenty-four hours since my visit to the Secret Service headquarters. Yesterday, I had concerns over last minute wedding plans; today, I had concerns over the destruction of the human race.

I left my apartment, deciding to walk and take advantage of the lambent sunshine and coastal views. It took me about twenty minutes to reach the station, clocking a response vehicle rallying out of the gates, responding to an emergency call with the glint of their blue lights and sirens echoing throughout the streets.

I swiped my access card to gain entry to the station, heading directly down a set of decrepit stairs to the dreary basement level, finding myself within the evidence store. Many officers refused to come down here alone at night, and I sympathised. There was a peculiar atmosphere in the depths, which would have made even the bravest of warriors scarper with fear.

Gladys Locke, the property assistant, sat at her desk, hunched over and typing one fingered onto her computer keyboard. A small, stout lady in her late seventies, who'd refused to retire, working for the Police for well over forty years. Her white hair was short and styled, with her half-rimmed glasses draped around her neck on a chain.

"Morning Gladys." I greeted her with a dashing smile.

She looked up at me from her work and reciprocated, her perfectly aligned prosthetic top teeth glistening in the artificial light.

"Oh, hello Marco!" she struggled up from her seat and waddled over to me, throwing her arms around me and giving me the tightest of squeezes. "I haven't seen you for ages my love!" Her broad Cornish twang was sometimes difficult to understand, but her soft tone made it easier. I had to sometimes remember that I was the outsider, and my west London accent may have seemed as alien to her.

Gladys was a mother figure to the entire population of the station, knowing the majority of the senior officers from their days as probationers. With no children of her own, she projected her maternal instincts on us all; always seeming to take an extra shining towards me.

"Sorry Gladys, I've been a bit busy on the top floor. You know how it is."

"Yes, love, I do."

"How's Tigger?" I asked, enquiring about her twelve-year-old Yorkshire Terrier her world revolved around.

"He's just fine. Still thinks he's a puppy!" she chuckled to herself, her cheeks turning rosy. "Anyway, as much as I love seeing you, what brings you down here?" she looked me up and down, taking an interest in my light, summery clothing. "And on your day off too I'm guessing?"

"That amulet we seized from the St Mary's arson. Has it been sent off for forensics yet?" I asked.

"No dear, it hasn't."

"Ah lovely." I said, relieved. "I need to check it out. I've got a specialist antique dealer to have a look at it, to check its authenticity, so I can see if it's been stolen."

I was secretly impressed that I'd managed to produce such an elaborate, fake excuse on a whim; to the point where I even started to believe it.

"Of course, dear." She smiled at me, not even questioning my excuse and shuffled into a cage which ran the entire length of the ground floor.

The store owned several aisles of metal shelving, with various bags of evidence, assorted into date order. There were copious amounts seized from multiple crime scenes over the years; no one would dare remove anything without speaking to Gladys first. She was a bubbly, friendly lady, but could instantly turn into a dragon if provoked.

Gladys took a couple of minutes before she fumbled out with a bag in her hand, the amulet inside glistening as it refracted the bright lighting. She handed me the bag and then made her way back over to her desk, painstakingly tapping in commands into her computer with one finger.

I always remember when the paper system was digitally upgraded – I'd spend hours on end trying to teach her how to use it, which is why she probably favoured me over most.

I looked down at the wrapped-up piece of jewellery. I stared at it, an instant connection forming, however, this manifested more intensely than on St Mary's. The jewel in the centre began to emanate a green glow, seemingly recognising me. It enveloped me in a friendly warmth, giving me a boost of energy; closing my eyes as I succumbed to it.

"Marco!" I snapped out of my magically induced trance with Gladys, bellowing at me. "Are you okay dear?"

"I'm fine." I smiled at her, hoping she didn't notice the magical display.

"I just need you to sign it out, then you're all done." She gestured down to a printed document she'd produced, holding out a biro. I took hold of the pen and signed it with my overly fancy signature.

"Thanks Gladys, as always." I smiled.

"You're welcome, dear. Just make sure you get it back by Monday evening - that's when the forensic van does the pick-ups to Truro."

"I'll make sure of it."

After exchanging goodbyes with her, I manoeuvred the stairs and corridors to the exit like a ninja, trying to avoid anyone who would notice me sneaking out a vital piece of evidence.

I managed to evade detection, heading out into the car park, and placing the bagged-up amulet in my pocket. I sprinted the final hundred meters or so, out of the gate and onto the main road, where I headed out onto the seafront and navigated back towards home.

I stopped off at a café in the town centre, during my walk back to my apartment, and ordered a cinnamon latte before parking myself in a cosy corner. I researched 'Doctor Yi Chang' on my phone to see if I could locate which hospital she worked at.

I'd managed to locate her LinkedIn profile which displayed the majority of her professional information;

she'd studied at London School of Medicine, where she'd received first class honours – which came as no surprise.

She formed part of the staff at the Royal Cornwall Hospital in Truro as an A&E Senior Consultant, covering the Air Ambulance as a volunteer. It concerned me how much information I'd managed to find out about her from social media – a reason why I kept my own personal accounts locked down to close friends and family.

Truro wasn't far away for me to drive, a little under half an hour.

When I returned back to my apartment, I immediately jumped into the car that MI6 provided me and inspected the inside. I caressed every surface, hot to the touch, with the summer heatwave we were experiencing.

I was amazed that the Secret Service agents managed to recover the majority of the little trinkets from my dashboard, which I parted with, believing they were destroyed in the wreckage.

I turned the soothing air conditioning up to full blast and sped away.

Twenty-Two minutes was the exact time it took me to get to the Royal Cornwall Hospital. It definitely did not live up to its name, appearing as clinical and sterile as any mainstream hospital.

I drove into the visitor's parking area, shaking my head in disgust at the extortionate prices, which were prominently displayed on various signs dotted around the car park. Once I'd parked up, I slapped my back pocket, to feel the bulge of the magic necklace, and marched with purpose over to A&E.

I passed through a set of revolving doors, which held me captive, after a disobedient five-year-old decided to throw himself across the floor.

Upon my escape, I noticed a young dark-haired lad sat closest to the entrance. He appeared to be barely eighteen, dressed in a blue and red football kit and covered in mud. He held a blooded towel over his right eye, an injury I assumed he'd obtained from the pitch.

There were further patients speckled around the waiting area, all with their own painful story to tell.

I walked up to the queue-less reception desk, the woman staffing it sporting a straight blonde bob cut and took no prisoners with her vacant bedside manner.

"Yes?" She barked.

"Good morning!" I enthusiastically chirped, counteracting her mood. "Is Dr Chang working today?" I asked.

"I'm not at liberty to disclose that information." The woman appeared as cold and impersonal as her colleague.

I reached into my pocket and pulled out my warrant card, flashing my unflattering mugshot at the woman. I know it was a slight abuse of my power, however, I was desperate. She looked up from her computer, lowered her glasses, and studied it.

"How about now?" I asked, with a slight smug look on my face.

I could feel her icy gaze peering at my casual outfit.

"Oh. You're a Detective."

"I am. I just need to speak with her about the potential Murder I'm investigating. She covered the Air Ambulance that night." That didn't feel like a lie, maybe a slight stretch of the truth; I did actually need to speak with her about the events of that night, but not in relation to Agatha's death.

"Certainly Sir," The woman perked up, seeming to miraculously discover her personality. "I'll page her."

As the woman tapped away at her terminal, I stood to one side. I prayed that this time, the dear Doctor would be a bit more amicable than our first encounter.

Yi loudly burst through the double doors from the main triage area, alerting the entire waiting room to her presence, and strutted over to the desk. She still retained the same stone-cold facial expression that I remembered from Wednesday morning, however this time she'd kitted herself out in mint green smocks, her neck decorated with a baby pink stethoscope.

The receptionist pointed her in my direction, and she approached, folding her arms tightly; already creating a hostile barrier between us.

"You wanted to see me Detective?" she sternly greeted, judging my outfit. "I take it It's dress down Friday at work." Her voice oozed with sarcasm.

"Is there anywhere we could go in private?" I whispered.

"Why?" she raised an eyebrow.

"Please," I pleaded with her. "I can't really discuss things here."

She gave me a half-hearted nod and pointed me in the direction of a nearby office. She closed the door behind her as I sat on one of the swivelling chairs, marvelling at the posters of various human anatomy. As I expected, she refused to sit, standing with her back to the door like a gate keeper.

"So, what is it you want?" she inquired, sensing a slight bit of frustration in her voice.

"Well, I don't know where to begin." A wave of dread overwhelmed me.

How the hell am I going to tell her this?

Do it, Marco.

"You may remember me from St Mary's Island a few days ago?"

"Yes." The air froze around her. "You couldn't wait to get your hands on the crime scene and ended up nearly being a victim of your own arrogance."

Taken back by her snide comment, I paused for a moment, angrily redrafting my reply in my mind over a dozen times.

"Did anyone ever tell you you're slightly rude?" I asked, rhetorically.

"I don't care to be honest. I'm not here to make friends, I'm here to do a job."

"You don't say…"

"So, are you going to sit there and exchange these wonderful pleasantries, or do you actually have something worth my time?" her disparaging remark bubbled my stomach with slight rage.

I was tempted to up and walk out; I was here, trying to save the world, and my first recruit hurled abuse at me, getting as far under my skin as she could.

I discreetly composed myself and took a deep breath and

dispelled the hate I began to feel for the dear doctor. She made me doubt my ability to deal with conflict, even with my vast amount of experience; I gave myself an inner pep talk and tried to shake of her negative aura.

"This is all going to sound very strange." I hesitated for a moment, still mentally tweaking my recruitment script. "As soon as I tell you all this, you're going to request I see a psychiatrist."

Yi harshly rolled her eyes, to the point where I thought they were going to roll into the back of her head.

"This isn't filling me with much confidence."

"No, I'm sure it isn't." She lost her thread of interest in our conversation; if words alone wouldn't sway her to my side, I would have to show her.

I reached into my pocket and pulled out the amulet, still neatly packed in the evidence bag, and held it out in my palm towards her.

"What's that?" she asked, staring at it intently; I'd succeeded in getting her attention.

"Just take it." I thrust it towards her.

Yi unfolded her arms and reluctantly took it from me, shaking the bag around and examining the contents. The amulet reacted to her touch and began to glow a brilliant white, conjuring a small gust.

The wind began to intensify, circling around the Doctor, her hair, tied up in a ponytail, loosened over the sheer power of the vortex. She looked at me, her mouth widened in shock as the draught intensified and lifted her off the ground; a mere few centimetres but enough for both of us to notice.

CUSTODIANS: THE PROPHECY

As the wind subsided, Yi gently landed back on the ground. She threw the bag at me in fear and cowered towards the door.

"What the hell was that??!" She cried out in terror, clearly disturbed by the experience.

"I can explain." I held both my hands up in a calm attempt to reassure her, tucking the magical locket in my back pocket.

"Well, I suggest you do, quickly!" she yelled.

"Look. This is going to sound insane, but I hoped this would help convince you I'm telling the truth." I cleared my throat, choosing my next words carefully. "You're a Custodian."

"A what??"

"A Custodian. A supernatural being prophesied to help save the world from a legion of evil demons."

I heard myself in my head; if roles were reversed, I would have probably reacted in the same way.

Yi scrunched her arms tightly into her chest.

"This is utterly ridiculous!" she barked; an appalled look painted her face; I didn't need to be a telepath to know she thought I needed sectioning.

"Exactly what I thought when I was first told." I tried to show some empathy towards her, recalling my reaction when Harriet informed me, I was a wizard of the elements.

"I am reporting you to your superiors. This practical joke, or whatever you may call it, has gone too far, detective." She scolded. "I have patients that need to be seen, and you are distracting me from them."

Even though I understood her reaction, I began to lose

my patience with her. It was a race against time to locate and gather the rest of the team, so I needed to get her on board quickly. It felt the appropriate time for a different approach.

"Look! What I am telling you is true!" I raised my voice slightly. "That amulet has just given you your power. You may not like it - I mean, I'm not exactly over the moon about it all - but I need you to try and accept this."

"I think now is a perfect opportunity for you to leave." She muttered, opening the door, stepping to one side, and gesturing with her hand. "You've taken up quite enough of my time."

"Doctor Chang." I tried one more time. "You need to believe me. We are all in grave danger. There are beings out there that will hunt you down and try to kill you."

I was exhausted. How else was I supposed to convince her? I couldn't get past her stubbornness.

"Inspector. I am giving you one last chance." She gritted her teeth. "Leave now, or I will have you escorted off the premises."

I admitted defeat and concluded I wasn't going to get through to her.

"Fine." I said, shaking my head. "At least let me give you this if you change your mind." I reached into my pocket and pulled out one of my business cards and a pen. I'd prepared this as a Plan B, hoping that she would eventually come round to the idea and give me a call. I wrote my personal number down on the back of it and offered it to her. She ripped it from my hand.

She stood there, her eagle eyes glaring at me to exit.
I left the hospital, having accomplished nothing.

SIX

I sluggishly drove back home, lacking any motivation, and decided to call Harriet to update her on the events at the Hospital. It surprised me when she answered, as I expected to be greeted with her voicemail.

"Good afternoon, Marco." She sang, her voice resonating through my car.

"Afternoon H."

Fond of a nickname, I'd decided to call her by her initial that she'd signed off in the letter she'd sent me. I thought it very 'James Bond', particularly with her working in the country's Secret Intelligence Service. She didn't correct me, so I assumed she'd endorsed it.

"How is your mission progressing?" She asked.

"Not very well." I sighed, disappointed with both me and the situation. "I was able to get hold of the amulet and locate Yi Chang but saying she's unreceptive is an understatement."

"Did she touch the amulet?"

"Yes."

"Then you've accomplished all you needed to. Everything else will fall into place once you've found the other two."

I was relieved that my efforts weren't in vain.

"It would help me out a lot if you could tell me who the they are?" I asked.

"Well, you're in luck."

"Oh?"

"According to my researchers, The Custodian of Water, Sarah Turner moved back to Australia twenty years ago. Her son, Brandon, moved to the UK last year and took a job as a seasonal lifeguard in Cornwall."

"Did you say Brandon?" I asked.

"Yes."

I immediately recognised the name, and my frown dispersed into a smile.

"I think I may have already met him..." I said, struggling to contain my excitement.

I remembered the young lifeguard who approached me on St Mary's. "I took his details at the scene, so he shouldn't be hard to find. What about the other?"

"Unfortunately, we have nothing on Thomas Stevens' descendants."

I stopped for a moment, trying to reproduce the experience of Wednesday morning, trying to recall anything that felt odd that day.

Grudgingly recalling my first meeting with Doctor Chang, I remembered the unusual static shock appearing when we shook hands. Aside from her lack of social skills, it was the only thing which seemed out of place.

The spark also took place with Brandon, come to think of it – surely that was no coincidence.

I recalled another person that I shared the experience with - a rather handsome, buff, firefighter, *Jack*.

Or was it, *Jamie*?

Johnson?

Jarod?

No, it was *Jayce*.

"I may have an idea," I chirped.

"Go on?"

"A firefighter called Jayce?" I told Harriet. "I know it's not much to go on, but I'm sure there's only one firefighter in the Cornwall district with that name?"

"Stand by, I'll get one of my aides to check it out." She left me hanging momentarily.

Whilst I waited for her to get back to me, I forcefully veered to avoid a fox that dashed out into my path. I was near to having a head on collision with an oncoming car, who duly responded with a long drone of their horn as I straightened into my own lane.

My heart hammered deep in my chest and my breathing laboured, as I bounced back from my near-death experience.

I took a deep breath in to calm my nerves before Harriet returned on the line.

"We've got a potential match from social media records and the Fire Service attendance log from the night in question." She advised. *"Jason Stevens. A relief firefighter for South Cornwall and the Isles of Scilly. He lives in St Ives. He's the Owner of a gym in the town,*

Kernow Fitness."

"Thanks H." I mumbled, still slightly disturbed from my fox mishap.

"Looks like we're getting somewhere. I'll send all the details through to you. Good luck Marco. Let me know if you need anything else."

I drove to the parking garage at home, relieved to see Grayson's space still empty; not that I didn't want to see him - I knew he'd interrogate me over why I was late home and why I'd been scurrying off to various places around the country.

When I entered, I made a bee line to my work bag, which lay on the floor in our office. I rummaged through it, finding my notebook hidden among folders of needless paperwork.

I placed it on my desk and swiftly flipped through pages to try to find the notes I'd drawn from the arson.

I winced and hauled back my left arm, as a sharp pain shot over the very top of my right forefinger. I glanced down to see a clean paper cut tricking with blood. I intuitively tried to soothe it with my mouth.

The pain subsided, and I watched the small injury miraculously heal itself. To me, it was the only pro of being a supernatural being, the remainder being much more of a con.

I continued my task at hand, succeeding in locating the pages I needed and skimmed through the rows of my negligible notes to eventually find Brandon's details. It was a little hard interpreting my own handwriting, but I squinted my eyes, as this seemed to help me translate it:-

CUSTODIANS: THE PROPHECY

Brandon Turner
74 Cliff Road
St Mary's Island
Isles of Scilly
Cornwall
TR21 0zX
07877-76543

I rang the number in my phone, and a young man answered.

"Brandon?" I inquired.

"Speaking. Who is this?"

"It's Detective Inspector Marco Ramirez from Cornwall Police. We met on Wednesday Morning." I started. "I don't know if you remember me?"

"Ah yes mate. I do!" He yelled, like an animated puppy.

"I wondered if you could pop over the mainland for me to ask you some questions?" Another lie. This began to evolve into an addiction.

All these years of being a Police Officer, I have never been dishonest; right now, I spouted out lies as if it were second nature to me. I despised myself for it, but I continued replaying my encounter with those evil satanic creatures, which quickly emphasised the reasons why.

"Funny you should say that buddy, I'm actually over here for a few days visiting a mate in Newquay."

I nearly leapt for joy when he'd said it, saving me the gruelling task of travelling miles across the county.

"Brilliant. Well, I don't need you to come to the station or anything. I'm more than happy to meet for a coffee. You wouldn't be free early this evening, would you?" I asked, as I looked down on my watch. It turned three-thirty in the afternoon.

"Me and my mates are going for beers in Walkabout later. I can always meet you there?"

A trip to a local boozer wasn't what I'd anticipated, but then I didn't really care where we met; the content of that meeting concerned me more.

If I got a pint out of it, then so be it!

"Sound's great. Is seven thirty any good?"

"Yeah mate. That's awesome."

"See you then."

I'd dropped Grayson a quick courtesy message informing him I was heading into town for drinks, knowing he too was out with a selection of colleagues from his firm. Thankfully, we were that type of couple who didn't need to be in each other's pockets every waking moment.

We each bragged our own group of friends, along with our mutual ones, both enjoying time by ourselves as we did together. Grayson messaged me back with his usual plethora of affection, romance not exactly being dead between us.

I'd changed into some smart jeans, a long, chequed shirt with sleeves rolled up to my elbows, and sprayed on a dash of my favourite aftershave. I walked into town, passing families out for an evening walk as part of their summer break. Newquay always buzzed with tourists during this time of the year.

Once I arrived at *Walkabout*, a large bar with views over Towan Beach, I could already hear the rumble from groups of people who'd gathered to begin their venture into the night life.

I scoped the room, spying for Brandon; even though I'd only encountered him once, his distinctive messy blonde hair and bronzed skin would set him apart from the remaining onlookers.

I heard a voice come from up behind me.

"Detective." A strong Australian accent took me by surprise.

I turned around only to discover Brandon with a full pint of beer in hand, smiling at me with his bright teeth. He seemed to have a habit of sneaking up to people from behind.

"Ah Brandon." I greeted him, taking his outstretched hand in a solid shake. "Thanks for meeting me."

"No drama's at all mate." He sipped his beer. "What did you want to speak to me about?"

"Is it okay if we go to a quiet corner?" I asked, the background noise of the bar's patrons becoming more vocal by the influx of customers.

"Sure mate." Brandon agreed, taking me to a discrete, less loud table in a remote corner. "You look like you're ready to hit the town mate!" he remarked.

"I'm not on duty." I confessed to him, sensing he was a little more open and more friendly than his previous conscript. "I just thought as you were in town, I'd have a chat with you tonight."

"Well in that case I'm getting you a beer." He grinned, diverting to the bar.

Brandon asked me for my choice of beverage, which I always chose San Miguel when it came to beer. It wasn't due to the fact that I had Spanish blood, but simply because I preferred the flavour of it over others.

Both with a drink in our hand, Brandon accompanied me back over to the table, where we made ourselves comfortable.

"So, Detective…....." He began, pausing for me to tell him my surname.

"Please, call me Marco." I said, holding my arm up.

"So, Marco. Why did you need to speak with me?"

I figured that on this occasion I would be a little more tactful, particularly after my experience with Yi. I pulled the amulet from my pocket, the evidence bag around it now somewhat worn, and placed it on the table.

"Do you recognise this?" I asked him, knowing full well he wouldn't.

"I do actually, mate."

What?

How?

I'd been so taken back by his reply that he would easily have seen the expression of shock over my face.

"You do?"

"Yeah."

"Right." I blinked in quick succession, unsure of what else to say.

This was a stark contrast from my encounter with Chang. "So, if you know about the amulet, you must know that…."

"…. I'm a Custodian. Yeah mate. I knew you'd find me at some point."

I didn't expect any of this.

"How did you know?" I asked, intrigued.

"My mum was a Custodian. She filled me in on everything from when I was a kid. She thought it would be better for me to know everything than to be kept in the dark about it all."

"I knew nothing." I divulged to him, slightly envious that he'd a lot more of a lead on this than me. "My father died when I was a child, and his death was covered up."

"Your dad's Serafino, right?"

My eyes widened.

"How did you know that?"

"Your dad and my mum knew each other well. As did all of them. She's got a book back home with pictures of all of them together."

"I guess my dad wasn't as sentimental." I sighed, churning the remaining drops of beer around in my glass.

"To be fair mate, my mum broke a lot of rules keeping her scrap book. Agatha found out about it, and they had a big fall out - which is why she went back to Australia."

This all seemed too easy. Following my run in with Hellions the previous night, I needed to be sure I could trust him.

"How can I be sure you're not a Hellion? I mean you seemed to have no idea what was going on a few days ago." I asked.

"It was all an act on St Mary's, mate. I know who Agatha

was. I knew who you were as soon as I met you, especially when you gave me that static shock."

"Did Agatha know who you were?"

"No, she didn't. I only moved there so I could keep an eye on her and the amulet. My mum knew she was getting old and frail, so I got a job as a lifeguard there - standard for us Aussie's." He laughed, the expression on his face quickly becoming subdued as he stared outside the window, which provided a view of the sea. "I should have seen that attack coming."

"Don't blame yourself." I comforted him; I myself being a victim of my own hindsight on numerous occasions.

We talked for another twenty odd minutes, trading stories of our personal lives. We instantly clicked, seeming like familiar friends who had known each other decades. He also cast in the conversation that I, being the Earth Custodian, had the responsibility of leading of the team.

No extra pressure then!

When it came the time to give Brandon his gift, he suggested we should walk down to a remote area of the beach, ensuring there was no one in sight of the magical theatrics we were about to endure. He knew he was the Water Custodian, so predicted things may get a bit wet.

Towan beach was deserted at that time of night, and the sun set in darkness, so we were both confident we were would not be overlooked.

I added a little bit of humour to the situation, getting on one knee and bowing my head as I presented Brandon with the amulet in both hands.

"I, Marco Ramirez, present to you, Brandon Turner, the power of the Water Custodian!!" I broke out of character as I fought to keep a straight face and laughed together with Brandon, who already found it all entertaining.

"Just give it here, you knob!" he chuckled, grabbing the amulet out of my palm.

I watched on as the amulet glowed once more, this time with a light blue colour; my assumption it represented the element of water. The familiar gust that I came to know, enveloped him.

There stood a distinction between himself and Yi; he was expectant of our destiny, embracing it. A small whirlpool of water started to circle around his feet, gradually rising, until his body was at the centre of a miniature waterspout. It took seconds for the water to dispel and reveal the newest Custodian.

"How do you feel?" I asked him.

"Tingly." He responded, clutching his fingers together in each hand. "Let me try something."

With that, he turned his attention to the sea and extended out his arm, closing his eyes. I looked on in astonishment as a section of the ocean began to part either side, exposing the seabed and a collection of underwater vegetation. He pulled his arm back to his side and the water gently receded back to normal.

"Amazing." I whispered. "How did you grasp that so quickly?"

"Like I said, mate. I've been preparing for this since I was a kid." He handed me back the amulet. "Who's left to go anyway?"

"Jason Stevens, a gym owner in St Ives. He was one of the firefighters there that night."

"Want me to come with you?"

"That would be great, thanks." I grinned as a slight weight lift of my shoulders. I didn't feel alone anymore. "I planned on paying him a visit tomorrow morning."

"Sounds awesome, mate." Brandon chirped. "But let's let our hair down tonight. You can hang out with me and my lifeguard buddies."

My immediate reaction was to refuse, however, I deserved to have some fun after the three days of chaos I endured. I accepted Brandon's invite, and we headed back inside the *Walkabout* pub, where he dared me to drink him under the table. Brandon's friends were extremely welcoming, albeit a bit boisterous.

As soon as the Walkabout called last orders, we drank the remainder of our pints and began to leave, somewhat inebriated. I'd offered Brandon our spare room for the night, as he explained he currently shared a room with six lodgers whilst staying in Newquay.

I told him that wasn't ideal, and it made sense if we were heading to St Ives in the morning.

We both staggered back to my apartment, very intoxicated, Brandon signing the Australian national anthem at the top of his voice, constantly requesting the inhabitants of Newquay to take part as they walked past.

I'd been able to refrain from being as disorderly.

Grayson informed me via text that he'd safely deposited himself home, so I requested for Brandon to remain silent as we creeped in. I gave guest a brief tour and laid a towel on the ready-made spare bed.

"If you need anything, help yourself." I instructed him, ever so slightly slurring my words.

"No problem bud." He said, with a strong husk.

I poured two glasses of water in the kitchen and provided him with one, then took myself to bed.

Recent days, Grayson and I were like ships passing through the night and I'd only seen him whilst asleep or in bed. Fortunately, even in my drunken state, I'd managed to sneak into the bed without causing even a stir. Once I'd got comfortable, I rolled towards him and positioned my arm around him; he subconsciously moved in closer, and I drifted off into the world of slumber.

The Saturday morning sun rose on day four of my new Custodian life. I woke up with a pounding headache, this time alcohol at fault, rather than a host of demon attacks.

Grayson was day off, so he still laid next to me, deep asleep and enjoying his well-deserved lay in. I examined the clock on my mobile - eight thirty.

I'd set an alarm clock for an hour past that, slightly frustrated my body clock had other ideas.

I forced myself up, leaping straight into the shower, eventually popping a couple of paracetamol with breakfast. Brandon roused at a similar time, meeting me in the kitchen in just his boxer shorts.

I kept my glances to myself; however, I couldn't help admiring his strong, athletic physique. My cheeks blushed slightly, hoping he hadn't noticed.

"Coffee?" I asked him, in an attempt to distract myself.

"Mate. Yes." He wearily replied, working on an itch on the blonde mop of hair on his head.

As I boiled the Coffee Maker, Grayson walked in, a bit less naked than Brandon. He fired me with a confused look, pointing and blushing in a comparable manner to me.

"Oh, sorry Gray." I apologised. "This is Brandon Turner. Brandon, this is my partner, Grayson Blackford."

"Nice to meet you, Brandon." Grayson offered out his hand, which surprisingly took him a moment to accept.

He weakly gripped Grayson's hand, assessing him with narrowed eyes.

"Yeah… You too." He said, with a distinct lack of enthusiasm.

I'd only known him for one evening, but even I could tell he subdued his bubbly and infectious personality.

I shrugged it off as a hangover.

"Brandon's a friend of Louisa's at work, he's visiting from Australia and needed a place to crash for the night as Louisa's been called away for PSU. I hope that's okay." PSU or 'Police Support Unit,' was a phrase for 'Riot trained Police.'

In truth, Louisa was in attendance her obligatory two-day annual refresher training sessions. I wasn't due mine for another six months, which I was thankful of with my current situation.

"No bother for me." Grayson smiled, pouring himself a mug of coffee. "Remember we've got lunch with my boss today, Marc."

Damn it!
That's right!

How could I forget?!

Sweat began to form on my brow as my body filled with panic.

"Shit!" I exclaimed. "I'd totally forgot about that! I've offered to drop Brandon off in St Ives today."

Grayson looked angry, pursing his lips, a vein on his temple starting to protrude. He didn't shout at me, knowing we had company.

A single word exited his mouth.

"Fine."

I was in deep trouble.

I guiltily planned ways in which I could make it up to him. He'd been looking forward to this lunch for some time, due to it being a steppingstone to a significant promotion to partner.

He was always supportive of my professional career, and I'd failed him.

There are bigger issues though.

"Why don't we move it to dinner instead?" I proposed, sensing absolute fury from Grayson. "I'll easily be back for then."

"Okay." He muttered, refusing to meet my eyes.

Another one worded answer.

I was in the doghouse with certainty.

Avoiding any more conflict, I diverted my focus to Brandon, hunting for a spare toothbrush for him to freshen up.

Luckily, he didn't take long to get ready so, I could swiftly escape from the tension that formed between myself and my partner.

As we leaped into my car, Brandon turned to me, a look of unease on his face.

"How long have you been together?" he asked.

I met his gaze as I started the engine. "Fifteen years. Why do you ask?"

"Nothing." He stared out of the window, into the empty car park, clearly holding something from me. "Don't worry, It's fine."

"You don't seem so sure. What is it?"

"Honestly, It's nothing." He turned back to me and shot the single biggest fake smile I'd ever seen. "Let's go and get this fire guy!"

SEVEN

I'd only been to St Ives a handful times since we'd relocated to Cornwall, yet it was one of my most favourite towns within the south-west of the county. Built on a large hill, the streets and the pathways were steep, however, the scenic landscape made up for the high altitude.

I parked at the main car park at the top of the town, which required a lengthy stroll down adverse slopes and steps into the main town centre.

Brandon navigated us using his phone, yet somehow managing to take several incorrect turnings; acknowledging he struggled with his sense of direction – something else we had in common.

We'd finally escaped the labyrinth of alleys and found the place for which we were searching. I looked up at the neon blue sign made out in the letters of *'Kernow Fitness'*.

It was a charming little gym, previously home to an Indian restaurant in a prime location of the town centre. As we both walked in, we were amazed at the sleek and contemporary interior and ultramodern fitness equipment, a contrast with how it looked from the outside. I spotted Jayce within seconds, towering above everyone, me included – and I stood at a looming six foot two.

He wore a white polo top, dark sports shorts, and a pair of vibrant coloured trainers. The right breast of his polo shirt featured the gym's logo, and he carried a clipboard, feverishly circling around various exercising members.

He returned to the reception area, where me and Brandon were stood, tentatively waiting. His receptionist, a young woman wearing what appeared to be sprayed on leggings, chattered rapidly on the telephone. He fired us a smile, exposing perfectly lined up teeth which I must admit, did make me go slightly weak in the knees.

"Morning Gents." He said in his heavy accent. "How can I help?"

"Morning." I began. "I don't know if you remember me. My names Marco and I was one of the Police Officers at the fire you went to a couple of days ago?"

He eyed me a crossed brow.

"Vaguely. I'm rubbish with faces, so you'll have to forgive me."

"Don't worry. I'm not here to interview you. We were actually looking to join a gym and your fire boss, Dave, recommended yours." I said, thinking quickly on my feet again.

"Ah, that bloke. Always looking out for me." He smiled. "Unfortunately, we're not taking on any new members at the minute. We're at capacity. The best I can do is to put you on the waiting list?"

"Yeah, sure." I said, looking over his shoulder and noticing one of the members, who'd been using a treadmill, looking at me intently. I gazed back at her.

"If you fill in this form, I'm hoping to extend the membership next month. We've not long been open and with this being the only gym in town, I'm a bit inundated at the minute."

I smiled at Jayce and took the form that he supplied me. Not even vaguely interested in joining, I skimmed the details and grabbed a pen from the desk.

The woman in the main gym area still stared at me.

I looked up at her again. She'd been standing, like a statue, no longer running, unnervingly glaring at me.

What is she looking at?

"Marco." Brandon whispered. "I don't have a good feeling about her." He motioned discreetly across towards the same woman, noticing she was paying us both a lot of attention.

"Me either." I muttered back, continuing to fill in the form, whilst keeping a close eye on our stalker. "Who's that woman?" I asked Jayce, casually.

"That's the Assistant Manager, Jo. She helps run the place when I'm off fighting fires. I don't know what I'd do without her." He smiled.

"I see."

We handed back our forms and stood, watching whilst he briefly looked through them.

"Newquay?" Jayce looked at me confused. "I'm sure there are closer gyms than here?"

"It's close to where I work." I bluffed.

"Cool." He shot me those pearly whites once again. "Would you like a tour of the place anyway?" he asked.

"Yeah, why not." I grinned; it would get us away from that weirdo of a woman.

"Follow me then gents."

Jayce led us around the main equipment area, showing us all the different modes of the exercise machines and the broad range of dumbbells, we would be able to use if we joined. I wasn't really paying attention as the Assistant Manager continued to stare at me and Brandon, her eyes tracking us as we walked the perimeter.

He then took us in the empty men's changing area, providing us with a well-rehearsed speech about the prices, facilities and which package deals he was able to offer - even throwing in an Emergency Services discount. He stopped mid-sentence as Jo broke through the doors and stood, staring at us again.

"Jo?" Jayce seemed baffled. "Are you okay?"

She didn't respond to him. Instead, she opened her mouth and expelled a large screech which punctured our ears. I instantly recalled that shriek from days before.

Jo began having metamorphosis, growing two times her size in height and body, her clothes tearing as her muscles burst through the seams. Her complexion turned an ash white and her long, dark hair in a ponytail became thick and wiry.

She was a *Hellion*.

"Jayce, get down!" I yelled as she launched towards us. I instinctively held out my hand and a variety of vines materialised from underneath the floor tiles, constricting around her waist, in time for her long talons to miss Jayce's chest.

"What the fuck is going on?!" Jayce shouted, understandably terrified.

"Mate, come with us!" Brandon commanded, as he rushed to the exit. Jayce and I followed suit, and we raced outside into the street, creating as much distance between ourselves and demon Jo. We continued to sprint, dodging various tourists who looked aghast as we weaved in and out of them. I looked round and could see Jo appear from the front of the gym, back in her human shape as she started to chase after us.

We'd managed to form enough space to take refuge in an alleyway, where we all needed a moment to catch our breath.

"Will one of you tell me what the hell is happening?!" Jayce demanded.

"There's no time," I snapped, pulling the amulet bag out of my pocket. "Take this."

I presented Jayce with the package, and he accepted it without questioning me. His hand touched the bag, the jewel in the centre turned a fierce red. The expected breeze appeared, this time materialising into a vortex of ember, which surrounded him.

Jayce tried escaping, but got caught in the whirlwind of flames, which danced gently around him. As the fire subsided, it dissipated with a great blast of energy that ripped through the surroundings, astonishingly not causing any harm.

As the wave hit me, a sudden surge of power flowed through my body, stimulating my energy. I turned my attention on Jayce who looked completely perplexed.

"I know you're totally confused by all this, but you need to listen to me." I took hold of his arms and peered directly into his eyes, attempting to stop him from flailing around like a car dealership inflatable. "Jo isn't Jo. She's a demon. She's trying to kill us."

"This is insane." Jayce shook his head and laid his hands across his face.

"I know mate." Brandon chirped up. "This is insane, but that doesn't make it any less real. You've got a power now too, mate. You'll need to use it."

"What?"

"That amulet I gave you. It's given you a power. Kind of like magic I suppose." I explained.

"There's no such thing as magic!" Jayce scolded.

"I thought that too only a few days ago." I said, softly. "But it's true. You have to believe me. The fate of the world depends on it."

I could tell this began to be too much for him.

"What 'power' have I got?" He asked, the look on his face matched Yi's when I informed her of her new destiny – he thought I was mad.

"You can control fire." Brandon interluded.

"Fire?" He began to intricately examine his palm.

"Over there." I pointed over towards a pile of discarded cardboard about six foot away from us. "Hold your hand out and think of setting that alight."

"This is absolute dog shit." Jayce protested.

"Please, try it. If it doesn't work, then you can walk away, and we'll never bother you again." I pleaded.

"I can't believe I'm even considering doing this." He mumbled to himself.

He extended his palm at arm's length, towards the heap of rubbish and taut his brow. It took a minute or so, but the pile began to set off a cloud of smoke, prior to erupting in a small display of flames.

"This has got to be a trick." He said, his eyes widened.

"It's no trick." Brandon interjected, before materialising a stream of water from his hand which instantly extinguished the blaze.

"How did you do that!" Jayce leapt back a step.

"That's my power mate. I can control water."

"I must be in a dream."

"I wish it were." I said, sympathetically. "Now do you believe us?"

"I don't know what to believe."

I peered from behind the wall and looked back over from where we'd run, witnessing Jo closing in on us, pushing innocent members of public out of her way when they crossed her path.

"She's coming!" I yelled to the others. "We need to try and divert her away from all these people."

"Let's get her to the beach." Brandon suggested.

"Great thinking. We need to make a run for it."

All three of us ran into the main street, where Jo spotted us instantly. She brought up her pace and started pursuing us again. Brandon led the pace, being a better sprinter than me, snaking past the harbour and down on the main beach.

It was busy, especially being peak holiday season, nonetheless, I noticed a small bay tucked in the corner, with scarcely anyone nearby - the ideal place to battle with a demon.

When we got to it, we all turned and faced Jo. She converted back to her creature form and then let out a further unworldly scream, before attempting to strike us with her claws.

Brandon stuck his arm out at her and covered her in a bubble of water. This time however his power appeared significantly stronger, as Jo struggled to flee her ocean tomb. Harriet did say we'd be stronger together.

Demon Jo eventually freed herself from Brandon's creation and ran over to Jayce.

"Please Jo! What are you doing?" He begged her, holding his hands up.

"She's not who you think she is!" I yelled at him. "She'll try to kill you!"

As she pulled closer to him, her screeching intensified, all of us covering our ears, struggling to withstand it.

"Jo!" Jayce screeched at her.

I'd no idea of their relationship, but he seemed to care about her a great deal. I assumed she was his partner.

"Jayce!" I yelled, the sonic screaming still cutting through me like a knife. "Use your powers!" I bade him.

"No!" He shook his head. "I won't do anything to hurt my sister!"

His sister!

Shit!

Thinking about it, she did have similar facial features to

him, when she wasn't an evil demonic assassin.

Was she always a Hellion?

Have they killed his sister?

I could only begin to imagine the way he felt; I don't know what I would have done if that demon masqueraded as my sister, or even – God forbid - Grayson.

I drew my hands off my ears and took the brunt of Jo's shrieking. I threw my palms out in the direction of her, and a bunch of tree branches magically manifested from the sand and wrapped her arms and legs in a shrubbery constraint, which immediately stopped her screaming.

"Jayce, you have to use your power!" I cried, continuing to hold Jo's trap with my hands still drawn.

I looked over to him and tears ran down his cheeks.

"I can't." He murmured. "I just can't."

"Jayce listen to me mate." Brandon knelt next to him. Jayce crouched with his head in his hands, finding it difficult to understand what was happening. He looked at him and wiped tears away from his eyes. "Look! That is *not* your sister! That is a *demon*! Marco needs your help! We *both* do!"

"Hurry!" I gasped as I sensed Jo push against my strength, and I fought to keep a hold. "She's breaking free!"

Jayce tentatively got up on his legs and gradually raised both of his palms, directing them towards Jo, in her cocoon of magical branches.

"What do I do?" He asked quietly, an errant tear running off his lip and onto the sand.

"Just shut your eyes and think of fire." Brandon instructed. "Imagine it lighting up the branches."

Jayce obliged and loosely shut his eyes, whilst extending

his arms outstretched. It took several moments, but the branches I created began to release a scorching glow, strengthening by the second. As the blaze grew stronger, it overwhelmed Jo, causing her to scream in horrific agony - upsetting Jayce even more.

Her skin turned charcoal, and began to turn to ash, her remains slowly accumulating as a pile of soot on the beach.

As soon as she'd gone, Jayce fell to his knees and broke into tears.

"What have I done?" He muffled, hardly able to hear him through his clasped hands.

"You did what you had to do." I consoled him, lightly placing my hand on his shoulder.

"What, kill my own sister?" He looked at me, his eyes puffy. He quickly went from sorrow to anger. "You've turned me into a freak!" He yelled, standing up and storming off.

"Wait! Jayce!" Brandon ran ahead of him and prevented him from walking off. "I know this is all weird, but you're not a freak. We're all part of some prophecy."

"Believe it or not, we've been chosen to help rid the world of evil demons." I interjected. "I'm pretty sure that was one of them posing as your sister."

"Well, if she was an imposter, where is the real Jo?" He asked.

"I couldn't tell you." I cowered my head. "I don't really know much about them."

"How am I supposed to trust you?" Jayce's top lip quivered. "How do I know you're not the evil ones?"

"Sorry mate, did you see bloody She Hulk?!" Brandon

exclaimed, sarcastically.

"Brandon!" I glared at him.

"Sorry."

"Look," I spoke in my soothing tone of voice, one that I usually reserved for work, when I needed to show a bit of care and compassion. "I know you're scared. I know this is a lot to take in, but it's all real Jayce.

"And we need you." Brandon added.

"So what, I'm supposed to just accept this!? My sister is fucking dead!"

I placed my hand at Jayce's back as he broke into tears, sharply pulling away from me. I found it difficult to know what else to say.

"I promise you; we will find out what happened to her." I assured him. "That wasn't your sister. She may still be out there somewhere."

His eyes wandered between both me and Brandon, his expression contemplative.

"Fine." Jayce muttered, wiping away another stray tear.

"Once we get the other on board and seeing sense, I'll take you to meet Harriet." I suggested. "She's the one who's been guiding me through the last week."

"Who's the other Custodian?" Brandon asked.

"A doctor called Yi Chang." I answered. "She was there that night at St Mary's with us. I went to see her yesterday. Let's just say things didn't go well."

"Yi? I know her." Jayce sniffed.

"You do?" I asked.

"We've been to jobs together when she covers the Air Ambulance."

"Do you think you might be able to sway her?" I asked, hopeful.

"She's stubborn."

"You don't say!" I tittered.

We arrived back at Jayce's gym after a semi-leisurely walk. I could tell he was still dubious of the whole 'Custodian's' situation, but he did well, considering.

He made us all a coffee, whilst we made ourselves comfortable in his office. I'd filled him in on my experiences over the week and how this all came to be, including my trip to MI6 and my peculiar introduction to Harriet. He was taking it in far better as time passed.

"Sorry gents." Jayce began. "I'm trying to get my head around it all. I mean, that version of my sister. I wouldn't have known any different. It was only this morning we were talking about our childhood holidays up in Scotland."

"We'll probably get more answers from Harriet." I assured him. "Our main focus now is Yi and getting her to remove the stick from her ass and get on board."

I managed to get a slight laugh out of Jayce.

"She'll be a tough one." He said, taking a sip of his coffee. "She's always been a bit of an Ice Queen."

"That's an understatement!" I exclaimed. "I don't think I've met anyone quite like her."

"Once you get under that frosty exterior, she's not too bad." Jayce tried to assure me. I wasn't convinced.

I sent Harriet a message to update her on my successful recruitment of Brandon and Jayce. Not long after, she started to video call.

I accepted and she appeared on my screen, as I placed my phone on Jayce's desk, so we were all in view.

"This is Harriet." I introduced her. "She's who I've been telling you both about."

"Gentlemen." She acknowledged us with a gentle nod. *"Anything to report?"* she asked, getting straight to business.

"Not only are Hellions posing as humans, but they're also posing as people we know."

"What?" Even from a seven-inch screen, I witnessed Harriet's expression sink.

I glanced at Jayce - his head held in his hands. I was conscious I needed to be sensitive.

"Jayce's sister. She was a Hellion."

"Sorry?" her tone worried. *"His sister?"*

"I didn't know any different." Jayce cut in. "It wasn't until she turned into that creature…."

His eyes surged and I placed a gentle touch on his broad shoulder.

"This gravely concerns me." Harriet rested her hand on her chin. *"If they knew where to infiltrate operatives, this means they know more than we think."*

"This is worse than we thought" I commented.

"Very much so." she agreed.

"What do we do now?"

"Return home, stay out of sight. We need to wait until Ms Chang is ready to come on board. I will contact you all when it's time."

The restaurant where Grayson selected for the meal with his boss was beautiful - Lewennick Lodge, close to our apartment and buried in the far side of Fistral Cliffs.

I'd managed to get home with hardly any hiccups - dropping Brandon off at one of his friends on the outskirts of Newquay.

Racing into the flat, I rushed into the bedroom and changed into my favourite shirt, before slapping on a smidgen of expensive aftershave.

It took me around five minutes to make my way to the restaurant, as Grayson left before me; something we would argue about later.

When I entered, I immediately spotted him in his tight-fitting tweed suit, which I adored on him. His mousey blonde hair was styled perfectly, and he wore his stylish top brand glasses. I fell in love with him all over again.

As I neared the table, I stopped short, looking over at his boss; a slim, dark-haired woman in her late fifties, although appeared more in her forties.

"I'm sorry I'm late." I said, planting a small kiss on Grayson's cheek.

"Ah hello, you!" He greeted me with an enthusiastic smile. I wasn't sure if it was for display or genuine. "Clara, this is Marc. My fiancée."

"A pleasure to finally meet you." I manoeuvred to her and pecked her cheek.

"Likewise." She smiled. "Grayson has told me so much about you."

"Oh dear." I winced, jokingly, as I made myself at home on the spare seat between them. "Nothing too embarrassing I hope."

"I've saved those stories for later." Grayson winked.

The evening presented a hit. The meal utterly delicious, the red wine flowed, and the conversation didn't stop. I played the part of the perfect 'trophy husband,' laughing at all Clara's jokes on cue and only divulging tales of Grayson's better moments.

He was bound to get the promotion to partner.

When the night finally concluded, we helped a very tipsy Clara into a taxi before we walked home.

"Sorry I let you down today." I said, bashfully.

"It's okay. You more than made up for it this evening." He took hold of my hand and pulled me in front of him. "I love you."

"I love you too."

He embraced me, and we kissed, the light of the moonlight reflecting in the ripples of the ocean waves.

We were rudely interrupted by my pocket vibrating. I looked down at my smartwatch, which tickled my wrist in unison. A number I didn't recognise.

"Who is it at this time of night?" Grayson asked. "You're not on call."

"No idea."

I answered it anyway.

"Hello?"

"Inspector." A familiar stern voice echoed from the other end. *"It's Yi Chang. We need to talk."*

"I'm listening." I replied, walking out of Grayson's earshot.

"I believe you."

EIGHT

Sunday morning, I'd been called into work by Carole. I'd abandoned Grayson at home in bed, suffering from the effects of the red wine we'd consumed, at *Lewennick Lodge*. I experienced a slight ropiness, but still legal to drive.

After Yi's surprising phone call, I was pleased to see things were all beginning to click into place. We were able to begin our mission to free the world of these menaces and hopefully go back to living a normal life.

It wasn't particularly enjoyable having to lie to my friends and family, and even less so using my newfound powers to cause serious harm. I know it was towards malevolent beings from another realm, but it still went against everything in my nature as an officer, where I'd sworn an oath to protect.

I quickly shook off any doubts, as I knew it was all for the good of mankind.

Our conversation the evening before, continued for

about forty-five minutes, much to the annoyance of Grayson.

Yi had much to tell me. The morning after our disagreeable encounter, she'd woken up, levitating three foot off of her bed. She still remained quite sceptic, until inadvertently manifesting a tornado within her hospital, wreaking havoc to visitors and patients alike.

Fortunately, no one was harmed.

I'd arranged to meet her at some point in the week to speak with her face to face, unless we were summoned to MI6.

When I eventually hauled myself into work, I parked in my designated space, my name proudly embossed on a golden plaque. I swiped my access card to enter the building and made my way to the investigations floor.

Carole sat in her office, tapping away one fingered at her computer, her lavish nails impairing her speed. The central office was desolate of staff, a weekend shift always being resourced by a handful of detectives.

My boss had been very coy on the phone when she'd called. I knocked at her door, and she looked up at me with a stern look, her usual infectious smile absent.

"Come in." she commanded, gesturing me inside.

"Morning boss." I discreetly suppressed yawn from behind my palm.

"Mornin.' I know it's a Sunday, but I needed to get you in. After what I've found out, it's very serious." She manoeuvred from behind her desk and offered me a seat before closing the door shut. I was suspicious of the lack of her vivaciousness. "This can't leave this room."

"What's happened?" My stomach sank. *Had she found out about my encounter with Thames District Police?*

Carole leaned on the edge of her desk, towering above me as I sat nervously in front of her with my arms folded.

"I couldn't tell you this over the phone, due to how sensitive this is."

My palms started sweating and my leg became restless with angst, her stare slicing through me.

"It was a shock to me when I first heard about this." She continued, every word causing my heart to thump harder.

"Heard about what?" I quivered.

"The terrorists."

"Terrorists?" I asked, slightly confused. *Did she mean the Hellions?*

"I've got the London Met's Counter Terrorism team here, telling me they're linking the St Mary's murder to a terrorist cell."

My whole body untensed with relief.

"I thought you were going to give me a bollocking for something!" I sighed.

"Why would I give you a bollocking?" Carole raised her eyebrow. "Have you done something for me to give you one?"

"No, not at all." I shook my head. "It's just you were giving me that vibe."

Carole lowered her head and looked at the floor for a few seconds, before heading back around to her ergonomic chair.

"Sorry babe." She rubbed her eyes. I sensed she was

under a lot of pressure. "Since they declared this a terrorist incident the Chief has been on at me every five minutes. He wants to know why we missed this."

"Missed this?" I rolled my eyes in disbelief. Unfortunately, it wasn't uncommon for the executive officers to make unjustified demands. "How could we miss it when we didn't know what we were looking for?"

"Exactly what I told him, but you know what he's like."

"I do." I agreed. "So, what do you need me for?"

"They want to do a warrant on a potential suspect's address." Carole went on to explain. "I need you to sort out a team and go and assist."

"How did they find out about this being a terrorist cell anyway?" I asked.

"From a DNA hit from the crime scene, believe it or not."

"How have they managed that? I thought the water from fire would have wiped out any forensics."

"Your guess is as good as mine."

"How long have I got until they want to hit this address?" I looked down at my watch. It was already half past nine and warrants would usually be conducted at a more unsociable hour, to give the element of surprise.

"About an hour? They've set up in the briefing room darlin' so feel free to go and consult with them."

"Thanks boss." I smiled.

"Best of luck Marc, if you need anything give me a shout."

I walked over to the conference room, situated off an

adjacent corridor to our office. As I peered through the slither of unfrosted glass, I saw a group of plain clothed officers all dressed in individual black 'Northface' jackets, which was the unofficial uniform for specialist teams.

I pressed my face against the window, gestured to enter by one of the officers sat closest to the door.

"Afternoon." I greeted as I walked in. "My name's Marco, I'm one of the Detective Inspectors for Major Investigations. I believe you need help with a warrant?"

"Ah, hello sir." The man smiled, in his thick Welsh accent. "I'm Gruffydd Evans, one of the DS's in the London Met Counter Terrorism Team. These are my colleagues, DC Rushinda Kaur and DC Jenny Matthews."

Gruffydd purposely approached me and shook my hand firmly. Both Rushinda and Jenny followed suit, albeit their handshakes a little less forceful.

"Nice to meet you all." I grinned. "Please don't call me sir by the way. Marco is fine."

I took a seat on one of the empty chairs which encircled the large oval shaped conference table, away from their plethora of laptops and documents.

"If you could fill me in, that would be great. I'm one of the Senior Investigating Officers for the Lockwood Murder. I understand you think there is a potential terrorism link to this?"

"That's right." Gruffydd nodded. "There was a tiny strand of DNA located at the scene, which flagged up with us when it was run through the Police National Computer."

Gruffydd tapped a compilation of commands on his laptop and the still image of an unkempt, middle-aged man appeared on the projector screen at the far end of the room.

"This is Jeffery Hutchins." Rushinda interposed from her seat, splitting her attention between me and the screen. "He's the leader of 'Category-Z' which is an anti-establishment and anti-government group. They're very well-funded and have been responsible for several terror attacks over the last ten years."

"Hutchins is believed to be living in Crantock, under an alias of 'Michael McCrory." Gruffydd continued.

He brought up a street-map view of the address where he was believed to be residing. It was a normal, semi-detached house in a charming, suburban area.

"Hutchins' DNA was located at the scene on St Mary's, close to Ms Lockwood's remains." Jenny enlightened me. The three of them clearly worked together for a significant amount of time, as they contrasted one another perfectly.

"We still don't know the connection between your victim and Hutchins, but it's clear from reading the fire officer reports that your arson wasn't suspicious." Gruffydd said.

With most of my attention diverted on my mission to save the world, I'd slacked on my professional duties – I'd not even a chance to read the fire reports, relying solely on Louisa to bring me up to speed with anything significant. She left me a number of voicemails over the prior days, but I barely had any time to breathe, let alone listen to them.

I'd no choice but to pretend I knew what Gruffydd was talking about.

"Yes, I wondered about the connection myself." I bobbed my head in pretend agreement.

"Have you any questions, gov?" Rashinda asked.

"Are we considering armed response if this is a terrorist cell?" I challenged. I understood that these were the experts, however, my skills as a trained tactical firearms commander, provided me with another angle to look at.

"Apart from on St Mary's, there's nothing to suggest that he's directly involved in the other attacks himself." Gruffydd explained. "We need a Police Support Unit and Taser officers to assist."

"Well luck be have it that I'm both of those." I smirked. It wasn't often that I had the chance to flex my specialist policing skills, but when the opportunity arose, I jumped at the chance. "Any further intelligence that points to any threats?"

"Nothing. We've had the house under surveillance for the preceding three days. We're not expecting anyone to be in there, but you can never be too sure." Rushinda replied.

"Fine. If we meet in an hour, will that suit all of you?"

"That sounds perfect, sir. We'll see you in a bit." Gruffydd concurred.

I winced at that horrendous title.

"Marco, please."

I needed to beg, borrow, and steal from Response and Neighbourhoods to gather the specially trained officers I required. The Duty Inspector, Nadine Tanwell, a close work ally, agreed to relinquish the officers to my command.

I'd kitted up in my riot gear, which at this time of year, was hell to wear; not to mention that the plastic guards that covered my limbs always dug into my skin and the balaclava sent my head into an itching frenzy.

I'd managed to obtain of one of the remaining tasers; a bright yellow energy device that incapacitated people with a jolt of several thousand volts. I'd never discharged it; however, I was pleased to have it as an addition to keeping me safe during the rare occasion that I left the station in uniform.

I'd requested all the officers to attend the conference room, so the Counter Terrorism officers would be able to deliver a briefing, and I could divulge my plan of action for our arrival at the address, and sternly remind them to keep this operation confidential.

Upon leaving the briefing room, we all formed an orderly line in the car park, splitting into several teams to go in convoy to the address in question. I sat in the lead van, being the most senior officer of the operation. It took us about ten minutes to reach our destination, stopping yards before the street where Jeffrey's house was situated.

The London officers gave a signal over the radio, and my team rapidly alighted the vans, gathering in single file along the pavement, impressing me with their discipline.

One of the officers on my serial carried a large red metal cylinder, with a handle on top, affectionately known as 'The big red key'. He stood first in line. I held my hand up and gave the signal for the unit to move forward. The visor on my riot helmet materialised a vision impairing mist, which made things a bit more difficult.

I could only just see up the street, guiding my team, weaving through the members of public going about their daily business. As my visor cleared, I noticed the curtaintwitchers peering at our snake of officers, as we encroached on number Forty-Two Elm Road.

Two of my team automatically ventured to the rear of the house, before I directed the officer with the red key to break down the door, with another of his colleagues reinforcing it. It only took three bludgeons of the door, and we were in.

Officers yelled as they ran in one by one, notifying any occupants of their presence. I went in last.

I instantly picked up a pervasive smell of mildew - even through my visor. The kitchen was modern, yet unsanitary, with mouldy plates of food scattered across the worktops. The living room area occupied a sofa with décor that placed it in the seventies and rust covered springs protruded through the cloth. The drawn curtains helped fester the musty aroma.

Someone'd been here, albeit not for a while.

Nothing really jumped out at me as I continued to inspect the house. There were no mass explosives or toxic chemicals. I wasn't concerned at all; until I heard a voice directing me upstairs.

"Boss. You need to see this." It was Gruffydd, with an uneased infliction in his tone.

I climbed upstairs and tracked his echo into one of the rear bedrooms. The curtains were tightly drawn and fixed into place with an extensive amount of duct tape. The room was dank and dingy with no natural light. I pulled out my torch to investigate the walls, the house being barren of any electrics.

The entirety of the unit would have surely heard me

gasp, when I came across a startling black and white photograph of me, shot from a distance, pinned up on the wall. It presented amongst hundreds more, some with fierce red crosses and others linked together with pieces of string.

I followed the path of the chord from my image which lead up to a still image of an old woman, with long wiry hair, sporting the Custodian pendant on her neck. It too had a large red cross penned over the top of it.

Agatha.

I traced several links of string…

Brandon.

Jayce.

Yi.

What the fuck?

My already elevated anxiety levels increased; my chest pounded so hard, the blood rushed to my brain, as I fought to keep myself upright.

I focused upon all mugshots of my supernatural team to help me concentrate, and noticed they were also blissfully unaware they'd been 'papped'.

Jeffrey Hutchins was sure to be a Hellion; It would have been negligent of me to not place him as a prime suspect in Agatha's death.

It seems that the demonic regime knew about us this entire time.

"Is that a picture of you, boss?" Gruffydd asked, his brow arched in confusion.

"Looks like it." I muttered, trying to act as surprised.

"Why is it here?"

"I have no idea." An obvious lie, but I played along with

the charade, investigating the remainder of the portraits.

No. It can't be.

A remarkable familiar face jumped out at me, directly underneath mine.

How did I not notice it until now?

Grayson.

My heart instantly shattered.

Why was he there?

My mind warped into overdrive. If they did anything to Grayson, then I would gladly seek out every single one of these arseholes out and elicit my own revenge.

I continued to peruse through the hive of images, creating an exhibit of conspiracy theories in my psyche. I needed to stop, but I couldn't.

Jo, Jayce's sister had a place on the display, placed underneath her handsome brother, circled in a vibrant green scribble.

I didn't draw any conclusions on the symbols or colourings, leaving the task down to Harriet's research team.

I studied the wall, silently for another five minutes or so.

The chilling photo of Grayson remained engrained in my brain, my eyes overwhelmed with a mixture of unease and fury as a tiny teardrop trailed down my cheek.

The adjacent wall housed a more political theme, with world leaders linked to their national flag. A handful were struck out with the fatal cross.

The United Kingdom flag stood out proud, our Prime Minister, Gail Holton MP, circled in green. Harriet reported directly to her, so she'd need to know that her ultimate boss had been compromised.

Gruffydd and his team left the room, as I pulled off my padded riot glove, and fumbled my phone from my pocket. I attempted to snap a discreet picture of the collections, but my flash had other ideas. Luckily, I remained inconspicuous, grabbing a selection, and forwarded them to Harriet, accompanied by a brief message;

> **Me +447877892365   11.21**
> H. I'm at a warrant in Crantock. 42 Elm Road. Address of Jeffery Hutchins, who I think was a Hellion. Saw these. Concerning to say the least.

My phone returned to its snug home in my pocket before I ventured back downstairs. Hutchin's home had been cleared and secured, my presence no longer being required.

"Can I leave this all with you?" I asked Gruffydd.

"Of course, boss." He shot back at me with a thumbs up.

"They're a great bunch of officers. I take it you'll want a full search team put together?"

"That would be great, thank you."

"I'll head back to the nick and get it sorted."

I couldn't leave without preparing some sort of rationale as to why I appeared on a terrorist suspect's bedroom wall. Harriet would surely help clear me from any Counter Terrorism investigation, after all, time was not the essence.

"I'll look into that picture of me. I reckon it's because

I'm the SIO." I said.

"How would he have known you're the SIO?" Gruffydd abruptly questioned me. "It just strikes me as very strange. You have to see it from my point of view."

I was a detective. I knew exactly the tactic that Gruffydd attempted to pull. I saw him eyeing me as a piece of meat on his investigation dinner plate, contemplating how I was linked to all this.

"Detective Sergeant Evans." My authoritative, Inspector tone released. "I know exactly what you're thinking. Feel free to question me about this, but through the right channels. Issue the correct Regulation 15 paperwork and allow me to contact my Federation Rep. Is that perfectly clear?"

Gruffydd reminded me of a petulant child who'd been scolded. I was discreetly proud of myself for standing up to him.

"Yes sir. I understand. I apologise."

"Well. If there's nothing else, I'll head back to the station." I scorned.

"No sir. Thank you." Gruffydd nodded diffidently, as I walked away.

I changed back into more comfortable attire upon my return and sprinted up the labyrinth of stairs to the investigations floor.

Carole remained buried in her computer, her extravagant nails catching the keys as she typed. I gently tapped with my knuckle on her office door.

"Have you got a minute?" I asked.

"Oh darlin! How did it go?" She looked up at me, her contagious grin returning in all its glory.

"It went well. No one inside, no hazards. Everyone kept safe."

"That's good to hear."

"Yeah." I was slightly distant, still overwhelmed by what I'd seen. "There were couple of worrying pictures on the wall though."

"Oh?" She clasped her hands together, resting her chin.

"Yeah. There was one of me, linked to the Victim. Then there was one of Grayson."

"What?!" She shrieked.

"I know.. He must know of my connection to the St Mary's case somehow."

"We need to get an alarm put in your house ASAP."

Carole, in a frantic state, picked up her desk phone and barked at the Duty Superintendent. The conversation was extremely heated, and I covered my eyes in embarrassment.

"Done. It'll be installed later on tonight." She smiled with accomplishment.

"You really didn't need to do that boss."

Carole glared at me with one eyebrow arched and her lips pursed.

"Whatever!" She scoffed. "I also want you escorted to and from work by Armed Response."

"Carole!" I protested. "Don't be so ridiculous! I'll be absolutely fine. I'll take the alarm and make sure I change my routes home."

I appreciated she was only being protective of me, but it wasn't in her pay grade to authorise such an extravagant and resource intensive contingent.

A sequence of vibrations stemming from my smart watch interrupted us.

Harriet was calling me.

I excused myself and meandered over to my office, closing the door firmly behind.

"Hi H." I whispered. Being aware the walls to my office were paper thin, and often lacked privacy.

"Afternoon Marco."

"I take it you've seen the photos?" I asked.

"Yes, I did. I've forwarded them to my intelligence officers to see what they can dig up."

"Good." I paced around the room. "The biggest thing that concerns me is..."

"Grayson?"

"Yes, of course it concerns me." I said. "But the even bigger worry is it looks to me that the Government has been infiltrated."

"What makes you think that?"

I referred her to the markings on a selection of the images, and divulged my theory behind the symbols, inferring that the green circles were potentially converted demons.

"I wouldn't place all your bets on that until we know more, but it's something to consider."

"I hope they haven't infiltrated MI6." I commented, half joking.

"It could be a possibility. However, I would sense if any of my team had been compromised. One thing I'm certain the Hellions haven't mastered, is a way to hide themselves from us telepaths."

"I think we need to get a plan together and meet at MI6."

"I agree."

"Tomorrow?"

"Yes. I'll send transport for you all at 8am."

"I'll get the rest of the team to meet me at my apartment."

"I shall make the arrangements. Take care Marco, and please stay safe."

"See you tomorrow H."

The call ended, and I created a messaging group between the four of us Custodians, naming it 'Myst' to try and keep it covert from prying eyes.

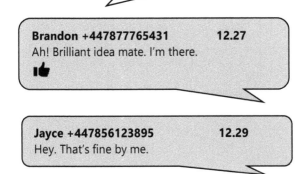

Me +447877892365   12.26
Hey. Thought I'd set this up so we can keep in touch. Spoken with Harriet. We've got a meeting with her at MI6 tomorrow. Be ready for 8am at mine as we're getting picked up. Marco.

Brandon +447877765431   12.27
Ah! Brilliant idea mate. I'm there.
👍

Jayce +447856123895   12.29
Hey. That's fine by me.

Yi +447862516455   12.29
I'm working tomorrow.

Me +447877892365   12.34
Take leave or phone in sick then. It's not as if the fate of the world is at stake Yi.....

Brandon +447877765431   12.36

Yi +447862516455   12.36
Fine. But inform her I shall be claiming for compensation for loss of earnings.

Me +447877892365   12.40
I'm sure she'd love that...... Anyway. My address is:

12A Fistral View, Newquay, TR7 3WY.

See you all in the morning.

I returned to Carole's office, where she dismissed me, affectionately shoving me out of the investigations room and ordered me home.

"I'd better not see you for at least three days." She added.

"Don't worry, you won't!" I waved at her before descending the staircase towards the exit.

I patted down an uncomfortable bulge in the back pocket of my jeans.

The Amulet!

A bout of nausea filled my mouth with saliva. Gladys had been abundantly clear that she required it back by Monday evening.

I slipped it out of my pocket and examined it, desperately figuring out how I could keep hold of it without upsetting her - which no one in their right mind would ever want to do. I'd also be investigated for tampering with vital Murder Investigation evidence.

I needed something similar in appearance to the amulet.

The Station Clerks didn't work a Sunday, due to the crawling back of Police funding, so there would be no one at the front office guarding the Lost Property box. I managed to sneak downstairs and found the *'Box of Goodies'* as the Clerks affectionately named it.

I rummaged through. To my luck, a gold necklace with a locket on the end lay amongst the trinkets. It was smaller in size, but it didn't matter. As long as there was something inside that bag that resembled an amulet, I didn't really care.

I took the necklace down to the depths of the evidence lock up and carefully cut open the bottom of the bag, concentrating hard to counteract my nerves. I gently removed Agatha's amulet and placed the imposter in its place, before sealing up the bag and leaving it in the mound of weekend evidence, for Gladys to process in the morning.

I knew this was a job-loser, but I kept thinking to myself, that it wasn't a malicious or criminal reason I did this, but to save the whole bloody world.

I sauntered out of the station, navigating a maze of secret corridors to remain undetected by my colleagues, and breathed a sigh of relief as I made it to the car park.

I climbed into my car, burying myself into the driver's seat, and placed my hands on the steering wheel. I placed the key into the ignition, and heard a deathly growl originating from the rear.

I glanced up into my rear mirror, noticing nothing but my deep brown, tired eyes.

A strong arm emerged around my neck, pulling me back and constricting my throat. I glimpsed at the mirror again, in a desperate bid to identify my attacker.

It was *Gruffydd*.

NINE

"Get off me!" I strained to yell as Gruffydd continued to choke me. I grasped for breath as my vision blurred and the world darken around me. I clenched my fists, hitting on his arm in a panic, not knowing if I'd contacted any part of him.

"I've got you now, Custodian." He roared in my ear, the fiery warmth of his breath danced gingerly across my earlobe.

As he squeezed tighter, my throat closed, and my lungs struggled to maintain their rhythm. In my state of panic, I couldn't build up the strength to use my powers. Using the remaining energy of my fiercely pumping adrenaline, I hit the car horn with my knee.

I pressed down as hard as I could, willing to get the attention of anyone nearby. Unbeknownst to me; Carole had left the station and headed over to her car. When she heard me sound the horn, she gravitated towards the noise.

Despite suffering the effects of oxygen depletion, I

could make out her silhouette peering into my car window. Stepping into action after discovering me in distress, she tried to open the rear driver's side door, but Gruffydd locked my car from the inside.

She repetitively banged on the window, calling Gruffydd an array of colourful names, some of which even I'd never heard before. I recalled her barking orders at a response officer who ran over to her aid, smashing the car window with his baton.

At this point, Gruffydd transformed his hands into his demonic talons, swiping at the poor, unsuspecting officer. Luckily, it was enough to distract him, for him to release the grip from my neck, to which I coughed and gasped my way back to consciousness.

I swiftly alighted my car and grabbed hold of the young PC's collar and pulled him away from Gruffydd, protecting him from the London Met officer's true, evil nature.

"Keep back!" I yelled at my colleagues, which included a small crowd of officers and civilians who'd gathered around us.

"Marco! What is going on?!" Carole shouted, the confusion and fear noticeably clear in her expression.

"Just get everyone to safety Carole - now!" I demanded, waving them back inside the building. This was no time for rank or pleasantries.

I watched on as Gruffydd clambered out of my car, morphing the rest of his body into his malevolent form, growing several inches in height and stature, and meeting my gaze with his piercing, green eyes.

Carole and the audience of officers frustratingly chose

to ignore my directions, screaming and cowering at the Hellion's transformation.

"What is that!!??" Carole shrieked, holding her hands over her mouth in disbelief.

"Carole!" I yelled, losing my patience. "Get everyone away from here now!"

She nodded, rustling up colleagues and ordering them back inside. A squadron of Taser officers disobeyed, pointing their bright yellow devices at Gruffydd, barking commands at him to subside, whilst the red guidance lasers danced around his chest from their nerves.

He ignored them.

They deployed the electrified barbs which pierced the skin of his chest.

Zzzzzzzzap!

They deployed their weapons, the fifty-thousand volts of electricity clicking through the conducting wires.

The shock from the Taser's were futile, as Gruffydd ripped out the wires in anger, launching them back towards the two terrified officers. They activated their remaining cartridges, their efforts remaining fruitless, only fuelling his anger.

The officers looked in horror once they concluded they weren't going to subdue this demonic creature. I heard the chirp of an emergency button from one of them, which would deploy all available officers from the county, towards the station.

I faced a conundrum; use my powers and be exposed to my fellow officers or refuse to use my powers and be killed along with them, and the Hellions would take over the world.

I had to do something. I yelled at the two remaining officers, still clutching their Taser's tightly, to get to safety.

I thrust out my arm, my magic flowing through my veins, my thoughts focusing on conjuring the elements and willed for Gruffydd to stop.

I could feel a small vibration emanate from beneath my feet which trans-versed into a rumble, and the tarmac started to crack like a broken iced over lake. I conducted the branches to create a path around his arms, pinning him to the wall of the station.

Gruffydd fought to escape the containment and kicked his legs back, causing the wall of the station to crack, helpless colleagues scurrying out of the emergency exits, screaming in terror. The sirens in the distance encroached on us as officers responded to the urgent assistance call.

My audience all observed, as I wrapped Gruffydd's legs in another foliage constraint. I was conscious to the fact that I'd exposed magic to the world.

I continued to subdue Gruffydd's evil persona, as he endeavoured to counteract my sorcery.

Knowing that he was hell-bent on killing me, I had to strike first. Just as he was about to break free of his bark like chains, I conjured a branch from the ground, this version having a sharp tip. I continued to orchestrate the branch, piercing it through his chest, taking a wild guess as to the location of his heart.

My lunch rose to the surface as I heard it squelch through his organs.

Gruffydd let out a gut-wrenching scream, which

drowned out the singing of the police cars that arrived.

As more officers arrived, they hastily ran into the rear yard, and stopped in their tracks as they witnessed the supernatural being crying out, before evaporating into a cloud of dust.

He'd gone.

The onlookers watched in awe as I commanded the branches to return to their dormant state beneath the concrete.

"What are you?!" one of the officers gestured at me in horror.

"Where did he go?" another colleague yelled.

"Did you kill him?" a voice from bellowed from behind me.

I decided to make a sharp exit.

My excitable comrades were attempting to rationalise what they'd seen, and some were starting to hold me responsible for it.

I sprinted to my car to evade the continuous questioning, and my imminent arrest.

In a frenzied state, I threw myself into the driver's seat and turned over the engine, forgetting to put on my seat belt.

I drove.

I drove as quick as I could, as far away from the station I could get.

I couldn't go home. People would know to find me there. Harriet was too far away, and I couldn't call Grayson as I didn't want to put him in any danger. There remained only two people I thought I could trust, even though I'd only known them a day.

I picked one to call.

"Marco. Are you okay?"

"Not really."

"What's happened?"

"It's a long story. Are you at home?"

"Yes mate."

"Would you mind if I came over?"

They must have heard the tremble in my voice.

"Of course, you can, I'll message you the address."

"Thank you, Jayce."

I didn't even pull over to look at the address, I tapped in the post code and aimlessly followed the route to his house.

It took me slightly under an hour to arrive at Jayce's, a small two bed house located on the outskirts of St Ives.

I'd only known this man for a day, but he'd a familiarity about him, as if I'd known him for years. It also impressed me how he quickly grasped our newfound saviours-of-mankind situation – his handsome looks were a bonus.

I was conscious that he still grieved for the loss of his sister, but like with many of us within the emergency services, we cope and deal with it; sometimes desensitising ourselves from these difficult emotive situations.

Despite his loss, Jayce still managed to answer the door with his warm, inviting smile. He put on a convincing front as I could tell he was still mournful inside.

"Hello mate." He greeted me.

"Sorry." I held my head down. "I didn't know where else to go."

"Come on in. I'll get you a coffee."

He took me through to his kitchen; cosy, chic and not the typical taste of a six-foot eight bodybuilder. I admired a picture frame with the words 'A Heart of a Home is in the Kitchen' which fit the theme of the room.

As Jayce boiled the kettle, he leaned with his back on the work top and asked me what had happened.

I told him *everything*.

At that moment, a woman walked in. She and Jayce shared the same emerald eyes and button nose, albeit not as joyful.

The woman appeared weathered, and I could tell from the remnants of tears on her cheeks, she'd been crying.

"Marco, this is my Mum, Michelle." He introduced her.

"Hello." She muttered, barely making any eye contact with me. This did, however, explain the décor of his house.

"I'm sorry for the loss of your daughter." I said.

She looked at me and gave me a light smile.

"Thank you." She nodded, sorrowfully walking over to the kettle area, and pouring herself a mug of coffee.

"She knows about everything." Jayce said. "What my dad was, what we are."

"Really?" I asked, intrigued.

"Yes." Michelle interrupted. "You're Fino's son, aren't you?" she asked, intricately studying my face as she took a sip of her steaming java.

I hesitantly nodded, wondering how she knew my father's name; especially 'Fino' which was a version only known by close friends and family.

"Oh, you've grown. I haven't seen you since you were a

child."

Michelle's eyes brightened slightly, especially upon her realisation of who I was.

"You know him?" Jayce turned to his mother in awe.

"Yes." Michelle stated. "You do too, Jason."

I stood there in an array of confusion. I'd never seen Jayce or his mother before in my life.

"That old bag wiped your memories when your fathers were killed. She told us widows left behind to pick up the pieces, to never speak to each other again. I protested, but Adelina convinced me it was for the best." She hung her head slightly when she mentioned my mother's name. "I'm sorry to hear about her."

"You knew my mother too?"

"Yes, we were incredibly close. Although we lived far apart, we kept each other company when your father and Jason's father went on missions together. You always used to visit us here on holiday."

"Mum? Why have you never told me this before?" Jayce asked.

"I was sworn to secrecy. She told me that if anything was to happen to your father, then you would automatically be next in line to get the powers."

"By her, you mean?" I interrupted.

"*Agatha*. That old bitch. You can tell her that she's not treating my Jason the same way she did his father. I can't lose any more of my family."

"Michelle." I paused, my throat drying up. "Agatha's dead."

I realise it wasn't the most sensitive of ways to inform

her, but she needed to know, before she said anything else about her that she would regret. She inferred a lot of hatred towards her.

Michelle stood for a moment, in silence, contemplating her thoughts.

"Oh." She swallowed hard, trying to fight back another group of tears. "How did that happen? I thought she was invincible!"

"I don't know." I said, unsure of how much I should be disclosing to her. "I've been led to believe that it was probably a Hellion that killed her."

"I see." Michelle took another sip of her coffee, clasping the mug tightly between her hands, the tip of her fingers turning white.

"What happened to the two children she took in?" she inquired.

Michelle shut her eyes, tilting her head around in differing directions, trying to recall their names.

"Henry and Ruby?" she sighed. "I think were their names. She took them in when their parents died. Telepaths they were."

"Did you mean Harriet?" I interjected.

She shook her head. "No, definitely a boy and a girl. Absolutely beautiful they were. Their parents were too. She didn't really want to take them in, she did it out of guilt."

"It's definitely Harriet." I corrected her. "She's carrying on Agatha's work and she's the one that's brought us all together."

"You mean *he* is *she* now?" Michelle scoffed.

"Maybe you're a bit confused Mum." Jayce placed his

arm around his mother's shoulder and held her close. "You've been through a lot."

"Maybe you're right."

She looked extremely fatigued and gaunt. Jayce look at her with some concern as she closed her eyes and almost fell asleep with her half-filled mug of tea in her hands.

"Why don't you go and lay down for a bit. You're exhausted." Jayce suggested, his tone soothing and caring.

Michelle gingerly nodded and shuffled out the kitchen, not before throwing her arms around me in a surprising hug. She squeezed me tightly.

"It's so good to see you, Marc." she said, nuzzling into my chest. She was only five foot eight, so I towered over her. "Please be careful. I couldn't bear to lose anyone else. I know what you and Jason must do, but bring him back to me, please."

She pulled away, her eyes raw.

"I will." I whispered.

Jayce ducked down to allow his mother to plant a kiss on his cheek, before she dragged her slippers up the stairs to her bedroom.

"So that was unexpected." Jayce commented.

"I know." I shook my head. "I thought you seemed familiar."

"Me too." He laughed.

"I don't think my brain can take any more of this surprise information." I joked, rubbing my temple.

"What are you going to do about the situation at work? Have you spoken with Harriet?" He asked.

"Not yet, I just needed to get somewhere safe first."

"What made you think of here over your own place?"

"Well, I didn't want to bring Grayson into all this,"

Ah, *Grayson*.

I'd abandoned him, but I kept him safe from the disarray that was my life currently.

Jayce handed me a beautifully smelling, steaming cup of coffee. I sniffed it, taking in the fragrant aroma, before I drank it, piping hot. I could feel the warmth of the beverage envelop me from within. I needed that boost of caffeine.

"I had to get somewhere where people wouldn't look to find me." I explained.

"Did you want to stay over?" He asked, taking a loud sip of his own coffee.

"I don't want to intrude. You're going through a lot." I said, compassionately.

"I'd appreciate the company to be honest." He sighed. "My Mum isn't really dealing with things well."

"Understandable."

"Yeah, I know. It just all feels a bit numb. She spent all yesterday afternoon and this morning in bed."

"Everyone grieves in their own way, Jayce." I could sense his struggle to understand his mother's reaction. "Remember she's just lost her daughter."

"I know." Jayce swirled the remnants of his coffee around in his mug.

"Why don't we get something to eat?" I suggested.

"Ah yes! There's an amazing Chinese Takeaway round the corner." He pulled open a drawer in the corner and rummaged through, extracting a worn, folded menu. He playfully threw it at me, and I impressively caught it with my spare hand.

We both threw each other a cheeky smile, I blushed from being smitten.

Stop it Marco!

Why was he making me feel this way?

I coyly opened the menu, hastily selecting my choice, whilst Jayce dialled the restaurant.

When our food arrived, I took no time in devouring my chow mein with crispy chilli beef. Jayce was even more of a food connoisseur than me, as he wolfed down two plates of a concoction of different exotic dishes.

Jayce scavenged a couple of beers from the back of his fridge, which complemented our meals perfectly. We got re-acquainted with each other, in a desperate attempt to recall our lost memories. Apart from the increasing familiarity with one another, no memories from our childhood together resurfaced.

"Where does your partner think you are?" he asked, changing the subject.

"I told him I was staying over in Exeter for work."

"Why don't you just tell him the truth?"

I paused for a minute, contemplating my answer.

"It's not that I don't trust him," I replied. "I just don't want him tangled up in this whole supernatural web. I mean it's not even been a week and look at how much we've all been through already. Throw Grayson into the mix and it would just complicate things."

"I get it." Jayce mumbled, still working on a mouthful of his food. "I didn't really have to explain things to my Mum, once I told her the truth about how Jo died."

"You seem fine about your sister." I observed.

"I've dealt with a lot of death in the Fire Service." he said. "I mean, I'm devastated, obviously. But there's no point in dwelling on things. You have to move on. That's what my father always taught me."

"That's a great analogy to have." I nodded.

"Besides. I still hold hope that my sister is still alive out there."

"I hope so."

After dinner, we sat in his living room watching a film on Netflix, one of my favourites - Guardians of the Galaxy. Jayce confessed that he'd never seen a Marvel film, so I quickly enlightened him into the infamous comic world.

I glanced over him, mid-film, glued to an action scene and immersing himself in the story. It was like watching a child opening presents on Christmas Day.

I couldn't really concentrate, still processing the tales about my parents and my life before I lost them. For the first time in a long while, I felt them both close, sensing they were watching over, guiding me.

This made the past week a bit easier to contemplate, especially realising that my father would have gone through a similar experience of becoming a supernatural saviour overnight.

The film ended, and Jayce let out a mammoth yawn, hoisting himself to his feet with athletic grace.

"I think I'm gonna hit the hay. I'll get you a duvet if you're okay with the sofa?"

"Of course."

In truth, I loathed sleeping anywhere but a bed, however I couldn't exactly be selective.

Jayce provided me with a mound of seventies patterned bedding and wished me goodnight.

I tried to make myself as comfortable as I could before shutting my eyes and trying to sleep. Initially I struggled, but after trialling various positions, I finally found one that felt most comfortable.

My dream that night was of my father.

We were back in our old Town House in Hammersmith, a mysterious, eerie haze surrounding us. I was nine years old and playing football with him in the garden.

My sister, Lucie, and my mother were sat on the patio furniture watching over at us.

I must have smiled in my sleep, as I was content and happy.

My father stopped mid score, staring at me, possessed.

"Marc." He said, with a ghostly whisper.

I screamed with terror in the body of my younger self, as I witnessed his eyes glow a pale white, his pupils disappearing.

"You are in danger. You are all in danger." His voice reverbed much like the Hellion's did in their creature form.

"When the time comes, you must do what must be done. Only that will save you."

I was terrified.

Who was this?

Was this my dad?

I didn't like this scary man.

As quick as he'd been transformed into a soul-less zombie, he reverted to his normal, smiling self, continuing to kick the football around the garden.

I sharply stirred in a sweat, bolting upright.

The dream felt real.

Jayce burst through the living room door with Michelle in tow, switching on the light. Michelle was wrapped in a fluffy, pink dressing gown, whilst Jayce brandished a pair of pyjama shorts and top, which accentuated his strapping frame.

"Marco? Are you okay?" He asked, catching his breath.

"I'm fine."

"Are you sure? You were screaming."

"I was?" I assumed it was part of the dream, I didn't realise it transcended into reality. "I had a strange dream."

"What was it?" Michelle asked, intrigued.

I explained the dream to them and recited the words the apparition of my father had spoken in his zombie trance.

"Take that seriously." she warned. "I think that was your father contacting you from beyond."

"How?" I asked.

"I don't know. Jason's father used to have similar dreams. He said it was something to do with the connection to the amulet that all the Custodians have, whether living or dead."

"I hate that damn Amulet." I exasperated. "Nothing good has come of it so far."

"You're preaching to the choir." Michelle remarked. "I'd hoped it'd been lost."

"Mum, you don't mean that." Jayce said.

"Of course, I bloody mean it!" she yelled. "What's that damn thing ever done for me?! I've lost your father, your sister and now you're going out there to confront the very things that killed them. I can't lose you too Jason, I just can't."

Michelle exploded into an erratic display of emotion, collapsing onto Jayce's chest.

"I promise you; I won't end up like them, Mum. I've got Marco."

Our eyes met from over his mother's shoulder, the corner of his mouth raising into a half smile, which hurled me into an infatuated state.

I need to stop feeling like this! I have a partner!

"Don't worry Michelle." I spoke. "I'll protect him with my life."

TEN

I remained awake for the rest of the night, not being able to shake the chilling message from my deceased father out of my mind.

Brandon sent an early ecstatic message in our group.

> **Brandon +447877765431   05.30**
> Guys! I have a huge surprise for you! Can we meet at about 9.30. At a beach would be good...

> **Me +447877892365   05.31**
> Brandon, do you have any idea what time it is!! Besides, we've got the car picking us up at 8am from mine?

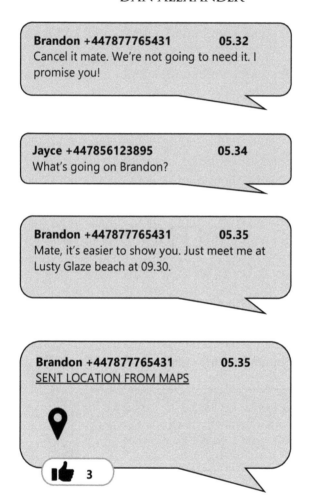

Brandon +447877765431   05.32
Cancel it mate. We're not going to need it. I
promise you!

Jayce +447856123895   05.34
What's going on Brandon?

Brandon +447877765431   05.35
Mate, it's easier to show you. Just meet me at
Lusty Glaze beach at 09.30.

Brandon +447877765431   05.35
SENT LOCATION FROM MAPS

👍 3

Jayce and I were the first ones down to the beach at about quarter past nine, followed by Yi not long after. This was the first encounter we'd had in person since I'd stalked her at the Royal Hospital in Truro.

"Gentleman." she greeted us, slightly warmer than usual,

however a slight frost still lingered around the edges of her tone.

"Morning Yi." I smiled. "I'm glad you've finally joined us."

"Well, I didn't really have a choice." she grumbled.

"You did." I reminded her, lifting an eyebrow in mild protest. "We all did. We just all made the right one."

"That's debatable. Do you know how much money I'm going to lose out on today?"

I wanted to punch Yi's scrunched up face. I wasn't a violent person, but her negativity had an unexpected effect on my temper.

"For fucks sake Yi! Will you stop with your moaning!" I scolded, my face turning a bright shade of scarlet.

"Marco!" Jayce reprimanded.

"Sorry, but I'm just so fed up with all her negativity!" I shrieked, my vocal chords straining under the intense pitch. "She needs to understand that the world doesn't revolve around her!"

I couldn't help myself, the words were involuntary spewing from my mouth.

"Look." Jayce seized hold of my flailing arms and linked our gaze. "You need to calm down. She's here. That's all that counts. You can't lose your head now, otherwise we won't stand a chance against the Hellions."

Jayce was right. For someone so young, he contained a treasure of wisdom.

"You're right." I peered at the floor, then rotated to Yi. "I'm sorry. This is all starting to take its toll on me."

"The main thing is you're here now," Jayce smiled at her.

"It's nice to see you, Stevens." She nodded.

"You too Chang."

I spotted Brandon from the corner of my eye, bouncing towards us across the sand. His bright yellow vest mirrored the morning sun, which expelled an extreme heat in the cloudless sky.

"G'day mates!" He chirped. "What a beautiful fine day it is today!"

I introduced him to Yi, who welcomed him with her standard bleak greeting.

"What's this exciting news you have for us?" I asked.

"Guys, you are going to freak... out…!" he shrieked, his overzealous positivity clearly inciting some annoyance in one particular member of the group.

"Oh, please just get on with it." Yi demanded.

"I can make water portals!"

"Water portals?" Jayce asked.

"Yeah mate. My Mum wrote down everything I needed to know about being a Water Custodian, like a manual. I don't think I could get us as far as Oz, but I'm sure I could get us to London."

"You mean you haven't tried this?" Yi scolded.

"Not with actual people. I tried it last night and managed to send a can of beer from the kitchen sink into the bathroom."

"I'm not sure about this, Brandon." I said, apprehensively.

His enthusiasm was infectious, but I kept mindful we were all still incredibly lacking in experience, despite his head start and guidance from his mother. I would have preferred a four-hour journey to London.

"Mate, it will be fine. I promise." Brandon desperately assured me. "I'm not going to let anything bad happen."

"Well. We're here. I suppose we've got nothing to lose." Jayce cut in.

"Apart from drowning!" Yi exclaimed. "I hate water."

"Is there anything you actually do like?" I teased her. She replied with a glare.

"I say do it." Jayce smiled. "After everything we've all been through, I think we can manage this."

"Go on then Brandon." I gestured to the ocean. "Show us what you can do."

"That's too out in the open." He shook his head, walking over to a small rock pool, tucked away into a cove, as we snaked behind him.

Although hugely pessimistic, part of me wished for Brandon to succeed.

We all gathered around him as he held his arms over a metre deep rock pool, housing a variety of tiny crustaceans and anemones. He made a circular motion with a palm and shut his eyes before taking a deep breath.

As he gestured, the water awakened into a small whirlpool, which expanded as Brandon accelerated. I couldn't help but ogle at the enthralling commandment of his element.

Now at full strength, he positioned his palms stationery over the newly materialised portal and turned to us.

"Who's gonna be the first one to jump in?" He smiled, his platinum blonde hair wavering in the turbulence from his creation.

The remainder of us all glanced at each other with trepidation.

Yi pressed her arms tighter into her chest and shook her head definitively.

"Not me. Marco. You're our leader. You should go first."

Now she sees me as the leader.

"All the more reason for me to remain behind if it all goes wrong!" I remonstrated. "I vote Jayce to go first. He's the strongest out of us all so I'm sure can withstand it."

"Hey!" Jayce chirped, playfully. "This maybe the first time ever that my muscles have given me a disadvantage."

"Hurry up!" Brandon bellowed; his face scrunched. "I can't hold this for long!"

Yi shoved Jayce to the forefront, volunteering him as tribute.

"Oh. I see how it is." He nervously chuckled.

"You'll be fine." I sarcastically grinned. "Think strong thoughts."

He cautiously stepped up to the edge and looked deep into the centre, the remnants of the pool racing into a black abyss.

This led him to look back at me and Yi, his lip quivering with dread.

"C'mon Turner you're a fireman for goodness sake!" Yi yelled through strands of her sleek mane covering her face from the portal's draft.

Jayce took one further look at the watery chasm and closed his eyes, holding his nose and breath at the same time.

He hesitantly took a large leap into the pool, and instantly vanished, absent of any screams or signs of difficulty.

That put me slightly more at ease.

"Your turn." Yi gestured at me.

I rolled my eyes at her self-importance and paced a few meters away. Channelling my inner athlete, I focused my attention and sprinted towards the swirling pool of water, taking a fierce dive as I approached the edge.

I immersed myself into the vortex, a slight warmth enveloped me as my surroundings darkened, panicking for a split second that I'd been blinded.

I moved at a rapid speed, violently thrown into a whirl of turbulent velocity like a flume at a swimming resort.

A pinprick of distant light magnified as I raced closer towards it, signifying my journey was nearing an end.

The light shrouded me as I propelled through it, landing on a cold, stone surface.

When I pushed myself to my feet and brushed off some needy pieces of lint, I scoped the room and investigated a pool of water from a weathered fountain I'd materialised from. The portal diminished.

The section of the mysterious building I ended up in, was sparse of any people, so my supernatural secret remained intact.

I expected to be greeted by Jayce's pearl white smile, but he was nowhere to be seen.

I explored the building further, the taps of my shoes reverberating with each step on the cracked marble floor, and grimaced at the condition of the barren building.

I could tell this was once a grand and vibrant place, as snippets of metallic gold paint shimmered through the rubble.

I freed my phone from my pocket, and looked down at the screen, hoping one of the team tried to contact me. I tutted with frustration when I realised that the screen was flickering, tapping it viciously with my index finger, willing it to work.

I shoved it back in my pocket and started to look for an exit.

I couldn't see any signage which would give me an indication where I'd been warped to.

I came across a large archway which led into another section, which was the only route, so I followed it.

As I blindly navigated the maze of the decrepit corridors and collapsed hallways, I'd succeeding in getting myself lost; the building deserted and extinct of people to ask for help.

I'd eventually discovered a reception area, which contained two piles of burnt wood loosely resembling a desk. As I studied the remains, I noticed a damaged computer screen, hidden within the mound of rubble.

I surveyed the pile of debris and picked up a cracked and chipped plastic sign buried within, wiping off a thin layer of dust with my hand. I coughed as stray particles caught the back of my throat.

I could just about make out the text.

'National History Museum.'

Being a child of London, we frequented here on family visits, but this wasn't the museum I felt familiar with.

I studied the decrepit reception area and spotted two

rectangular shaped voids which looked out into the street, unusually silent for the peak of summer.

The daylight light crept in from the openings, putting a spotlight on the waste land that that should have been a magnificent building. The hall was expectant of a hustle of tourists, yet it remained bare. I bubbled with confusion.

My curious nature ventured me outside into the open air, stepping out onto the peak of the outside steps, scanning the sight of the London streets.

My heart sank.

What was once grass, now stood dry soil and debris of collapsed buildings. The apocalyptic sight sent chills down my spine, the hair on the back of my neck standing to attention.

Where the hell has Brandon sent me?!

I'd no idea if the remainder of the team had been transported with me, but I made it my mission to try and locate them.

"Marco!"

I sighed with relief at a familiar voice echo from behind me. I sharply spun to see Yi walking towards me with a purposeful stride.

I would usually find her presence cold and lifeless, but I was so pleased to see someone I knew, I temporarily put that feeling to one side.

"Yi!" I shouted back, heading inside to meet her.

"Where in the world are we?" she asked, glancing around the entrance hall.

"London." I replied. "Welcome to the National History Museum."

"What?!" she exclaimed.

"Yep." I scrunched my face up in disbelief. "Brandon's portal worked, we're in London, however *which* London is the bigger question."

"Where's Jayce?" She asked, still scoping around the ruins.

"No idea. I haven't come across him yet."

I turned back to head out of the exit, Yi following suit. I looked out to the London skyline, still bewildered by the lack of vibrancy.

Yi stood at my side as we both remained silent.

"This isn't right." she shook her head. "Where is everyone?"

"If I knew that, I'd tell you." I replied, focusing on the remains of a burnt-out Mercedes in the road.

I trailed down the steps, continuously sweeping the horizon to try and discover anything appearing to have life. Yi followed close behind, and we ventured out onto the remnants of Cromwell Road, passing through the rust coated gates.

The London streets were a desert, with twig like trees, cracked pavements and rows of crumbled architecture, like a nuclear wasteland.

As we explored deeper into the city, a family of malnourished rats scuttled across the roads, rummaging through the debris.

We tiptoed around a pack of feral dogs viciously fighting each other for scraps of food, avoiding detection, in anticipation of being their next meal.

Wandering around aimlessly, we searched a number of

decrepit and derelict buildings, trying to unearth even the most minuscule shred of evidence about how our capital had transformed into an apocalyptic nightmare in the blink of an eye. We continued our search up Brompton Road, an area I knew well, with ten years of policing the Kensington & Chelsea Borough.

It took us no longer than ten minutes to walk through the waste land, before stopping outside the former Harrods, one of the most iconic landmarks in the area. Much of the magnificent structure had caved in on itself, leaving but a shell of its former affluent glory.

I briefly took myself back to my childhood, recalling my annual Christmas visits with my father and sister, arguing with them on which tree ornament to buy - a tradition which continued until he died.

I'd not dropped by since his death, as even the happy memories were too painful to relive, even more so now they'd symbolically been reduced to a pile of rubble.

"Are you okay?" Yi asked, noticing the well filling my eyes.

"Just memories." I choked.

This was the first time I sensed any form of empathy from my woeful teammate. I hoped this began the start of a more civil comradery between us.

We walked for going on two hours, dehydrated from the fierceness of the beating sun. Craving water, I led us both to the nearest riverbank of the almighty Thames, which still surged through the desolate city. Yi took one look at the murkiness of the water and eyed me with detest.

"I'm not drinking that!"

I agreed. The unsanitary river looked as if it would do us more harm than good.

"We're close to MI6." I noted. "Let's head there and see if that's still intact. I bet there's a nuclear bunker in there or something."

Yi nodded as we continued our expedition.

The journey on foot to Vauxhall was painful, with the absence of any public transport.

As we approached the site of the iconic government palace, I gave up any hope when I saw it too had been reduced to a pile of debris.

Out of all buildings in the capital, I was hopeful that it would have been left standing, provided it was the securest of premises in the United Kingdom.

I snapped out my trance of disappointment, startled by the sound of an unworldly growl from behind us.

We both turned one-eighty, to be greeted with a demonic creature, which I could only describe as a Hellion on steroids.

They'd the familiar white skin and deep green eyes, but their gigantic, bulbus stature dwarfed their previous incarnations. Their talons were more extended and razored with skeletal spikes protruding down their spine. A row of elongated needles for teeth jutted out of their mouth, embodying evil.

Yi and I instantly prepared ourselves with a defensive stance, ready to counteract any attack.

As the Super-Hellion delivered a much more supersonic screech, they darted at us with lightning speed.

Yi held her palm out in front of her, attempting to use her elemental enchantment of the air to help subdue our enemy. I could see the concentration in her face; her brow crossed, dripped with sweat.

Nothing materialised.

We scurried out of the creature's path, barely missing a swipe of the bladed talon.

I thrust out my hand, with an aim to create an earthquake to knock the Hellion off balance.

Nothing.

I investigated my hand, puzzled as to the sudden lack of magic.

"Run!" Yi yelled, as the demon tracked us.

We sprinted towards the remnants of MI6 as the Hellion swiftly closed on us.

A crudely crafted arrow soared the narrow gap between us, striking the Hellion in the chest which collapsed on the ground, shrieking in agony.

I scanned around, trying to uncover the origins of this mysterious arrow, sighting a young woman holding a makeshift bow, perched on top of a statue, in an aiming stance.

As we ventured deeper into the secret service ruins, I was grabbed by an unsuspecting hand, a cold, sharp object held up against my throat. I discreetly turned my head, taken back when I identified my attacker.

"Harriet!" I gasped.

"Who the hell are you!?" She yelled, her voice trembling with anger.

A couple of extra lines adorned her face, and stark

streaks of grey trailed her unkempt, wiry hair. She dressed in tattered jeans and a soiled leather jacket which was a sheer contrast from her usual formal two-piece suits.

"It's Marco!" I screamed back, realising the metallic object pinned to my neck was a knife, which she pressed further into my skin, the tip piercing a miniscule wound.

"Bullshit!" She growled. "You Hellions are getting sloppy if you think that I'll believe that crap! Posing as the dead does not play well with me!"

"Dead?!" I muttered.

"Seriously, you are trying my patience!" Harriet appeared more edgy and intense than she did a few days ago.

"Harriet! Honestly it is me!" I protested.

Before I had time to even say another word, the blade vaulted to the floor with a perfectly timed kick from Yi, who stealthily approached from behind. A small struggle ensued between the two women, ending with Yi pinning Harriet's arms behind her.

"Look, I don't know who the hell you are," Yi uttered through clenched teeth. "But you need to tell me what's going on. Right, now."

It escaped my mind that Yi had never encountered her.

"Finally come rushing back have we Chang?" Harriet laughed manically. "Good enough for you now, are we?" She'd matched Yi's level of sarcasm.

"Harriet." I held my hands up in front of her, indicating at Yi to loosen her grip. I cautiously approached her, noticing a crowd circling around us.

They wore similar styled rags to Harriet, in possession of an artillery of handmade bows and spears, aimed at Yi and me.

"It is me. Marco. I'm telling the truth." I pleaded. "We went through a portal Brandon created. Next thing we knew, we ended up here." I gingerly placed one foot in front of the other, decreasing the gap between us.

"Well, that's fucking bullshit if I ever did hear it!" She shouted, stirring murmurings from the eclectic audience. "Marco died seven years ago!"

"What do you mean seven years ago?" Yi queried.

Is this the future?

"What's the date?" I asked, a grave hunch twisting my stomach.

"This is red-"

"THE DATE!"

"The 12th of August 2032."

I glanced at Yi, the same look of trepidation clear on our faces.

I walked over to her.

"It all makes sense," I said aloud. "We're in the future. Ten years into the future."

"How?" Yi asked, closing her eyes, and shaking her head in scepticism.

"It must have been something to do with Brandon's portal."

Future Harriet approached us, whilst I continued to make sense of everything.

"Prove to me you aren't a Hellion." she commanded, holding out a golden dagger, which had a ceremonial guise. "Cut your hand with this. If it bleeds black, you're *evil*. And you *die*."

This incarnation of Harriet was vastly different from her counterpart in my time, being much more confrontational and aggressive. I could sense she wasn't going to let anything get her way of whatever it is she'd set out to do.

I hesitantly accepted the dagger, turning over my palm to expose the flesh. I allowed the tip to penetrate my skin, as I drew the blade across my open hand, wincing as the cut seared into my pain receptors.

Even though I'd no doubt, I was relieved to see bright red blood seeping out of the wound. I assumed Future Harriet cleverly implanted those slight doubts into my mind; I assumed from her telepathy, which was ten years more advanced from my perspective.

As soon as I passed the test and she realised I was not a demonic imposter, Harriet hastily embraced me with a strong squeeze.

"Marco, It's really you." She whispered in my ear, lightly rocking from side to side for several minutes. "How can this be?"

She stepped back and studied me, a slight twinkle of hope manifesting in her deep hazel eyes.

"I have no clue. One minute we were in Cornwall, jumping in a pool of magic water, and the next we're in apocalyptic future London."

Wiping away a strain of delicate tears with the back of her hand, Harriet cleared her throat and nodded at the spectators that gathered around us, signalling we weren't a threat.

They immediately retreated and withdrew their armaments.

"How far in the past have you travelled from?" She asked.

"Ten years. We're from 2022."

"So, you've not long had your powers?"

"We've only had them a few days."

Harriet began pacing in pensive circles, a trait I recognised from her past self.

"What's happened H?" I asked, moistening my dehydrated lips with the tip of my tongue. "How did all this happen."

"Approximately three years from your perspective, you died in a Hellion battle." She looked down at the floor, then back up at me. "This caused a cataclysmic chain of events which resulted in them apprehending this world. Only a handful of us survived and continue to resist them, but it gets harder as each day passes. The more human life force they absorb, the stronger they get."

"What happened to the rest of us?" Yi asked, her counterpart notably absent.

"You disappeared without a trace." Harriet sharply jeered at Yi. "Mr Stevens was also killed in battle, whilst Mr Turner went back to Australia to help with their resistance fighters."

"All this, from them wiping me out?" I struggled to contemplate my significance in this war of the realms.

"You didn't have any children to pass on your powers to, so the Custodian prophecy ended with your death." Harriet said, with a blunt, factual tone.

"I hadn't even factored any of that in." I muttered. "I mean, we are thinking of having kids someday, but not any time soon."

"I'm not one to get involved in personal matters." Harriet shrugged; her broad shoulders perfectly accentuated by her moth-eaten jacket.

"Do you know how we get back?" I asked.

"I don't know. There is next to no magic here now. I've not been able to use my telepathy for years."

"So, we're stuck here?!" Yi piped up from behind me.

"I'm sorry."

"You don't sound very sincere. Surely there's something here that can get us back?" Yi challenged, her prickly exterior beginning to emerge once again.

"Yi!" I snapped.

"I'm not having it, Marco!" She crossed her arms tightly in dissent, creating a metaphorical barrier between her and Harriet. "If this Harriet is so brilliant like you suggested, then she must be able to help."

"Look, Chang." Harriet scorned. "Don't you start all this 'high and mighty' shit, especially you of all people. Turner is thousands of miles away. We have little magic. Certainly not enough to attempt to send you back. I'm powerless to help."

"'High and Mighty?!!... Just who the hell do you think you are?" Yi roared back, before leaping forward to grab her. I swiftly interjected and bear hugged my comrade, preventing her from doing anything she would later regret.

"Pack it in!" I yelled, struggling to detain a very sweaty and feisty Yi.

"Let her at me, Ramirez." Harriet tauntingly gestured her hands. "That's all she's ever wanted. This is all her fault anyway. If she believed you from the start, then none of this would have ever happened!"

"No! Stop it! Both of you!" I ordered, freeing Yi, who ceased her squirming. "This isn't helping anyone, is it?"

"Just keep her away from me!" Yi barked, her index finger sharply cutting through the air towards Harriet.

"Fine. Stay out of each other's way." I said, attempting to dampen the hostile atmosphere. I was somewhat alarmed at the rapid flaring of Yi's temper, willing the cause being her anxiety of our unexpected visit to the future.

"Let's hope our Brandon knows where to find us." Yi uttered before walking away.

"Sorry about her." I turned to Harriet, who was tracing Yi's every movement with a prominent glare.

"Don't apologise for her, Marco." She insisted. "You're not to blame for her selfishness."

"What caused all of this anyway?" I asked her, referencing the dystopian surroundings.

"It all started not long after you received your powers. The world leaders met at a conference in the United States. Unbeknownst to any of us, the majority were infiltrated by the highest ranks of the Hellion regime. This conference converted the remainder of the world leaders, which eventually spread to local governments and councils across the globe. Police and Military establishments were also replaced, causing the start of World War Three as different Hellion factions all fought towards global domination. Over half of the world's population were wiped out."

Harriet perched on a large mound of rubble, as she recalled the horrors of the next decade.

"I helplessly watched as they became stronger.

Overpowering all the world's natural and supernatural resources. Then your death came. That was the catalyst for all this. Total destruction."

"How did you survive?" I asked.

"I kept hidden. Utilised what resources I could. I banded together with other supernatural beings, fighting off as many attacks as we were able. We called ourselves 'The Resistance.' The people you see around you are former telepaths and sorcerers." Harriet scowled at Yi. "At least *some* of us stuck together."

Yi, noticing the detesting glance, furied into our conversation.

"What is your problem? Don't look at me like that!"

"I'll look at you however I wish. You're only going to abandon us all again anyway."

"You're blaming me for something I've not even done yet!" Yi scolded her.

"You're the same in any time, Chang. Selfish and out for yourself. You've not changed, and you never will." Harriet stood and headed towards a group of her resistance fighters.

I led Yi throughout the ruins of MI6, which had been converted into a refugee camp, or 'Camp Freedom' as Harriet's people affectionately named it. Although out in the open, they made clever use of resources to try and secure it from any unexpected attacks.

We weaved passed makeshift beds constructed from discarded wood and rubble, and an assortment of small fires danced on piles of kindling, which radiated an orange aura as darkness drew near.

The resistance prepared a meal for us, containing

severely out of date tins, scavenged from derelict supermarkets.

Our hunger and dehydration clouded our rational thinking and devoured our food as if we'd starved for months.

A brief demonic ordeal interrupted our dinner, breaking through the defences, swiftly concluded by the skilled and zealous members of the resistance.

Afterwards, me and Yi ventured down to the riverside, looking up at the vibrant stars, which were so unusually clear for the skies of London; a decade of no pollution restoring the constellations to their former glory.

Although she began to grow on me as a person, Harriet hit the nail on the head about the Yi Chang that I'd first encountered. I remained hopeful that this was a wakeup call for her to illicit some change.

"Do you think I'm selfish, Ramirez?" She asked. "Honestly?"

We both simultaneously sat on a heap of waste that managed to fit us side by side. Yi hung her head low, humbled by the feedback she'd been provided by future Harriet.

"Look," I said, my hands sliding into the small gap between my thighs. "You do come across as a bit cold when people first meet you. We didn't exactly have the best interaction when we first met, but, when it came to it, you put all your feelings aside and pulled through for the greater good."

Yi shrugged her shoulders.

"To be honest. Neither you nor Harriet are the first

people to tell me that." She looked up at me, her sorrowful eyes beginning to weep. "I don't really have friends. I seem to push people away."

"Why?" I asked, slowly chipping away at her tough exterior.

"I was raised by my extremely strict and stubborn grandfather in Hong Kong. He told me that emotion was weakness, and to never get close to anyone." She portrayed her best old man impression and changed her affliction to that of a native Honk Kong accent. "*Never get close to anyone; they will abuse your loyalty and take your kindness for granted.*" We chuckled at her mediocre imitation of her grandfather. "That always stuck with me, I've let it take me over."

"Don't worry, my grandmother in Spain is the same, she's very traditional and old fashioned."

I recalled my Abuela for a brief moment, a short, tubby and highly spirited woman. She was my last living relative next to my sister, living in a small apartment on the beautiful island of Majorca.

She'd somewhat archaic views on the LGBT+ community, which caused our relationship to be somewhat volatile, but I persevered with her, wishing for her to eventually come around to a more modern way of thinking.

"Are your parents still alive?" I asked, wondering if she too, was an orphan.

"Yes, but I don't speak with them. They sent me over when I was a baby. I always thought they didn't want me, but I'm assuming they wanted to protect me from all of this."

"Well, maybe if we ever get back, you can make amends

with them." I smiled, clutching her hand, reassuring her she did have a friend, desired or not.

She squeezed my hand in return and smiled back, wiping away a solitary tear.

"Thanks, Detective Inspector Ramirez."

"You're welcome, Doctor Chang."

Our touching moment was interrupted by members of the resistance rushing in mass over to the shore of the Thames, a stone throw away from where we were sat.

We upped on our feet and followed the excitable crowd, curious as to what attracted them to the bank. I pushed through the barricade of rebels, before peering over a set of decayed railings.

Yi joined me seconds later, gripping the barrier tightly, gazing deeply into a chaotic patch of the river.

"What's that?!" I turned my attention to the unfamiliar voice next to me, realising it was the blonde archer, who'd earlier protected me from being mauled by a Hellion.

She pointed down to the strange phenomenon in the water.

"I'm hoping, our way home."

ELEVEN

Harriet approached beside me, studying the spontaneous swirling vortex of water, the wake turbulence causing Yi's hair to mimic the mane of Medusa.

"That's one of Mr Turner's portals. I'd recognise that handy work anywhere." she half smiled.

Harriet's arm draped lightly over my shoulder, guiding me close to her, our heads pressing against one another.

"It was good to see you again Marco, even if it was only for a short time."

"Don't worry H. We'll do whatever we can to make sure that this future doesn't happen." I assured her.

"Please stay safe." she whispered.

She relinquished her arm from around me and focused on Yi.

"I don't take back what I said to you." Harriet's tone transiently shifted. "But I know you are capable of change. You don't have to live by your grandfather's rules. Open your heart, as you'll get nowhere by shutting everyone out."

Yi nodded, as Harriet extended out her hand in peace, which she accepted in return. They stood silently, welcoming each other as powerful, independent women.

"Now go." Harriet commanded us both, nodding towards the edge of the railings. "That portal won't last much longer."

I climbed over the threshold, looking vertically down towards the watery abyss, overcome by a wave of justified apprehension.

What if we end up in prehistoric times? Or in a time where the world doesn't even exist?

I recognised the idiocy of my imaginative assumptions, but my experiences over the previous four days taught me to strongly consider my gut instincts.

Yi stealthily appeared next to me, her unkempt hair still flailing from the portal as she struggled to keep her eyes open from the force of the wind.

"Ready?" She squinted, formulating her jump, her arms extended behind her and clutching tightly to the railings.

"As ready as I'll ever be." I grimaced. "After you."

I gestured my head towards the vortex, signalling for Yi to take her dive into the ethereal.

She didn't hesitate.

I looked up at future Harriet, perfectly poised, watching me with a caring smile, signalling with a gentle nod for me to leave.

I released myself from the railings and fell into the portal.

The travel through was as vicious as it'd been before, with

an aura of multicoloured lights and patterns dancing in a choreographed display around me.

The opening raced towards me, causing me to defensively shut my eyes and prime my exit into whatever time period I would emerge.

I launched out of a body of water and landed face down on a bank of sludge, right next to Yi, who slowly submerged into the unstable terrain.

I scanned my surroundings, seeing we were on the shore of the Thames, marginally below the MI6 building. I secretly celebrated the eclectic sounds of London residents and commuters scurrying about their business.

I looked up to the base of the intact secret service building, where Brandon and Jayce stood at the spot where future Harriet had been only moments ago, calling down to us both.

We were back in 2022.

I struggled to release myself from the sludge, my feet immersing deeper into the sand, which accelerated the more I tried to force myself out.

I held my palm down to the floor and willed for the ground to remain solid and take my weight. As I tried once more to wriggle out of my muddy prison, I crawled on the sand in front of me and managed to hoist up to my feet.

Much to my relief, I didn't penetrate through the sand, the ground beneath me as solid as concrete. I looked back at Yi, who still sunk at a snail's pace.

I cupped my hands around my mouth.

"My powers are back! Just follow my path!" I exclaimed; my voice projected by my improvised amplifier.

Yi grunted as she wriggled herself free from the sludge, which stained her bottom half in a layer of thick mud as he emerged.

We navigated our way back up to the side of the bank, where our teammates were hesitantly waiting for us.

Jayce reached down and offered out his hand, the bare skin of his muscular arm lined with protruding veins. I grabbed hold and another twinge of attraction instantly panged when he pulled me up over the railings without any hint of sweat or difficulty.

Once Yi had been hoisted up, we both tried to scrape off as much sludge from our clothing with a discarded tree branch.

"What happened to you two?!" Brandon asked.

"You tell me!" Yi said, annoyed, frowning at the youngest member of our team.

"What she means is…." I interjected, frustrated that she'd already disregarded our heart to heart. "……. That we don't know. We jumped in right after Jayce, but somehow ended up ten years in the future."

"Future?!" Brandon gasped. "Dude, I didn't even know I could do that!"

"Well, you can!" Yi barked, desperately trying to scrape of the remainder of mud from her boots.

"We spent the best part of a day there." I explained. "How is it daylight already?" It'd only occurred to me that the night sky had transitioned to broad daylight.

"We left Newquay only minutes ago." Jayce informed us, looking bewildered.

"I'm not even going to remotely try to understand it all."

A slight headache began to manifest as I attempted to make sense of the time paradoxes. "If you didn't know where we were, how did you know to send a portal after us?"

"I didn't." Brandon said. "I made the portal to get here, that's it. You came out this end only minutes after us."

"Then who was it?" I asked, looking down at my soiled smart watch, noting that our appointment with Harriet was drawing near.

"Well, it definitely wasn't me. I'm certain of it." Brandon shrugged his shoulders, one of the straps of his summer vest almost loosening down his bicep.

"We'll figure it out later." I said, setting out towards the nearby Vauxhall Tube Station. "We'd better get going, or we'll be late."

I checked out the towering glass building enroute, the command centre for the secret service, surrounded by armed guards, with an abundance of reinforced chain linked fences, protecting it from anyone who to intended to foolishly penetrate the defences.

I scanned around for a big, metal abstract building which was just shy of the entrance to the station, where I needed to seek out a set of double doors, as instructed by Harriet.

I eventually located it, giving off an impression of a large, American tin caravan. There were two signed emergency exits, with the numbers '13251920' embossed on the side.

"There's the entrance." I pointed out to my entourage. As we sneaked towards the doors, I tasked Jayce with scoping the area to ensure we didn't draw any attention. Luckily, the crowds of the surrounding streets camouflaged us.

I couldn't pinpoint any locking mechanism or access point - Harriet only advised me of the location of the clandestine entrance, nothing else.

I pressed my palm against the cold door, a sudden warmth emanating from beneath it, seeming to react to my touch. A light green glow radiated around the seal as the door opened inward, exposing a bleak corridor.

Focusing back on my teammates, I noticed the recurring look of anticipation painted across their faces, which I attempted to suppress by digging out my best poker face – the one thing they didn't need was a leader who appeared weak.

I gingerly stepped inside, the soles of my still muddied Adidas' chiming as they hit the metallic floor. I faded into the darkness, the team following close behind.

The door slammed behind us, engulfing us in a dark void, lacking any form of light. I froze, too terrified to move, an unexpected spell of claustrophobia taking control.

I expelled a log drab of air I'd seized in my lungs in relief, as a sequence of brilliant white lights lined up along the ceiling, tracing a path to a sharp left turn at the end.

We hesitantly tracked the corridor of this unknown territory, stepping through a variety of security measures, relived when we finally reached the central office of Operation Myst.

Entering through a set of sliding glass doors, activated with the most innovative of recognition technology, I studied the diligent operatives bustling at their desks, spotting a more sophisticated Harriet conversing at the far end of the room with a colleague.

She was a direct contrast of her future self, wearing a two pieced fitted suit and a floral silk blouse. Her hair lay comfortably on her shoulders, with a styled curl. A pair of high stilettos polished her look off nicely.

Once she acknowledged our arrival, she trailed the centre of the office, slaloming around her employees and stopped short of our group.

"Marco, welcome." She smiled. "Ms Chang, Mr Turner and Mr Stevens, welcome to Operation Myst."

The others were still taking in the brilliance of Harriet's department, mirroring my first visit. She extended out her arm to my comrades, greeting each of them with a firm handshake.

We pursued her into a large meeting room adjacent to the central office, where abstract leather chairs encircled a sleek oval table. Harriet offered us a seat.

I was the first to accept her offer, not prepared for the deceptive comfort of the apparent sterile chairs – I even let out a slight pleasurable groan.

Jayce raced to get the available seat next to mine, whilst Yi didn't hesitate to isolate herself from the rest of us, on the far side of the table.

"Can I get anyone a tea or coffee?" Harriet asked, expectantly.

"Have you got anything stronger?" Yi chuckled.

"I'm afraid not Ms Chang."

"Then I suppose coffee will have to do."

Harriet commissioned a member of her team to provide us all with our choice of beverages, the aroma from my mug of coffee tickled my nostrils, providing a much-needed jolt of endorphins.

A cinematic screen mounted at the forefront of the conference room, controlled by a small circular device affixed to the peak of the table, where Harriet was positioned.

She waved her hand over the device to project an image of Jeffery Hutchin's house, where I executed the warrant only days ago.

"Thank you all for joining me here today." She began. "It's great to have you all together. You would all make Agatha immensely proud."

"Agatha?" Yi asked. "The arson victim from St Mary's?"

"Yes, Ms Chang. Agatha was my mentor, my teacher. She taught me all I needed to know about the Custodian prophecy."

"What exactly is our prophecy?" Jayce asked. "Marco explained it to me when we first met, but so much happened, I didn't a hundred percent understand it. No offence mates." He playfully placed his hand on my arm, a rhetorical spark forming between us.

"None taken." I smiled at him, smitten. I needed to snap out of this crush – I was perfectly happy with Grayson.

Harriet possessed intimate knowledge of our supernatural destiny, so it was only right for her to reiterate what was in store.

"That's quite alright Mr Stevens. I'm aware of your turmoil over the past week." Her tuneful voice carried across the briefing room, enticing us as an audience to her opera.

"Your prophecy has been destined for thousands of

years. The powers have been passed down from generation to generation, through your bloodlines. Your purpose is to help protect the world from the evil underground Hellion empire which come to light every few decades."

Harriet paced around the room as she spoke, our watchful eyes all tracking her in unison, her heels verberating on the steel floor.

"Each set of Custodians has prevailed, however every time the Hellion threat has reared its head, they have returned more powerful than before."

She briefly leaned against the end of the table, glancing at each of us in turn.

"This is the first time that the Hellions have been able to disguise themselves and take human form, so you definitely have your work cut out."

"This is all very inspiring." A sarcastic Yi rolled her eyes, scrunching her arms so tightly into her chest I convinced myself she was going to break a rib. It seems old habits die hard.

"Seriously Chang!" Jayce scolded, clearly annoyed. "Show some respect for a change!"

Silence hit the room as Yi wrinkled her face in displeasure and embarrassment. The newly formed tension very apparent, I tried to avoid any eye contact with anyone, and focused on a point on the wall.

"Ms Chang, I understand. You have been through a tough time. You like order and routine, and this has just brought disparity and chaos amongst your life." Harriet's wisdom began to defrost the atmosphere in the room. Attempting to be the peacekeeper, she turned to Jayce.

"I also understand your frustration, Mr Stevens. You are a man of honour and valour. You detest rudeness and disrespect, but you must appreciate that Ms Chang is finding this situation significantly more difficult than you."

Her natural talent for diplomacy seemed to work, as Yi stared down at the floor.

"Sorry." She muttered.

"I'm sorry too." Jayce said, directing a handsome half smile towards her.

Harriet completed a full circle of the briefing room and met us again at the head of the table.

"I appreciate emotions are high, and you will all have time to deal with that, however, we haven't much time." She steered us all back on topic and turned her attention to the still image of the semi-detached house. "This is forty-two Elm Road in Crantock. Mr Ramirez executed a warrant here yesterday." She waved her hand over the sphere remote and an image of Jeffery appeared.

"This is Jeffery Hutchins, the occupant. We have identified through our links with the Police and our intelligence sources that he is responsible for the death of Agatha. It is believed that he is very senior within the Hellion hierarchy, based on evidence gathered from this address."

"It's clear that the Hellions are looking at world leaders. Just about every country was represented on that board. Including the United Kingdom." I added.

"Thank you, Marco. What concerns me is that the Prime Minister is the only high-ranking government official that knows about this facility. If she has been compromised, then I don't need to tell you how dyer that would be." Harriet said, her tone representing the seriousness of our predicament.

"Surely if that were the case, we would have been sought out and assassinated by now? I mean the government has a whole army at their disposal." Jayce remarked.

"True." Harriet nodded in agreement.

"There's something you should know H." I began. "When testing out Brandon's portals this morning, somehow, me and Yi ended up ten years in the future."

"We met future you, and you were a badass!" Yi chuckled.

"It's safe to say that things don't end well." I explained, a hint of concern in my voice.

"How on earth did you end up in the future?" Harriet questioned, with demand.

Was she expecting me to know the answer?

"I don't know." I timidly replied.

"I am aware of Water Custodian's ability to open travel portals; however, time manipulation is a sacred magic which is only harnessed by the Time Custodian. As far as I'm aware there hasn't been one for over three hundred years."

It took me a minute to process what Harriet had said. I think she'd forgotten for a moment, that we were all novices.

"So, we have no idea who sent them there?" Brandon asked.

"Unfortunately, not. However, it would seem whoever did, wanted you to see the future in order to prevent it. Did you find out what the catalyst for this was?"

I recalled my conversation with future Harriet and tried to replicate her information as best I could.

"A world conference somewhere. That brings all the world leaders together. This led to their conversion to Hellions and ultimately the destruction of the world."

Harriet listened intently, before waving her hand over the device, turning her attention back to the screen. The next image depicted a large group photo, with a mixture of people of varying ages, genders and ethnicities, posed in uptight and militant postures.

They were dressed in formal attire and displayed perfectly placed pin badges of flags on the left side of their chest.

I recognised our Prime Minister, Gail, within the mass of world leaders.

"That actually brings me onto my next point." She paused for a moment, as she studied the image projected on the screen behind her. "For those that do not recognise this group, these are the current world leaders. They are assembling again in two weeks for the World Peace Conference, held in Las Vegas."

"Did you say Las Vegas?!" I asked, my eyes widened with excitement. "Amazing place. Me and Grayson have been no end of times!"

I wasn't joking. The preceding October was the seventh time we'd travelled within the last five years. I couldn't put my finger on what attracted us back; it was a place that required a visit in person to make judgement.

"Yes. The conference is being held in the Venetian hotel." Harriet maintained her straight-laced attitude, ignoring my excitable outburst.

"My counterpart in the CIA is closely monitoring the situation, but I have newly disseminated intelligence to suggest that the Hellion 'High Order' has plans to continue to infiltrate the highest of world governance."

"Does this mean what I think it means?" Brandon asked, almost leaping up from his chair.

"Yes." Harriet strutted elegantly over to a briefcase laid on one of the side tables that surrounded the room. We all watched on, expectant, as she popped the gold laced locks it and lifted open the lid.

She removed a collection of documents, cradling them with one hand against her chest as she ventured around each of us, supplying a personalised, plastic folder which she placed on the desk.

When I received mine, I examined the translucent folder and sighted a crisp and glossy passport neatly positioned between a driving licence and set of credit cards.

I was intrigued to see an austere portrait of me neatly laminated on the licence, with a name of 'Fabio Gonzalez' replacing my true credentials.

"These are your cover identities. Any official MI6 mission from here on out, you will need to use these. You should have everything you need - Passports, Credit Cards, Birth Certificates and National Insurance numbers. There is also a fact sheet of your cover persona, for you to study and get to know them intimately."

"Jessica Gonzalez. Nice." Yi raised her eyebrows and nodded approvingly as she examined her documents. I was pleasantly surprised that she accepted it without any argument or sarcastic remark. I realised we both had been given the same surname.

"Did you say Gonzalez?" I asked, my eyes narrowing.

"Yes, why?"

"That's my last name." I declared as I carefully held the edges of the laundered licence at Yi.

"Guess we're married then!" she laughed. "I've always wanted a gay husband."

"Watch it!" I playfully scowled at her, fond of her new sudden enthusiasm for our cause.

I looked over at Brandon, gleefully rummaging through his array of fake identity cards.

"Lucas Taylor. Easy to remember!" he chirped. "And what a great photo!" He laughed as he exhibited one of the photos around to show us all.

I loved Brandon's naive and innocent approach to life; he had a perspective of the world in a unique way to the rest of us, which was one of his pure strengths.

"Why did I get Norman Gusterford?" Jayce looked utterly displeased with his character. "Do I look like a 'Norman'?!".

"Unfortunately, the names are not for negotiation," Harriet quickly interjected, before any more of us could protest. "However, you may change some of the details on the fact sheet if it helps you to remember them easily."

"I'm fine with mine." Yi smiled. "Jessica is a socialite, married to a billionaire, with buckets of money and private jet. What have I got to complain about?"

"You'd better not be spending all my money." I joked, studying my briefing pack into Fabio's life. He was a successful entrepreneur, who'd become extremely wealthy from his own clothing line and married to his wife Jessica, the daughter of a Chinese ambassador.

Before I joined the Police, I formed part of an amateur dramatic society, where I thrived in being cast as the lead, performing theatrical productions for my friends, family and a sea of paying strangers.

I had to reluctantly retire due to the pressures of shift work, so I was extremely pleased to have the opportunity to be able to flex my thespian muscles once more.

I caught Harriet breaking her serious character with a slight grin, as we dived into our espionage characters.

I admired the craft of her team, who created intricate details of our personas, enabling us to have a fighting chance at infiltrating the conference.

She gestured over the dome, materialising an image of the Venetian hotel in Vegas, one of the more luxurious accommodations along the strip. The hotel mirrored the elegance and beauty of its inspiration, the quaint Italian city of Venice.

"This is the Venetian hotel. As you have anticipated, your mission is to infiltrate the conference and to defeat any Hellion infiltrators using any force necessary. Remember that the eyes of the world will be on this conference, so try not to expose yourself in public areas."

Harriet continued to brief us. Yi and I would use our personae to meet world leaders at the gambling tables, whilst Brandon and Jayce would pose as hotel staff, to gain us access to all areas.

Her counterpart in the CIA would meet prior to our

mission and provide us assistance where necessary.

"You have two weeks until you deploy. I suggest you get your affairs in order. Your flight leaves Heathrow Airport at 1245 hours, two weeks tomorrow."

"I've got to admit. This is all quite exciting." Yi said, surprising the entirety of the room.

"You've a change of heart." I said. "Two days ago, you wanted nothing to do with us, now you can't wait to get started?"

"He has a point, Chang." Jayce agreed.

"I get to be a rich and powerful socialite. What more could I want?" she grinned.

"It's only pretend!" I reminded her.

"I know." She uttered. "I told you I'd be better, Marco, I need to make a start somewhere."

"I'm sure you will all prevail." Harriet interjected, pushing her thick rimmed glasses back onto the bridge of her nose. "I'll keep in touch with you until then, but I wish you all the very best of luck."

"We'll do you proud, H." I assured her.

"I have no doubt that you will. You are *Custodians*."

TWELVE

For the next few days, I did nothing. The intensity of the previous week started to take its toll on me both mentally and physically.

Grayson worked long hours, so I'd a lot of solitary time to reflect, which consisted of several mile runs around the coastline and heavy gym sessions.

I'd no contact from work, which was a blessing. Although I was pleasantly surprised that I hadn't yet been arrested for Murder, what with the entire station witnessing me killing 'Gruffydd.'

I assumed Harriet used her powers of persuasion, as I wouldn't be able to accomplish any saviour duties from a prison cell.

I tried desperately to lock those events away in a deep corner of my mind, but they continued to resurface, and I'd no choice but to face them head on.

I eventually plucked up the courage to return to work on

Thursday morning, driving my car into my parking space where my plaque remained intact.

I made my way into the building, clutching tightly to the strap of my brown leather shoulder bag, my knuckles ghostly white from the sudden lack of blood.

I took the lift to the third floor.

I snapped out of a slight daydream when the lift doors opened, and Carole appeared; her contagious, scarlet-lipped smile shining at me.

"Mornin' Darlin!" she sung, as I stepped out.

There was no hostility. No questions. No demand for explanations. Harriet *must* have worked her magic.

"Morning boss." I replied.

"Feeling better?" She asked.

I was confused.

"Better?"

"Yeah darlin.' You went home sick on Sunday."

"Oh right. Yes. I feel much better, thanks." I forced a smile, pretending to know exactly what she was referring to.

"I'll catch up with you in a bit. I've got to go and meet with the Super." Carole said, scuttling into the lift.

"No worries, I'll see you later."

I meandered my way into our office, where Louisa sat at her desk. She displayed her hair in her typical messy ponytail and wore a striking, yet classy leopard print blouse.

"Morning Lou." I greeted, as I approached her.

"Morning boss." She turned away from her console and looked up at me. "Good days off?"

I took a calculated minute to answer. She'd witnessed the amulet blasting an energy ripple when I first found it, but she hadn't been privy to any of the chaotic events of the past week.

"Well apart from being struck down with man flu - busy." I replied. "What about yours?"

"Nothing exciting." she shrugged.

"How's things going with the St Mary Murder?" I asked.

"Sorry boss, the what?" Louisa looked at me blankly.

"The St Mary Murder." I repeated, surprised that she didn't recognise the name of our biggest case in months.

"As in Scilly Isles St Mary?" She asked, her face evolving into an even more confused look.

"Yeah."

"Boss. There's been no Murder there."

My eyes widened. Harriet had not only wiped the events of my 'Gruffydd' encounter, but the entirety of Agatha's death. When I fathomed that Louisa had no clue of what I was talking about, I accepted defeat.

"Ah sorry. Must have been another one I was thinking of. Sorry it's been a stressful week."

"No worries boss. I'd better crack on anyway." She turned back to her terminal, making it obvious she attempted to avoid any more conversation with me – understandable if she thought I was insane.

I went to my office and closed the door behind me, sitting back in my chair and liberating my mobile from my pocket.

I dialled Harriet.

"Good morning, Marco." She answered, the chaos of her frantic department evident in the background. I speculated if she'd a significant private life, as she always appeared to

be at work whenever I contacted her.

"H. Did you do something to my colleagues at work?" I whispered down the phone.

"What do you mean?" she asked, puzzled.

"They don't seem to have any recollection of this last week!"

"All I've done is advise my Police contacts of your incident, and to make any subsequent investigation disappear." she explained. *"I don't tend to wipe people's minds unless absolutely necessary, especially on a mass scale."*

"Then how is it no one here seems to have recalled anything?"

She paused.

"Unfortunately, Marco, that's a question that I am not able to answer."

Another mystery to add to my list.

"You must admit, this is all strange? Me and Yi getting transported to the future? All my work colleagues having no memory of the last week? What is going on?!" I minimised the volume of my tone but indicated to her I was frustrated.

"I understand this is unexplainable and that you want answers, but I all I can do is have my team look into it." she attempted to quell my concerns.

"Thanks H. Sorry to keep pestering. I'll speak to you later."

"Goodbye, Marco."

I ended the call and logged onto my office terminal, painfully watching as the usual unnecessary correspondence filled my mailbox.

Once I'd pain stakingly expelled my inbox of spam,

Louisa knocked on my door, before cautiously opening and peering her head through.

"Boss, sorry to disturb you." she whispered.

"You're not disturbing me, Lou, it's fine. What's up?"

"Just had a call from the Duty Inspector, there's been a potential murder. A body's been found on Crantock Beach with suspicious circumstances. I'm heading down if you want to come with?"

"Isn't Waldring the Duty DI today?" I asked, knowing I wasn't due on the rota for a week or so.

"He is, but I'd much rather you come. Please."

Louisa rarely requested anything from me, our professional relationship being much of a one-way street. It would take my mind off my alternate employment of battling demons.

"Fine. Meet you downstairs in five."

I was used to the ruckus that came with a serious crime scene. Masses of Police tape, an abundance of blue strobe lighting, hi-visibility jackets galore and every emergency service present known to man.

Louisa pulled up at the end of the car park, where I recognised one of the local Police Community Support Officers stood guard at the cordon.

It was twenty-odd degrees Celsius outside, so I didn't need to wear my brown suede jacket that I was known for sporting at crime scenes by the uniformed officers.

Instead, I rolled up the sleeves of my shirt, which co-ordinated with my chinos, the sand creeping into the crevasses in my boots.

"Morning Sir," the PCSO chirped, smiling at me as she scribbled our names into the logbook before lifting the tape over us.

I greeted and thanked her, before spotting Nadine. She always seemed to unluckily be the Duty Inspector when anything critical seemed to occur.

She was also present for the Hellion encounter at the station, so it would be interesting to see if she mentioned it.

"Ah Rambo!" she nodded, as she spotted me and Louisa wading towards her through the sand banks.

"Alright Tans!" I playfully greeted her; we'd both passed our promotion process the same year, so we'd gotten to know each other well; especially over our love of a decent cocktail. "What've you got for me?" I asked, getting straight down to business.

"Got a call in at six thirty this morning, from a dog walker, who found a deceased female on the beach. It appears she was mauled to death by some sort of animal. If it weren't due to a driving licence being found in her handbag, we wouldn't have a clue who it was."

"Who is it?" I asked, intrigued.

"You'll never believe this." Nadine dramatically paused. "Clara Buxton, of Buxton-Reeds Law Firm."

I instantly felt nauseous.

"What?!"

"Isn't that Grayson's firm?" Nadine asked.

I took a minute to answer, as my chest pounded hard with angst.

"Yeah. She's his boss." I revealed, swallowing a heap of saliva that congealed in my mouth.

"Shit." Louisa muttered. "Will you be okay with this one, boss?"

"I'll be fine." I said, pushing a stray sleeve back up my arm. "Where is she?" I asked, trying to remove my emotive ties and focus on the investigation.

"This way." Nadine manoeuvred the difficult terrain and walked towards a group of Crime Scene Officers who were all huddled together in forensic suits, flashing their cameras at various numbered cones on the ground.

As I approached the scene, the remains of Clara became apparent.

The scene was gruesome.

Her face barely recognisable from slash wounds, and the bottom of her left arm dismembered, lying two meters to her side.

Her ashen grey complexion puffed out, as if she'd been laid in water for a considerable amount of time.

I summoned the night I met her at Lewennick Lodge in my psyche, feeling even more below par when I recognised the shredded remnants of a black dress, to be identical to the one she wore that evening.

I couldn't be the SIO for this case, especially with me being one of the final persons to see her alive.

I walked up to one of the Crime Scene Investigators, a young woman named Ellie. Naturally pretty, she attracted a high population of response officers.

It was difficult to bat away volunteers for scene preservation when they knew she was on duty.

Even as a gay man, I could appreciate the attraction.

"Ellie, is it?" I made sure I'd the right person. I was

skilful with names against faces, but she was someone who I'd not often encountered.

"It is. Morning, Sir," she muffled as she removed her mask. "How can I help?"

"Any early indications of cause?" I requested; hopeful I didn't appear rude.

Ellie stood, pondering as she gripped hold of a clip board full of scribbles of notes, glossing over them.

"I'm guessing from whatever mauled her face." she shook her head and sighed. "What a way to go. We can't be a hundred percent sure until the post-mortem, but it would be an educated guess for now. She's not been here long, I reckon the murder scene is somewhere else, probably a local nearby beach."

"You think she was swept up?" Louisa asked, intrigued, furiously scribbling in a notebook cradled in her arm.

"I can't be sure, but that's what it looks like." Ellie replied. "I would have thought she would have been found sooner if she was attacked and left here."

"What caused those claw marks?" I was interested to hear Ellie's explanation; I already had a working theory.

"Call me crazy, but they look like bear claw marks. They're too big for a dog or any wild animal."

Hellion claw marks.

"Estimation of how long ago this happened?" Louisa inquired.

"Three days? I couldn't be certain." Ellie responded.

"Thanks Ellie. You've been a tremendous help. Let me know if you need anything." I forced a smiled, before hurrying away from the scene. Louisa attempted to catch me up.

"Boss!" Louisa yelled, as she struggled to navigate the sand dunes. "Boss!"

I stopped sharply in my tracks and turned to my Sergeant.

"Sorry Lou." I rubbed my temple, closing my eyes, an all too familiar headache beginning to manifest. "You crack on with this one. I need to let Carole know I can't be the SIO. It'll have to be Tim."

I could tell Louisa was disappointed.

"Really?" she protested. "Are you sure there isn't a way you can stay on the case."

"Afraid not. I'm too close to this, and it wouldn't be fair me continuing."

"Okay, I understand." Louisa said, disheartened. "Where are you heading now?"

"I need to make a phone call, then I'll get Nadine to take me back to the nick."

We parted ways and I made a beeline for a discreet part of the car park where I wouldn't be overlooked. I'd no choice but to dial Harriet again.

"Marco." She answered, instantly. *"Is everything okay?"*

"I know this is borderline harassment, but there's something strange going on here."

"What now?" she asked.

I took a deep breath, trying to make sure that I could get as much detail as possible for her, as I expected this would all eventually be recorded and held in a top secret, classified MI6 file.

"I need you to look into a Murder investigation for me.

Clara Buxton; Grayson's boss. She's been found dead, swept up on Crantock Beach with injuries consistent with mauling. I'm positive they are from a Hellion." I explained.

"Has this just happened?" Harriet asked.

"I've arrived at the scene, but it's fresh. Maybe a couple of days old?"

"Leave it with me. Are you leading this one?" she asked.

"Not this one no. I was one of the final people to see alive, as she wore the exact same clothing as when me and Grayson met her for dinner last week."

"In that case, we must be cautious. Whoever killed her, more than likely knows your connection to her." I came to the same grave conclusion.

I fixed my thoughts on Grayson's wellbeing, concerned he was being hunted by some sort of Hellion bounty.

"I'll try not to call you again, H. Although, I have no idea what else is in store for me today."

I looked vacantly out of the patrol car window as Nadine drove back to the station. I was uncharacteristically silent throughout the journey.

"You okay Rambo?" she asked.

"Fine. Just a bit upset about Clara." I muttered into my palm, my elbow resting on the window ledge.

"Understandable."

With my mind temporarily on leave from my body, I missed Nadine take the turning into the station.

"Marco." She prodded my consciousness to return. "We're here."

"Oh, right." I hazily fluttered my eyelids, like a new-born. "Thanks for the lift Tans, sorry I wasn't best company."

"No worries mate. We can compare wedding plans next time." She smiled, as we both parted ways.

I sluggishly voyaged up to Carole's office.

"Boss, have you got a minute?" I asked,

Carole ushered me in, and I closed the door tenderly behind.

"Are you aware of log fourteen of today, the body found on Crantock Beach?" I canvassed.

"Yes, darlin' we've been talking about it in our morning meeting. Any updates?" she inquired.

"You're going to have to allocate Tim as SIO for this one."

Carole clasped her hands together, deliberant, her inch long nails peeking out from between her fingers.

"Why?"

"The body has provisionally been identified as Clara Buxton." I disclosed.

"Yeah, I know. Why, do you know her?" Carole asked, her brow arched, perplexed.

I took in a deep, drawn-out breath before dropping the blow. "Clara is Grayson's boss. He works for Buxton-Reed Law Firm."

"Shit!" she exclaimed.

Carole rested her chin on the brim of her hand, intent in thought, before leaning back in her chair.

"Right. That's it I'm sending you home." She demanded, shaking her head.

I held my palms up in protest.

"No! You don't need to do that, I'm fine."

"Well. Someone needs to tell Grayson, as her employee. I'm guessing you don't want him hearing this third party?" she asked.

As usual, Carole was right. I'd much prefer it for me to break the news, rather than a complete stranger, I knew this would devastate him.

"When you put it that way..."

"Go on! I'm sending you home, now." Carole gestured me towards the door. "I'll get everything off Louisa when she gets back."

My hand was forced by her persistence, so I waved her farewell and headed home.

I stood in solitude outside our apartment door, plucking up the courage to insert and turn the key, eventually braving it after a minute or so.

I entered, startling a harried Grayson, who quickly grilled me as to why I arrived home early. I remained reluctant to appraise him before hand, knowing full well he would have tried to encourage me to part with the grave news of Clara.

I slipped off my boots in the hallway and placed my work bag on the kitchen counter, before planting a peck on his strained forehead.

"Coffee?" I asked.

"Please."

I collected our favourite mugs from the mug tree, laying them beside one another, then fuelled up the coffeemaker.

"When was the last time you spoke to Clara?" I probed him, pouring a splash of milk into each cup.

"Not since we went out to Lewennick." He replied.

"Have you wondered why you haven't seen her?"

"No idea. She doesn't come into the office every day; it's not unusual for us not to hear from her for a few weeks. Why do you ask?"

I stirred the coffee, which released an earthy aroma into the apartment, serving one to Grayson, who sprawled his case work over the dining table.

I sat in the vacant chair opposite him, clutching my mug tightly.

I gazed deep into his piercing, blue eyes, accentuated under the lens of his glasses, which made it increasingly harder to deliver the agony message.

Just do it, Marco. Rip off the plaster.

"I hate to be the one to tell you this," I said, my chest pulsing with each word. "But she was found dead this morning."

Grayson sat in silence, taking a sip of his coffee, not reacting in the slightest.

I was astonished.

"How was she found?"

What? Is he being serious?

"What do you mean?" I asked, taken back slightly.

Why is he not upset?

"Answer me!" I jolted in my seat as he yelled with a curt and alien pitch.

I'd never known him to shout at me in that way.

"Why?" I asked, just as shrill. "Why is that so important to you!?"

"Tell me, Marc." He glimpsed up from his stack of

papers, persistent in his desire to know that specific detail.

"Washed up on Crantock beach, with slash wounds all over her body. She was unrecognisable."

"I see." He said, subdued.

"I'm concerned you're not taking this all in." I said, referring to his surprising lack of grief.

"I am. I don't wear my heart on my sleeve like you do." He articulated. "I just wanted to know."

I couldn't help the anger that consumed me. I barely knew this man sat in front of me. He'd wept when our dog, Buster died, yet remained absent of any emotion towards the death of his friend.

"Bullshit!" I berated back. "What's wrong with you?"

"Nothing! Just because I didn't collapse on the floor in a sorrowful heap like you did when your mother died, doesn't mean I'm not sad."

"That was uncalled for." I pointed at him, through clenched teeth, my throat dry and quivering.

What has gotten into him?

"Do you know she was in the same dress she wore when we saw her that night?" I divulged.

"So what?" He huffed.

"So, what!" I shrieked, my face burning in anger. "We were one of the last people to see her alive Gray! We'll be the prime suspects! You of all people know how that will look!"

"You need to stop shouting." He uttered, as cool as steel.

"No! I won't stop shouting! This isn't you!" I continued to yell, the ground quivering under my feet as my rage increased.

Calm yourself, Marco.

"Did you have anything to do with her disappearance?" I accused him. I regretted it as soon as the words left my mouth.

"Why are you even asking me that question?" He jeered, his eyes narrowing. "After fifteen years of being together, you really think that I'm capable of doing such a thing. Especially to my own boss?"

"I really don't know what to think any more." I sighed, dropping my face into my palms in exhaustion. "Sorry. I've had a long week."

I filled my lungs to capacity and collected myself together, the gentle earthquake subsiding as my internal heat evaporated.

I don't think Grayson noticed.

"So have I." he huffed, focusing back on his work.

Maybe I was too expectant of him?

I got up, navigating around our circular dining table, wrapping my arms around Grayson's neck and planted a gentle kiss on the top of his head.

"I'm sorry." I whispered in his ear.

He reciprocated by taking hold of my arm and pushing his head tightly into my chest.

"I'm sorry too." He said. "It was a shock. I can't believe someone would do that to her."

"I know. Don't worry though Gray, I have every faith in my team. They'll catch her killer." I assured him. "The one thing I'm worried about is you."

"Why me?" He looked up, baffled.

I paused, mentally rehearsing how I was going to reveal the news of a threat to him, without exposing the secret fantasy world.

"There is a lead that this maybe targeted. I just worry as you work for Clara's law firm. For all we know it's a disgruntled convict who you helped to put inside." I fibbed. "Please be careful."

"I will" He smiled, his pearly whites glistening. "Thank you for looking out for me Marc."

"You don't have to thank me; you're my world."

Grayson meandered over to me and took me by the waist, pulling me close and passionately kissing me, reigniting the spark that was overdue a jump start.

He gently took my hand and guided me to our bedroom, laying me down on the bed, and whisking me away to a promiscuous reality where all my troubles and woes were suppressed.

For the next few moments, I was in ecstasy.

THIRTEEN

Two weeks passed in the blink of an eye.

The four of us met up throughout the fortnight, at an abandoned military base on Penhale Point, near to the small village of Holywell, a discreet space for us to practice harnessing our magical abilities as we were still all novices.

The training ground was perfect.

It kept out of the way of public, yet the vacated residential buildings and air hangers provided some realism as we battled each other in mock scenarios.

Any downtime between sessions was spent losing myself in the vista of the Cornish coastline, the serenity of the waves momentarily causing me to forget my Custodian persona.

The Hellions we were preparing to battle were more senior within their community, and we anticipated them to be much more brute and starker than the minions we previously encountered.

Harriet also maintained contact, updating with any intelligence, both from MI6 and her counterpart within the CIA.

We'd been informed by our American friends, that the High Order were expectant of our 'seek out and destroy' mission at the Peace conference.

No doubt the defences would be heightened.

I filled with apprehension the closer our departure to the States drew. We were inexperienced and unacquainted, which was only emphasised by the pressure to succeed.

I'd severe misgivings, but we were the world's sole hope.

The pristine black Range Rover that pulled up at the front of my apartment complex wasn't exactly inconspicuous, although slightly concealed by the early morning night sky.

The driver, a mature, chiselled man in his fifties with a silver skin fade, helped me pack my luggage into the boot.

My alibi to Grayson consisted of a work trip to America, to meet with a forensic specialist who was assisting with Agatha and Clara's murder.

He didn't question me.

I'd become an expert at forging the truth, weaving myself into an ever-growing web of lies and deceit.

It's for the good of the world. I reminded myself.

I'd fabricated so many fables, that I'd filled a note pad as a reference to prevent me from inadvertently slipping up.

I slept for the entire lengthy journey to Heathrow, the cosy appeal of the seats a natural anaesthetic, only waking as my George Clooney lookalike driver pulled into arrivals.

Yi, Jayce, and I were the first ones to arrive, whereas

Brandon turned up thirty minutes later.

"Sorry guys!" He apologised, alighting his blacked-out vehicle, a group of huddled women disappointed when the realised he wasn't anyone famous.

"Forget something?" Yi asked, her hand placed sternly against her hip.

"Only my bloody passport!" Brandon giggled, whilst the rest of us rolled our eyes into our palms.

"Trust you." I sighed.

There were times during the previous fortnight, that his scatterbrain had become evident, either forgetting his lunch or his wallet or on the odd occasion, both.

"You did make sure it was your MI6 one, didn't you?" I checked.

Brandon's face immediately dropped in terror. He swiftly swung his backpack from his shoulders and furiously buried himself through all the pockets.

He joyed at the discovery of the blue booklet, with 'AUSTRALIA' embossed in gold on the front, along with a Kangaroo and Emu stood either side of a shield.

Brandon closed his eyes and delicately opened it to the identification page. He looked down with one eye and exhaled a large sigh of relief.

"Thank god for that!" He dropped his arms, almost collapsing in a heap on the floor.

"You really need to get your act together!" An irritated Yi snapped, shaking her head.

"Come on, let's get checked in." I said, in an attempt to whisk us through to the departure lounge and diffuse any tensions.

As we entered the terminal building, an architectural masterpiece of glass windows and metallic cylinders, I veered us towards the British Airways section.

As secret MI6 agents, we were business class passengers, and had the privilege our own check in desk. It was such a surprising thrill to trundle my oversized suitcase past a disgruntled looking queue of economy passengers.

"Good morning!" A chirpy twenty-something check-in assistant greeted us. She'd a face full of make-up, with bright, almost luminescent red lipstick which would have made Carole envious.

Her sheen hair tied up in a radical bun, pulled tightly on her cheeks, as her immaculate smile radiated a brilliant glow.

"Morning." I mirrored, before arranging my counterfeit passport and flight ticket on the desk.

"Where are you travelling today sir?" She inquired.

"Las Vegas." I replied.

"Lovely!" she exclaimed. "I went there three weeks ago, and it was fabulous!"

"Unfortunately, we're there on business." I interjected, before she could suggest any of the exhilarating entertainment that the adult playground had to offer, which we wouldn't have time to experience.

The downside to being supernatural saviours, I guess.

"Oh, that's a shame. Hopefully, you'll get some downtime to explore."

"Maybe," I muttered, unenthusiastically, as I collected all my comrades' secret agent passports together and presented them to the check in agent.

Although loud and slightly annoying, the woman was

extremely efficient, checking us all in and depositing our bags in a time worthy of an entry into the world records.

Yi's case displayed overweight, but as we'd evened out between us, the check in assistant waivered any fees.

"We've got twenty-five kilos *each*, how on earth have you managed to go over?" Jayce asked, shaking his head in disbelief.

"My hair straighteners alone weigh three kilos!" She protested. "This hair doesn't straighten itself!"

I chuckled to myself as the woman handed me back our passports with boarding cards peeking out the top like a bookmark.

"Come on, I need a pint!" I declared, as I darted towards the security gates.

"It's only ten o'clock!" Yi looked at me in disgust, as if I'd asked her to walk on a bed of broken glass.

"It's an airport tradition me and Grayson have." I smiled. "And this is nothing. I've had one at three in the morning before."

Yi shook her head and held her palm up towards me. "Not for me. It's too early to be drinking."

"Ah live a little!" Brandon said, vivaciously. "You're on holiday!"

"We're not on holiday," I reminded him. "We're going out there to work. Or have you forgotten the whole 'saving the human race from extinction' clause of our contract?"

"Mate, it's Vegas. It's a holiday for me. Even if it does mean vanquishing some Hellions whilst we're out there." Brandon chuckled.

We made our way through the security section, which

wasn't as swift as our check-in experience. A large group of travellers, were queued up in front of us, who still hadn't quite mastered the art of the liquid restrictions, despite being in force for well over twenty years.

We were thankfully ushered over to an empty lane by a mute security officer. He sternly studied us and pointed over to a conveyor belt, where we patiently waited to place all our lose odds and ends in a tray.

Whilst the rest of us breezed through the detectors, Brandon lit up the dazzling bright, danger red indicators. The officer rolled their eyes, as they sharply pointed to Brandon's watch still wrapped around his wrist, receiving a vigorous frisk, before eventually being directed to pass.

We all dashed towards the newly refurbished business class lounge; the heady stench of the paint still fresh.

It was better than I imagined.

A large abstract buffet table presented a colourful myriad of pastries, meats, and cheeses with intricately decorated fruits; a watermelon carved into the shape of a swan took pride of place as the centrepiece.

Jayce raced up to it and shovelled as much as he could on his plate until it overflowed.

I walked over to the bar, where the young bartender presented me with an ice-cold pint of beer upon my request. The condensation dripped lightly onto my hand as I pincered it, the freeze of the glass seeping into my palm. The beverage instantly dampened my nerves as I necked it back, a euphoria expanding from my core to my extremities, forcing out a sigh of comfort.

"Nothing like an airport beer," I smiled, as I took my

place at a table that Jayce gestured me towards. Yi and Brandon also invaded the buffet, showcasing their impressive hauls of nutritious treasure which oozed over the rim of their plates.

"Here we are then." Yi commented, whilst chewing on a mouthful of a croissant. "How is everyone feeling?"

"I'm excited!" Brandon grinned. "I can't wait to kick some Hellion ass!" He announced.

Two elderly patrons at an adjacent table turned to us in annoyance.

"Brandon!" I hissed. "Be careful!"

"Sorry." He sunk into his chair, apologetically holding his hand up.

"I'm nervous, if I'm honest." Jayce admitted. "Believe it or not, I'm not really a fighter."

His comment didn't surprise me.

He was a gentle giant, a stark divergence to his ability to manifest one of the most destructive elements known to man.

"I wouldn't lie if I said I wasn't nervous either, but we have to keep our cool. It's all down to us." I reminded my team.

"I mean, I get to pretend that I'm a rich socialite." Yi laughed.

"Not to mention you have a stud of a husband." I playfully winked at her.

My share of the banquet sat uneasy in my stomach, as a multitude of bodily gasses bloated me – I'd already regretted consuming my bodyweight in meats and cheeses.

Yi convinced me to succumb to a small glass of gin and

tonic with her, downing hers instantaneously, before ordering a trio more.

"Save yourself for the plane!" I giggled. "I thought you weren't an early morning drinker?"

We chilled in the business class lounge until our gate appeared on the departure board screen. I took charge of our entourage, meandering around snail-paced passengers and the stray carry-on bags blocking the pathways - eventually arriving at gate ten.

We were ushered onto the plane after the first-class elite, striding past the economy queue that snaked around the entirety of the departure gate.

As we entered the airbridge, we were escorted through the first-class area, the passengers already comfortable in their individual cocoons.

Business class was still affluent, with lavish reclining seats laid in twos, facing opposite directions. Brandon rested himself closest to the window, coupled with Jayce, and I paired with Yi.

As the captain began to make her final announcements, and the cabin crew scurried along the cabin conducting their safety checks, the plane began to move backwards.

I noticed Yi's eyes were tightly shut, and her breathing laboured. I glanced at her hands, viced on the arms of her seat.

"Are you okay?" I asked, leaning over to her.

"I'm fine!" She uttered through clenched teeth. "Just don't talk to me!"

"Are you afraid of flying?"

"Be quiet!" She barked.

Jayce, also noticing the sudden fear of our friend, reached across the aisle and took hold of her hand. He winced in pain as she squeezed the life from his fingers.

A gust of chilling wind starting to circle the cabin, causing the hairs on my arms to stand on end. The doors were closed, and the aircraft was sealed, so I checked my overhead fan.

It was off.

Then it came to me.

Yi was creating the gust.

Shit!

"Yi, you need to focus." I calmly whispered to her, trying to prevent a hurricane from manifesting.

"I'm trying!" she snapped, as she tensed further.

The wind began to rage, with passengers screaming in terror as it fiercely tracked through the cabin. The attendants all looked in trepidation as the invisible force ripped through the aisles, springing open overhead compartments, and gathering the contents into a swirling vortex.

Panicked passengers unclasped their seatbelts and rushed to the exits, battling with cabin crew as they attempted to force open the doors.

"YI!" I yelled, straining my voice, as the plane came to a sudden halt, shocking her out of her anxious trance, rescinding the violent gust.

The entire population of the plane looked perplexed, as crew members ushered stray passengers back to their seats, ordering them to buckle up whilst the plane returned to the gate.

"Why didn't you tell us you were afraid of flying?" I asked. She sheltered her phobia of flying extremely well, but it concerned me it was at a detriment to innocent members of public.

I kept thankful that we hadn't been thousands of miles in the air.

"It's embarrassing." She mumbled, sheepishly bowing her head.

"Surely you realise by now that our powers are effected by our emotions? Did you not think to tell us in case something like this happened?!" I scolded.

"Marco, stop." Jayce intervened. "She obviously has her reasons. We need to help her through it and make sure it doesn't happen again."

I didn't respond to Jayce, a slight bout of frustration still bubbled in my stomach.

He was right though, we needed to help our teammate through it to prevent a re-occurrence.

The captain's voice echoed through the cabin, informing us she was returning the plane back to the gate due to an 'unknown cause.'

I secretly had an urge to protest and reassure that there was no fault with the plane, but I needed to keep up appearances and play along.

We disembarked in a matter of minutes, crowding the departure gate, whilst engineers examined every inch of the aircraft.

The all clear was signalled to the gate staff, who orchestrated our re-embark into the comfort of our opulent seats.

"I promise I'll control it this time." Yi whispered over to us. "I'm sorry guys."

"Honestly, it's fine." I smiled, having time to bestow some sympathy on Yi's predicament.

The plane pushed back and taxied to the runway with no complications. Yi had been provided a Xanax by a fellow passenger who noticed her unease the first time round. We took off, with a small rumble of turbulence and levelled off at our cruising altitude.

I slept for the majority of the eleven-hour flight, being disturbed at intervals to consume the extravagant food and drink served by the cabin attendants.

I took a minute to observe my comrades, seeing how they were passing the time.

Jayce was prised to the television screen, sporting a pair of over the ear headphones, reminding me of a Cyberman from Doctor Who. He watched the Adam Sandler and Drew Barrymore chick flick '50 First Dates' – not a choice I would have expected from him.

Brandon immersed himself in his Kindle, but took two seconds to appraise me of the plot. I think it was some sort of crime drama, but as usual he spoke at lightening speeds so I could only decipher parts.

The descent into Las Vegas was beautiful. With the time difference, mid-afternoon had encroached the western side of the states, the high Nevada desert sun glistening brightly between the geometric pattern of the strip.

Thud!

The plane screeched as the brakes worked tirelessly to bring us to a halt. Yi's magic expressed a gentle anxious breeze, but nowhere near as severe as before.

Passport control provided the next challenge.

We all queued up together, remaining quite sombre, a mixture of both fatigue and nerves. My palms dripped with sweat as I reduced the gap to the immigration booth.

A sour faced, mature security attendant waved me over and I handed my 'Fabio Gonzalez' passport to him. He intricately studied me over his half-rimmed glasses, comparing me to the travel document, the collection of minutes seeming to pass like hours.

My expression remained neutral, ensuring he didn't have any reason to question me unnecessarily, which made me sweat even more profusely.

I relaxed with relief when the stone-faced man handed me back my counterfeit passport, ushering me through the gates.

I waited expectantly across the border for my friends to appear, which again, seemed an eternity.

I internally celebrated, when they finally emerged through the set of glass doors that sectioned off the immigration hall.

Another lengthy wait endured at baggage claim, our luggage not materialising on the belt for over an hour. Yi complained to a local, blemished, teenage British Airways representative who rudely shrugged us off.

He regretted it instantly.

Yi dressed him down in front of an audience of equally disgruntled customers, her composed, yet stern tone sliced through the youngster like a knife.

His eyes welled up – at one point I expected him to erupt in tears.

He scurried off, head held low, and our luggage miraculously arrived minutes later.

I expected a CIA official to meet us outside arrivals. Instead, a small round woman, in her sixties, with colourful clothing and thick bottle rimmed glasses clutched a handwritten sign with my alter ego's name.

She didn't strike me as an official, but I assumed they were going for a more discreet approach.

I greeted the woman, who blew a bubble with the chewing gum she munched on, before taking my extended-out hand.

"I'm Deloris" she said, gruffly. "Welcome to Las Vegas. Follow me."

Deloris walked with a slight limp, so we stalked behind her. The others all shot me a perplexed look as we followed her into the parking area, stopping short of a silver saloon car.

A pair of pink fluffy dice sat dangling in the centre of the windscreen, as an array of scrapes and dents decorated the car doors.

We'd just about fit three cases in her deceivingly small boot; Jayce having to contortion himself in the front and balance his case on his lap.

Yi, Brandon and I all wedged ourselves onto the back row, broken seat coils protruding through the upholstery and digging into my backside.

It was the most uncomfortable car ride I have ever experienced.

Deloris drove exactly how I imagined she 0would.

I sat in the rear of a rally car, as she refused to adhere to any speed limits, or make use of her indictors, causing the irritated drivers to sound their horns in reply.

I tried to keep a bout of nausea at bay, as we flew past the extravagant strip hotels, eventually screeching up outside what I guessed was the Venetian – I felt too disorientated to know exactly where we had ended up.

I cradled my whiplash as I crawled out of Deloris' car, taking in the surroundings of the Italian themed hotel.

Her saloon vehicle appeared misplaced between the Mercedes and Limousines that were setting down, exchanging groups of Vegas tourists.

"Thanks." I said, through gritted teeth.

I hope she's not expecting a tip!

"Don't mention it." She said, hoarsely, from the driver's seat, where she remained whilst we struggled with our belongings.

As I waved her off, she flew away, off into the distance, a long-drawn-out horn echoed from her direction, which I could only assume was in response to her evasive driving.

"Well, that was an experience." Yi said, sarcastically, placing on a pair of Gucci sunglasses that she pulled out of her handbag.

"I quite liked it." Brandon chuckled, as we headed inside into the lobby area. "I felt like I was on a rollercoaster."

"I don't do well on rollercoasters, let alone whatever that

was." Jayce said, looking very green.

We entered the lobby, and I immediately recalled the astounding beauty from my previous visit.

Grayson and I never stayed at the hotel, but frequented the Casino and the Shopping centre, all renaissance themed to match the exterior.

Not another queue! I thought to myself as we came across the snake of people wrapped around the reception area, however, the check in assistants were working with haste.

It only took twenty minutes for us to navigate the queue and be allocated our rooms.

I noticed the heavy presence of Las Vegas police officers, patrolling in pairs throughout the hotel, some overtly carrying large rifles.

We arrived two days before the conference, but world leaders had started arriving with their entourages.

I was concerned at our lack of contact from any member of the CIA, as we'd no clue of the intricate details of the mission, or any subjects of interest we needed to be on alert for.

Being a senior Police Officer, I relied heavily on intelligence to help with making tactical decisions.

So, I was slightly uneased.

We unanimously planned to check into our rooms on the twenty-fifth floor, and fortunately, side by side.

I tapped the key card against the lock of my room door, opening the gate to a small slice of heaven.

A large emperor sized bed sat as the focal point of the room, with the continued historical Italian theme and gold accented décor rendered throughout.

My heart skipped at beat at the splendour view of the Las Vegas strip, being sharply interrupted by a booming knock at the door.

"Room service!" A light voice accompanied.

I didn't order any room service.

I headed for the door and peered through the spy hole.

I saw a man with his hands on a cart, a silver food dome placed on the top and proudly wearing a Venetian uniform.

I opened the door, him effortlessly pushing his cart inside.

"Mr Gonzalez?" He inquired.

I stood in silence.

Oh wait, that's me!

"Yes?" I replied.

I closed the door behind him, focusing my attention.

"I can't remember ordering any room service." I said, apologetically. "Are you sure this is for me."

The man's friendly expression transformed to a sterile look as he lifted the lid on the serving dome, revealing four tiny spherical devices.

He stood upright and silent – his blood shot eyes drying from the lack of blinking.

Another knock ensued.

I peered through the spy hole; relieved to see a set of familiar faces – my Custodian friends.

"What's so important Marco?" Yi questioned me. I'd no idea what she referred to, until she waved a handwritten note in my face. The note said:

'Meet in room 2584, immediately.'

"That note isn't from me," I said, gesturing over to the

living statue.

"I see." Yi replied.

"It's from *me,* honey.*"*

A mysterious southern states twang resonated from the far corner of the room, from an opulent, throne-like armchair facing the window.

A tall woman, with a mane of fiery red hair rose to her feet, circling around to face us.

"Welcome to the United States." She beamed.

How did I not notice her!

I instantly adopted a defensive stance, my hands flying up to swiftly conjure my element if required.

"Who the hell are you!" Yi yelled from behind me, her posture mirroring mine.

"Sorry to have startled you, darlin's." She chucked, delicately closing the gap between us. "I'm Deputy Director Rebecca Nguyen, head of the Supernatural Investigations department within the CIA."

"Prove it!" Yi ordered, with a harsh affliction.

The woman reached into her long, coal overcoat, and produced an identity card, the smell of the authentic leather cover it was encased in, tickled my nostrils.

I investigated every inch of the identity card, admiring the dazzling gold crest proudly pinned on the inside of the holder.

Don't worry Marco, I'm not a Hellion.

A rich voice appeared in my head. Although startling, it was kind, gentle, and oozing with assurance.

"Was that you?!" I asked, my head gesturing towards this new, mysterious woman.

"It was." Rebecca smiled.

"You're a telepath too?" I inquired.

She nodded.

"Last time I checked darlin'."

The room relaxed, apart from Yi – of course - who bundled her arms stiffly into her chest.

"Sorry for the hostile welcome." I apologised. "We've been deceived before."

"Well, that's understandable, honey."

"I'm actually quite glad you're here, to be honest." I said. "Our MI6 contact only provided us with so much information. I'd hoped you'd be able to fill us in."

Rebecca swept back towards the window, her coat lifting like a cape.

"Of course, darlin.' What did you want to know?"

The woman didn't bestow the presence of a director. She appeared very spirited and jovial, a stark contrast to Harriet's serious and melancholy character.

"As much as you can tell us, obviously!" Yi scoffed.

"Don't be so rude!" I snapped.

"Okay honey. I'll give ya'll as much as I have." She began, her eyes lost in the breath-taking Vegas scenery. "Y'all have been sent here to help neutralise the Hellion threat. We have operatives working around the globe, infiltrated in all forms of governments, providing us with up-to-date intelligence."

She turned to face us, lifting her arm up to chest height, pressing firmly down on a device wrapped around her wrist.

It deceivingly gave the appearance of a standard smart watch; however, the device projected a translucent image of the various shapes and sizes of the world leaders.

"Delegates have already begun to arrive and will continue through to tomorrow; the conference beginning the following day. We have reason to believe that this conference will be used to convert a significant amount of world leaders into High Order Commanders."

She switched the hologram to a portrait of a man, appearing in his seventies, with silver hair and a haggard face.

"We also have significant intelligence that Golubev, the Russian ambassador to America, is the co-ordinator for all of the current Hellion attacks. It is highly likely that he has been compromised." Rebecca took a significant pause.

"He will be your target."

"Sorry, did she say we've got to *kill* a Russian Ambassador?!" Jayce exclaimed, exchanging a glance with me.

"She didn't specifically say we needed to *kill* him, only that he was our *target*." I whispered in his ear.

"We are unsure how the Hellions are infiltrating the world powers, but our assumption is they are replacing them with undercover agents, rather than controlling them directly." Rebecca interjected.

"Therefore, you are authorised to use lethal force if necessary. I believe y'all have false identities for the duration of your time here. You will also be provided with the most sophisticated tech that the CIA has to offer."

"Interesting." Brandon muttered to himself. "I expected to be whisked away to Area 51 or something. This is all a bit anti-climactic."

"I thought the same thing." Jayce said.

"Oh darlin's. You've been watching too many spy movies!" Rebecca giggled, in her warm Tennessee twang. "The less y'all move around, the safer you are. Besides, it got me and Agent Bullimore out of the office for the afternoon."

The emotionless mannequin turned to face his superior officer and nodded, his expression remaining sterile.

"That reminds me." Rebecca snapped her fingers and hovered back over us, her motions full of grace. She removed the four spherical items from Agent Bullimore's silver platter, sharing them out between us. "These are your covert communications devices. As you don't have the joys of telepathy, these will help you stay in touch with one another, and with me if you so need it."

"This is more like it!" Brandon gleamed with excitement, wasting no time in placing his communicator directly in his ear canal.

"Only use them when you need to darlin'." Rebecca instructed, half smiling at Brandon's enthusiasm. "There is one more thing."

A strange alert emitted from my phone, which I slid from the cocoon of my pocket to examine. The peculiar sound echoed like a submarine beacon, cascading across the remainder of my team's mobile's.

A new application added to my home screen, with the title 'Obelisk.' Curious, I opened it, requiring my thumb print for security access.

"This is your agent companion." Rebecca explained.

"You can review mission briefings, communicate

securely with other agents or CIA headquarters and it contains detailed maps of the entire Vegas region and buildings within."

"This is so cool!" Brandon excitedly yelled, showing me the screen of his. "I actually feel like a proper spy now!"

"I've got to admit, this is impressive." I agreed.

Yi shoved her phone into her pocket, appearing unimpressed, and walked over to the minibar.

"I need a drink."

"I don't blame you honey. I know it's a lot to take in." Rebecca sympathised. "I have faith in y'all. I trust Harriet, and she trusts you. I mean you're God damn Custodians!"

"I have reservations." I admitted. "We're all very new to this, and I don't think we have enough experience to succeed."

"Honey," Rebecca cupped the top of my arms and met my gaze, her emerald eyes radiating an aura of tranquillity. "You can do this. I bet every Custodian before you had the same jitters."

"Most of them are dead." Yi gravely reminded us.

"Look. It won't be easy, I know. But y'all need to work together, and you can succeed in anything. Have faith."

"Thanks Ms Nguyen." I lifted the corner of my mouth in something that resembled a smile.

"Rebecca, please!" she scoffed. "Now I'm gonna leave y'all to have a rest. I've pre-paid all your minibars, so help yourselves. Just holler if you need me."

Rebecca encroached us all in a heartfelt embrace, before waving us off, dismissing Agent Bullimore upon her exit.

Silence filled the room.

We exchanged a myriad of overwhelming glances, the ominous reality finally hitting us.

"Well." Yi uttered. "Minibar?"

A light transcended on our faces at the thought of free alcohol.

Yi rummaged through the selection of wines and spirits, eventually discovering a large bottle of champagne, passing it to Jayce to use his brute strength in opening it.

The cork blasted off to the ceiling, narrowly missing a miniature chandelier, causing the bottle to erupt. Yi caught the champagne volcano in a row of glass flutes and distributed the beverages between us.

"To us, the Custodians!" she toasted. We raised our glasses in response. "And the battle we are about to fight."

"To the Custodians!" The remainder of us cheered in unison, before taking a sip.

"Who's up for some slot machines?" Brandon chirped, guzzling down the remainder of his champagne.

"I think we've got some time." I commented, glancing at my watch.

I downed the final millilitres of the dry beverage, my eyes sealing shut at the taut taste, before ushering the team out of the door.

"Let's hope we win big!"

DAN ALEXANDER

FOURTEEN

This all looks amazing!
My palate was elated by the taste of all the extravagant food
that the breakfast buffet had to offer, expected at $160.

We requested a quiet corner of the banquet hall, so we
didn't fret about being overheard by any unsuspecting
Hellions in human skin. The Obelisk app had the ability to
discreetly dampen any recording devices within a hundred
metre radius, providing us with extra protection from any
demonic surveillance.

"According to the mission log, the Russian Ambassador
is due to arrive at 1400 hours this afternoon. The United
States president will be hosting an evening reception in the
Ball Room." I intricately devoured the briefing before
heading down for breakfast. "The CIA seem to think this is
where the Hellion recruitment drive is going to take place."

"How are we going to infiltrate this?" Jayce asked.

"This is where Yi's alter ego comes in handy. Jessica is

the daughter of a Chinese Ambassador, so the CIA have made sure she's been put onto the guest list. As I'm her husband in this charade, I'll be accompanying her."

"What about us?" Brandon questioned.

"You and Jayce will both pose as wait staff, that way you can get access to the areas off limits to public."

"How do we know who is a Hellion, and who isn't?" Jayce inquired. "I mean I couldn't tell with Jo. If she hadn't have transformed into that creature I wouldn't have ever known."

"I can help with that." Brandon interjected. "I don't know why but I think I can sense them out. I'd a really horrid feeling about your sister, and I was drawn to Agatha's mansion because I could sense evil activity there. There was also G….."

Brandon stopped sharp.

"There was also… what?" I asked, my brow arched.

"Never mind." He shook his head.

He was definitely holding something back, but I didn't want to press.

"Why didn't you say anything before?" Jayce asked.

"I thought you would think I was crazy." He replied. "I mean I'm still not a hundred percent sure, but I suppose it's the best thing we've got."

"Why can't the rest of us do that?" Yi probed. "I mean we can all heal ourselves, so why can't we sense like you can?"

"I think it has something to do with my dad." Brandon explained. "My mum didn't really know him, but she had suspicions that he may have been a telepath."

"What do you mean she didn't really know him? He's your dad?" Yi said, her voice raising up at the end in inquiry.

"Not that I see it is any of your business Yi, but I was the product of a one-night stand." Brandon hesitantly confessed. "She'd only been dating him about two weeks then she fell pregnant with me."

"I see." Yi nodded.

"Well, getting back to business." I interluded, refocusing my comrade's attention back to our mission. "We need to somehow draw the Russian Ambassador away from the rest of the delegates."

"Leave that to me." Yi smiled. "I'll use some of my natural god given gifts for that."

I must admit, despite her prickly personality, Yi was an attractive woman. My pull towards the same sex didn't stop me appreciating her beauty and her athletic figure.

I juddered my head, shaking off an alluring trance towards Yi. If it worked on me, we would have no problems in distracting members the delegation.

"Jayce and Brandon, that will leave you two to scope out any other potential Hellion threat. I would assume you'd need to look at Russian aide and close protection officers." I directed them. "We have to remember, that we don't know how deep they've infiltrated, so suspect everyone."

"Even you?" Yi joked.

I rolled my eyes at her.

"Of course, not me!" I jovially exclaimed. "We've got until 1800 hours to prepare ourselves. I suggest we all take that time to do a reccy of the hotel and get to know our alter egos, intimately. I don't need to remind you of what's a stake here."

"We can do this people!" Brandon threw his fists up in the air, with a shake of encouragement.

"Let's get on with it." Yi muttered.

As the day passed by, I stayed clear of the enticing casinos and pushy touts attempting to sell tickets to the evening showing of 'Adele' at the Coliseum theatre across the road.

I had however, been seduced by the assortment of food outlets in the Grand Canal Shoppes, and spent a solitary lunch at a charming café, which perfectly overlooked the indoor canal, complete with replica gondola's that waded through the water.

In the evening, after a brief late afternoon nap, we all met in the lobby, sandwiched between a crowd of pruned and polished attendees, dressed in elaborate ball gowns and starched tuxedos, for the President's reception.

I'd scoped out any quick exits and made a mental note of any potential inconspicuous battle grounds away from public view, on the almost certain probability we would need to call upon our supernatural gifts.

I blended in well with my black tie outfit, with the slim fit trousers emphasising my swollen thighs and claves, which I acquired from being a member of the local Rugby team.

My eyes shimmered when I studied Yi's outfit. She exuded aristocracy with her slender, pastel blue, sparkled dress which accentuated her delicate curves, fitting her socialite role perfectly.

We approached the entrance to the welcome reception,

as Jayce and Brandon forked off towards the staff area.

"Jayce can you hear me?" I discreetly muttered, tapping the small device uncomfortably lodged in my ear.

"Loud and clear Marco." he replied.

"Brandon?"

"All peachy here, mate."

After a short queue, I escorted Yi through the security check point, pretending to clutch lovingly hold of her arm, where we were greeted with a security guard who made Jayce look tiny.

"Name." He requested, gruffly.

"Jessica Gonzalez." Yi replied. "Daughter of the Chinese Ambassador to the United Kingdom." There was no surprise to me that she'd manage to fit that in.

"You?" The man pointed at me.

"Fabio Gonzalez." I announced. "I'm her husband."

So far, so good.

The giant verified us on the guest list and nodded us through. We waltzed into the reception; held in the most extravagant venue I'd ever seen.

The towering walls accented with intricate hand painted golden leaves, as magnificent crystal chandeliers suspended from the pinnacles of the grand ceiling, decorated with the uniformed renaissance flair that was apparent throughout the hotel.

Delegates huddled tightly together in a variety of social and cultural cliques, an orchestra of exotic languages weaving together in a pleasing symphony.

I locked eyes with Brandon, who stood at the entrance, balancing a collection of champagne flutes on a silver, oval tray.

"Champagne, sir?" He said, presenting the beverages to me. He played his role effortlessly as he snubbed me as a stranger once I'd selected a glass.

"Thank you." I smiled, receiving one of the drinks, whereas Yi grabbed one from the server opposite. I began mingling with the crowds, introducing myself – or 'Fabio' – to a cheerful governor of Botswana.

It was surreal.

I was surrounded by people I'd only seen on television or read about whilst boredly scrolling on Google on my lunch break.

I pinched myself, in an attempt to wake from this bizarre dream.

Maybe this whole thing was a dream?

Maybe I wasn't a Custodian after all and this has been a long, drawn-out dream?

My emotions conflicted when I wasn't hurled back to my comfortable, familiar life.

This was my life now.

I spotted Gail, our Prime Minister, at the far end of the hall, conversing with a small group of delegates, nodding intently at conversation, and partaking in sporadic laughter that collectively ensued.

I couldn't help but admire her natural ability to command a social event, which she was accomplishing with ease.

I wasn't remotely interested in politics, but Gail won me over at the last General Election, with her mandate to significantly improve the emergency services – a cause obviously close to my heart.

Unlike her incompetent predecessors, she surprisingly stayed true to her word, appointing a personable Home Secretary who began to transform the Police Service back to how I remembered it, when I was a probationer in the London Met.

There was still a long way to go, but the foundations had been set and already I found my job becoming more enjoyable by the week.

I continued to scope out the distinguished Mr Golubev, but he was nowhere to be seen.

"We've not spotted him yet." I whispered, subtly itching behind my ear to check my communications device hadn't dislodged.

"Me neither." Brandon stated.

"Nothing from where I am either." Jayce added.

Yi and I continued to greet passing guests, whilst discreetly endeavouring to locate the undercover leader of the Hellion regime.

"Got him!" Yi quietly hissed, in a bid to not draw attention to herself. "Six o'clock."

I turned to where she indicated and spotted him instantly, tucked away in a corner of the hall, meters away from the buffet table, surrounded by his entourage of aides. At least they *looked* like aides.

Golubev was surprisingly handsome for his age, his mug shot not doing him any justice. His demonic controller managed to replicate his sophistication and suaveness, which I witnessed during his numerous press interviews.

"Brandon, have you got eyes on?" I discreetly asked.

"Yep. Give me two minutes and I'll move in and get a read."

Brandon weaved in and out of the chortling and chuckling guests, heading towards the Russian delegate. As he moved closer, he creased up his face, the entire tray of drinks he clutched hold of, succumbed to gravity and crashed to the floor.

A collection of gasps echoed throughout the hall as Brandon followed suit, falling unconscious with an almighty *thud.*

"Shit!" Yi exasperated through gritted teeth, scurrying over to him, compensating for her high stilettos, and lifting up her restrictive dress for agility.

I followed closely behind her.

We shoved our way through the audience that circled around him and knelt down either side.

It didn't take long before he came around and looked up at us with his vibrant blue eyes.

"Where am I?" he asked, extremely disorientated. "What happened?"

"You collapsed." I advised him. "Come on, let's get you up."

The guests surrounding us mumbled quietly to each other, producing a babble of incoherent noise.

I willed our cover hadn't been blown.

Yi and I pulled Brandon to his feet, escorting him through into the restricted kitchen area, out of view from the prying eyes of the crowd.

Jayce, who was pouring another tray of champagne at one of the many workstations, instantly rushed over to us.

Luckily, we were alone.

"What happened?" he asked, helping to prop Brandon down on a chair he managed to acquire from an adjacent office.

Brandon's eyes sealed shut again.

"No idea, he just collapsed." Yi answered. "He tried to get close to Golubev."

"Brandon," he vigorously shook his shoulder, in an attempt to rouse him.

I couldn't tell whether the amount of force was intentional, or if he genuinely didn't realise the power of his own strength.

"Brandon, buddy. It's Jayce." He said, softly.

After five minutes or so, Brandon became fully alert, pressing his temples and grimaced in pain.

"That was intense." He whispered.

"What was?" Jayce asked.

"The *evil*. So much *evil* in that room." Brandon muttered. "The more I opened myself up, the more overwhelming it became."

"Was it from Golubev?" I asked.

"I couldn't tell. It seemed to come from everywhere."

"You mean everyone in that room is a Hellion?" Yi asked, her voice slightly trembling.

"I don't know. All I felt was darkness, coming from all around me. I'm not sure if it's everyone, but whatever I sensed it was pure evil."

"Great. This makes things slightly more difficult." I commented. "Thoughts?" I turned my attention to Yi and Jayce for ideas.

"I could always do what I did on the plane?" Yi

suggested. "I'm guessing those that aren't Hellions would run for cover, and those that are, would fight back."

"An indoor hurricane? I can see it now on the six o'clock news." Jayce said, sarcastically.

"Well do you have any better ideas?" Yi barked back at him.

"Maybe an earthquake instead?" Jayce proposed.

I shook my head in disagreement.

"I'd be putting too many lives at risk. I don't want anyone to get hurt from falling rubble. Using our powers in public is too risky. I've done it once and almost got caught."

"Why don't we seek out the help of the Prime Minister?" Jayce asked. "She knows Golubev well, and I bet she'd be able to get him on his own."

"That's if she hasn't been compromised." Yi chimed in.

I thought for a moment, contemplating an array of scenarios, considering the risks they would pose to both innocent members of public, and to us.

"That seems like the best option." I stated. "I'd better check with Rebecca, to make sure there isn't anything else that we need to consider."

I released my phone from the inner breast pocket of my tuxedo, using 'Obelisk' to contact her, her cherub face instantly appearing on the entirety of my screen.

"Well, hello there darlin!" She greeted. *"How can I be of assistance?"*

I updated her with the events of the evening, with Brandon's experience and the difficulties we were going to have in getting Golubev on his own. I submitted the plans for utilising Gail to aide us.

After some careful deliberation, she eventually green lighted the plan, but warned us to remain discreet.

The next challenge was to recruit the Prime Minister into our circle. She knew about Operation Myst, but I was unsure how much knowledge she possessed of the Custodian prophecy and the Hellion threat.

Once Brandon regained his strength, we reconvened in the main hall, where a live band began singing vibrant, catchy showtunes, luring the majority of the delegation to the square dance floor in the centre.

Yi conceived a solution to obtain Gail's attention. Jayce was to take her a tray of freshly poured drinks, offering a glass of champagne, which he managed to fulfil.

I observed Yi glaring at the tray that Jayce held, motioning her index finger towards it, magically knocking a glass over, the contents spilling on Gail's dress.

Jayce looked horrified.

The Prime Minister squealed, jumping back in shock, remarkably maintaining the grip of the beverage she was already sipping.

"How did you do that?" I asked, astounded. "Since when do you have telekinetic abilities?"

"I don't." Yi revealed. "I used my power to blow the glass over."

"Clever." I commented. "But I think you should have told Jayce that's what you were going to do."

"But then his reaction wouldn't have been believable." Yi smirked, as she headed over towards the commotion. "Watch and learn." She directed, as she seductively swanned away.

I pursued her, but halted short of the commotion, observing from a slight distance.

"Oh no!" Yi exaggeratingly exclaimed. "Prime Minister! Your beautiful dress!" she turned to Jayce and shot him a disgruntled look, which we all knew was to deceive those not within our trustworthy family.

"Waiter! You need to be more careful! Now get her a towel!" Yi fictitiously scolded him.

"Yes Ma'am." He obeyed, after glaring at her in frustration. "Right away." He added, through tightly clenched teeth.

I slowly meandered over, passing a group of delegates jiving at the musical festivities, and joined Yi, who continued to pander to our head of government.

"I'm sure it will come out! If not, buy another one." Yi said confidently, shining in her starring role.

"I would, but this is a Vivienne Westwood original." Gail sighed. "This is the only one of its kind."

"Have you anything else to change into?" she asked.

"Unfortunately, not. I always pack light. I don't like spending government funds unless I need to. More for the worthwhile causes of the country."

Gail continued to make a humble impression.

"Well, you look like my size, I've got a spare dress if you want to change?" Yi suggested.

"Oh, that's very kind of you." Gail smiled. "You'll have to forgive me, I'm really bad with names and faces, have we met before?"

"No, we haven't, but I'm Yun Sing's daughter, your ambassador to China." Yi said, plucking her fabricated backstory out of thin air.

"I can't say I've ever met your father." Gail admitted. "I have heard great things none the less."

"Well, he thinks the world of you." Yi fibbed.

She whisked the Prime Minister away, off up to her room.

"Shit!" I uttered under my breath when I caught eyes on one of Gail's close protection officers, following the glamourous duo as they headed towards the lobby.

Tom Bailey.

A London Met Police officer.

A fellow Hendon graduate of 2007.

I cowered my head away from him, praying he wouldn't recognise me.

He hadn't changed much in sixteen years, apart from a whisp of grey, highlighting his slicked back dusky blonde hair.

We used to be quite close, trailing each other around Hendon like shadows – always lunching together, choosing each other as partners in the various practical exercises we had to endure.

Tom and I shared a drunken kiss the night we graduated. Our head of class organised a night out in central London, where copious amounts of complementary alcohol flowed freely.

It was the last time I'd seen Tom, as we were shipped out to differing boroughs shortly after, and he'd cut off all contact with me.

He'd obviously freaked out about our brief moment of passion – up until that point he identified as straight.

I continued to linger in the ball room, in anticipation for the Hellion movement to strike.

Yi returned with Gail after about half an hour, now dressed in a red, silk dress, pulling me to one side, away from any prying ears.

I shielded myself from Tom, who positioned himself near the entrance, fixated on a group of rowdy delegates from the United States.

"How did it go?" I asked.

"Well, she knows about us now." Yi cautiously explained. "She didn't at first, but I told her we were part of Harriet's team and she seemed to understand. She did phone her to check, mind you."

"I bet Harriet was pleased with that." I chuckled sarcastically, thinking about the eight-hour time difference between Las Vegas and London – it would have been at least 4am there.

"Like with most things, I don't think it phased her."

"So, is she in?" I inquired, trying to get back on track with our mission.

"Yes." Yi answered. "I gave her my earpiece. When she manages to get Golubev on his own, she'll send us a signal."

"I hope this works." I said, anxiously, electing to not declare my history with Tom.

I needed Yi to focus.

The hour passed at a snail's pace, containing speeches from President of the United States and various other world leaders who'd been instrumental in facilitating the conference.

Gail had still not managed to separate the Russian ambassador from his associates, however, not through any lack of trying.

A sequence of taps emanated in my ear canal.

I promptly hunted for Gail in her vivid scarlet dress, locating her just feet away from the jazz band that were enthusiastically hollering a rendition of Frank Sinatra's 'Fly me to the moon.'

She was *alone* with him.

I traded looks with Yi, and we cautiously approached the pair. I diverted my attention briefly towards Tom, who still luckily hadn't locked eyes with me.

"Mr Golubev." Gail greeted him, with her mature, attractive smile. "How are things?" she asked.

"Never better. And yourself?"

"Can't complain."

"Well, this welcome reception is invigorating." I heard Golubev sarcastically grumble, in his thick Russian accent.

"Really?" Gail said, taken back slightly. "I've enjoyed it."

"It's not my taste." Golubev huffed. "I prefer something a bit 'livelier'."

"I don't strike you as a partier Mr Golubev." Gail trifled.

"I love a good party. I've actually heard of one being hosted here."

"Oh, really?" Gail responded, trying to sound interested.

"Would you like to join me?" He asked her.

"Of course." Gail accepted the invitation and took hold of Golubev's arm, escorting her towards the exit of the ball room.

I observed Tom zipping towards her, whispering

heatedly in her ear, before she frustratingly dismissed him.

I breathed a sigh as he left.

The four of as all grouped together after I gave a signal, tactfully shadowing the couple to a vacant corridor, stealthily darting behind walls and awkwardly shaped furniture.

Golubev led her towards a closed, unelaborate door, with two sun-glass-wearing colossal guards, stood protectively either side.

"This doesn't look much of a party." Gail commented, as she studied the door, which appeared to lead to nothing but a janitor's closet.

"Trust me, you will think very differently when you get inside."

Golubev nodded at the two giants, and escorted Gail inside.

"Great! We've got those two Men in Black knockoffs to contend with." I whispered back to the others, as we hid behind an adjacent wall. "Are they Hellions?" I turned back to Brandon, who nodded back at me, his telepathy sensing their true, sinister identities.

"How are we going to get past them without going into full on battle?" Yi asked.

"Leave that to me." Jayce said, with an air of surprising confidence.

He inconspicuously held his hand out in the direction of the two demons-in-disguise, a drop of sweat jumping from his brow as he created a fiery vortex, which circled around their feet.

The ember quickly intensified, engulfing them in an

inferno, as they screamed in terror. This continued for no more than a minute, until culminating in a large blast, causing us to shield our eyes from demonic entrails.

When the smoke cleared, the two Hellions vanished.

"Wow Jayce." I said, my astonished eyes fully widened.

"That was for my sister." He grimaced, with a revengeful tone.

"Well done Stevens!" Yi congratulated. "Our powers are definitely getting stronger."

We darted over to the door, and I autonomously grasped the handle. I instantly flexed back as a sharp pain sliced through my palm, not contemplating the brass knob had conducted a small amount of residual heat from Jayce's fire.

A slight, putrid smell of burning flesh filled the air around me, before my hand mystically rejuvenated a new layer of skin, dispersing the pulsating agony.

Jayce, immune to any effects of heat – thanks to his Custodian ability – twisted the knob with ease, which opened up into a void.

As we all cautiously entered, our path morphed into a winding, downwards staircase, which was poorly lit; I could just about see my hand in front of my face.

A distressed woman's screech echoed from below us, amplified through my earpiece.

Gail!

We sped to the bottom of the staircase, conscious not to trip or miss a step with the distinct lack of any luminosity.

An orange glare acted as a homing beacon, as we entered a large cavern, strangely out of place underneath a billion-dollar hotel.

A harmonious chorus of droning hums, provided by an army of uniformed hooded figures dotted around the cavern, echoed throughout the void.

A large pit of fire, erupting violent flames, was positioned perfectly in the centre, with a rocky platform extended out above it.

I looked up at the podium, and saw Gail being restrained by two titanic humans, doppelgangers of the vanquished pair guarding the door. She let out another piercing scream, drowned out by the sudden increase in volume of the tribal droning.

"There is so much evil here." Brandon winced, dropping to his knees, clutching tightly hold of his head. "I can't…."

"Mate, you've got to." Jayce crouched down at his side, as he encouraged him, grabbing hold of his shoulders. "Concentrate; the Prime Minister's life is at stake."

Brandon's face turned a bright shade of pink, as he forced himself to overcome his inhibition.

"My friends!" Golubev, who stood on the overhanging platform to the side of Gail, greeted his disciples. "A millennia ago, we first raged an attack on this world, in an aim to expand our territory. Only to be stopped by the poisonous Custodian prophecy time and time again."

We concealed ourselves behind a jagged rock as we listened intently to his speech.

"This marks a new era in the Hellion rule, as we continue our conquest of the human race. Our new strategy of replacing world leaders is ensuring our victory. The Custodians will be powerless when we control their governments, their armies and their security forces. To celebrate, I present to you the latest sacrifice, the Prime Minister of the United Kingdom!"

The announcement of Gail erupted in cheer from the entire cavern, as the minions moved her closer to the edge of the platform, with the raging fire strengthening the closer they approached.

She let out a horrifying scream, which signalled for us to act, quickly.

It was *our* fault she landed in this predicament.

"Wait!" I yelled, launching myself from the rock we were shrouded behind, the entirety of the cavern revolved in malevolent unison to face me. "Leave her alone! It's us you want!" I demanded, my voice resonating.

Golubev was the last to set eyes upon me.

"Ah. The newest incarnations of the Custodians I presume?" he asked, a sinister tone. "I'm actually quite glad you're here. It saves me seeking you out!"

"We wouldn't give you the pleasure of the hunt, anyway!" Brandon roared, saliva spraying from his mouth in anger.

"Oh, is that the case?!" Golubev expelled a dark, menacing laugh. "You Custodians get more foolish."

"You won't win!" Yi yelled up at him, her battle stance at a the ready.

"I think I already have." He chortled, sinisterly. "You should be honoured. You're getting to see the end of the human race."

The monastery chanting rapidly increased in tempo, causing Gail's Hellion sentinels to tip her backwards, with her head directly over the fire pit.

She shrieked, as a stray flare creeped up from the depths of the crater and pirouetted towards her.

A group of the human-disguised satanists, transfigured simultaneously into their creature forms and hunted us with their beady, green eyes.

As they hurtled towards us at phenomenal speed, my chest tightened, and my neck throbbed from the instant rush of adrenaline that filled my veins.

This was it.

This was the big battle we'd been waiting for.

As one of the creatures descended on me, I stood as a statue, my feet apart, gesturing at a large boulder on the floor.

I focused on the stone, the harshness of the serrated surface scraping my mind, harvesting all my magical strength.

The rock lifted into the air upon my command, and I choreographed it towards the demon, impacting them and pinning them to the ground.

Yi levitated into the air, a strong gust spinning around her to keep her airborne. She glided towards the podium and thrust her palms out to Gail's captors, manifesting a set of intertwined tornadoes, hurtling them both into the fiery abyss, Gail inadvertently being caught in the stream and following them to her death.

I reached out at the edge of the fire pit, causing a thunderous rumble, enchanting a segment of the rock to extended up and seize the Prime Minister, where she fell unconscious.

Jayce directed embers from the mystical flames towards

a battalion of Hellions infringing towards us, ripping through them without even a scorch.

"What the!?" He yelled, as he examined his palm. "Why isn't it working?!"

"Maybe they're immune to this fire." Brandon suggested, throwing spears of enchanted ice towards a wrathful adversary. "Materialise your own."

Jayce swiftly created his own rapid inferno on demand and steered it towards the growling henchmen, who cried out in terror as they burned alive, eventually dissolving into a pile of rotten dust.

"There's too many of them!" Brandon bellowed, producing another set of piercing icicles.

He shot them at persistent group of demons, who were increasing in size and mass.

"Guys I could use some help!" Yi exclaimed from the ether.

I looked up to her, floating around in the air, dodging lethal beams of energy from Golubev.

The remainder of us obliterated the majority of the army, so we headed up towards the rocky platform to assist Yi in battling the leader of the Hellion High Order.

I made an attempt to magically create a series of vines to wrap around his feet, taking him by surprise, but his lightning sharp reflexes countered with a strobe of energy, which hit me directly in the chest and temporarily rescinded my power.

I hit the floor with force.

My ears overflowed with tinnitus and my entire body excruciatingly ached, eventually blacking out from the pain.

"Marco!" I awoke with Jayce crowded over me, slapping my face. "Wake up!"

The slight haze clouding my mind taking a couple of moments to clear.

"Wha…. Where…?" I uttered, as I finally came round.

"Marco, we need you!" Jayce yelled at me. "Come on, get up!"

He helped me to my feet.

Yi and Brandon coveted the entirety of their magic, and hurtled it at the Golubev impersonator, barely causing a scratch.

This sight of my friends in peril, shocked me back into the fight, as my accelerated healing abilities soothed my aches and war wounds.

"He's immune to our magic." Jayce gravely conceded. "We're going to lose."

"No. We're not!" I encouraged him. "We have to combine our powers together. Throw everything that we've got at him. Don't give him the chance to adapt."

Jayce nodded in agreement.

"Let's do this!!" He yelled, refraining from letting out a Spartan battle cry.

I stood firmly at the side of my comrade, throwing my arms forcefully towards the master demon, focusing all the energy and might from within me, my forehead straining droplets of sweat.

I sealed my eyes tightly, imagining a vicious plethora of flora surrounding Golubev, piercing through his skin and encasing him in a cage of poisoned vegetation.

The image in my mind's eye manifested itself into reality

and Golubev was finally inhibited.

Jayce materialised a gyre of flames, which caught fire to my constricting vines, bestowing them with an intense burst of power and strength.

Brandon added his touch with a mist of ice, creeping up from the base of our creation, freezing it into a glacier, refusing to melt even with the flames still flickering brightly inside.

Yi was the final one to impart her battle gift on Golubev, as she conjured a violent hurricane, which surrounded him, and fuelled the entirety of the magical prison, elevating it into the air.

Thump!

Crack!

Golubev drummed away in his cage in a bid to find any weaknesses he could exploit and burst out into freedom.

However, his efforts were futile.

I gasped as my skin glowed a brilliant green aura, sending an invigorating rush throughout my entire body.

I felt unstoppable.

I felt like a *Custodian*.

My comrades also developed this symptom, however, their aura's differed in colour; Yi a bright white, Brandon a deep blue and Jayce a fierce red, each shade representing the individual elemental power we harnessed.

The confinement emulated our display of vibrant colours and the atmosphere turned electric as our collective supernatural energy gathered momentum.

The ambassador exorcised a deafening scream, as his molecules began to separate from his body, disintegrating into ash, until he was left with just a head.

"This is not over, Custodians!" He choked. "More of us will come. You cannot stop us all!"

One ultimate agonising scream echoed, before a catastrophic, mystical blast filled the entire cavern, gathering debris from all corners.

When the fallout passed by and cleared, the High Order Hellion was vanquished.

We'd done it!

It was over - For now at least.

Yi delicately descended back down to the ground and rushed over to Gail, who laid unresponsive, but didn't appear to be seriously injured.

"We need to get her some help!" Yi ordered, as she cradled her.

The remaining three of us hurried across to them, and I studied the Prime Minister's lifeless body, coated in numerous scrapes and bruises, from being tossed around the cavern like a ragdoll.

I knelt beside her and briefly inspected her pulse, relieved as I detected a strong, punching rhythm from under her jaw.

"She's alive." I announced, the team exhaling a breath of relief.

My hand rested on her forehead, where unexpected ripples of golden magic appeared underneath my palm, basking her entire body in a mystical glow.

Her wounds miraculously dissolved and her skin returned to a healthy pink, with a slight rosy tinge accentuating her rounded cheeks.

She violently bolted up right, expelling an involuntary gasp, coughing up the contents of her lungs.

Was that me?

"You healed her!" Yi gleefully remarked, as she placed a hand of comfort on the Prime Minister's shoulder. "How?"

"I don't know." I shrugged, very non-cholent about my new ability to heal others – I'm guessing the overwhelming, intense last few hours, dampened my excitement.

"What happened?" Gail interrupted as she came to, massaging the tension from her temples.

"We did it." I replied. "We defeated him."

"Thank goodness!" she beamed. "I owe you all a great debt. The *world* owes you a great debt."

"You owe us nothing," Yi protested. "It's our job."

We helped Gail to her feet, journeying back to the stairwell, climbing back up to the main Hotel reception, where Rebecca expectantly awaited us.

A collection of her crew were stood around her.

"Darlin's! You're alive!" She paced over to us, gently caressing Brandon's arm in a friendly comfort. "You had me worried."

"They have been exceptional, director." Gail interluded; a proud expression rendered in the direction of the four of us.

"You know each other?" Jayce questioned, a hint of confusion apparent in his voice.

"Of course, Honey. Harriet introduced us."

"I knew who you all were right from the start," Gail spritely confessed, fully recovered from her ordeal. "I needed you to approach me first, otherwise there was a chance you would have been discovered."

"I had an inkling you were gonna wanna use her to help, so she was briefed in on the mission too." Rebecca clarified.

"You deserve an Oscar, Ma'am." Yi laughed, to my surprise. "You even had me fooled – and I'm a hard one to pull the wool over."

"I can second that." Jayce muttered. I chuckled internally to myself, as I agreed with him. Yi, although a vast improvement on her former self, was still on occasion, cantankerous and stubborn.

"I'm sorry to have mislead you all, but it was imperative that this mission was a success." Gail continued. "The conference can go ahead tomorrow, without any worry of a Hellion attack."

"I wouldn't be so sure." I cautioned. "These beings are relentless. I've experienced their determination first hand over the last three weeks. Just be careful tomorrow."

"That's all noted, Mr Ramirez." Gail nodded. "Ah Tom!"

I spun around on my heel, to where she diverted her attention.

There he was.

Tom.

"Ma'am." He greeted, stiffly.

"Everyone, this is my close protection officer. Tom Bailey." Gail introduced.

I locked on his ice blue eyes, and instantly blushed, veering my head away before he could recognise me.

"Marco?!" He queried, orbiting around me to connect with my bashful gaze. "Is that you?"

I froze, unsure of how to react. I endeavoured to avoid this man at all costs, but my kind nature took control.

"Oh Tom! It's good to see you!" I volleyed him the most over exaggerated smile I could muster.

"What on earth are you doing all the way over here?" He asked.

I contemplated how I was going to explain this to him, without compromising my secret.

"I was invited by the PM." I lied. "A few of us were asked to attend the peace conference as an honour for a nasty job we dealt with."

"Really?" His bemused expression exposed his disbelief at my tall tale. "The first I've heard of this."

My palms moistened, nervous that he was about to uncover my supernatural truth.

"Well, I'm sure you didn't want to be informed of absolutely everything. I know what it's like when you get a briefing overload." I anxiously smiled.

"Hmmm." He replied, still dissatisfied with my explanation. "What are you doing these days?"

I caught him up on my career path over the last sixteen years; my relocation to Cornwall, transferring to Cornwall Constabulary, and my promotion to Inspector.

Tom exchanged with me his path; marrying a girl from our training school class, Emma, having kids – two girls, and how he was going through a messy divorce.

"Sorry I cut off contact with you." He apologised, sorrowfully looking to the floor. "I was going through a lot at the time. Still am, I suppose."

"It's fine, honestly." I held up my hand, batting away any

regret he held.

"It's great to see you again Marco. *Really* great to see you." Tom unnervingly gazed at me, his piercing aqua eyes shimmering as they caught a glare from the chandelier above.

I remembered this look from all those years ago – the night we kissed.

His sudden infatuation made me feel uneasy.

"Erm… thanks….. er…..mate." I squirmed. "I've got to go though. I'll send you an e-mail and we'll have a proper catch up soon."

Tom flashed his perfect teeth at me, waving bye with a flirtatious wink, causing me to swiftly exit back to my entourage.

"Are you okay?" Yi asked, her brow crossed with concern.

"I'm fine." I fibbed, shrugging off the encounter with Tom. "I'm tired. I think I'm going to go to bed."

"It's only eleven?" Brandon said, looking down at his watch. "You're not coming out to celebrate?"

"I'll give this one a miss." I said, my exhaustion apparent from a sporadic yawn. "I'll see you all in the morning."

I was the first one down for breakfast, with Yi, Jayce and Brandon appearing at intervals over the course of twenty minutes.

All of them cradled their heads, moaning in unison at the after effects of their celebratory night exploring the strip.

"Good night?" I grinned, slightly superior with my

soberness.

"Don't talk to me." Yi grumbled, burying her head in her arms on the table.

"Mate. It was amazing." Brandon said, attempting to fight through the effects of his hangover. "We ended up partying at the Jewel nightclub in the Aria with some world leaders."

"Yi got friendly with a French ambassador." Jayce playfully smiled, his voice slightly hoarse.

"Mate, I don't know about you, but I've never stuck my tongue down my friend's throats!" Brandon chuckled.

"Doctor Chang!" I teased.

"Oh, shut up, the lot of you, and get me some coffee!" She vexed.

Brandon, Jayce, and I all scoffed away at our plates, containing concoctions of the rich and flavourful American cuisine.

I'd selected a bed of red velvet pancakes, smeared in a thick and creamy, white chocolate sauce.

Yi, sat stiffly at her seat, refusing any food and consumed five cups of strong, black coffee.

At eleven o'clock, Rebecca called us all into a debrief, hosted in an elaborate conference room, the golden, rustic Italian décor evident in the curvature of the large mahogany table and co-ordinating chairs.

I selected a seat close to the front, gazing up at the miniature chandelier, a fraction of the size of their ball room siblings.

Jayce, as usual, perched up next to me, whilst Yi and

Brandon sat opposite.

We all cheered when Harriet's sophisticated face surprisingly appeared on the television screen, positioned on a stand in the corner of the room, her ornate office featuring as her background.

I quickly calculated the time difference; it was seven o'clock in the evening back in the UK and no surprise that Harriet still beavered away at work.

"Outstanding work, darlin's." Rebecca began, visibly impressed with our achievements. "I must admit, I didn't believe Harriet when she said you would succeed."

"Well, thank you for your confidence." Yi interjected sarcastically, still suffering from the effects of her intoxication.

"Oh honey, I didn't mean it in that way." Rebecca apologetically gestured her palm. "I meant I was slightly apprehensive, considering all the intelligence we had on Golubev."

"I had faith in every one of you." Harriet said. *"But I think your work has just begun. The Hellions are the strongest we have ever seen them, and this new discreet tactic of them will make them harder to locate."*

"We're up for the challenge." I nodded. "How is the Prime Minister today?"

"Safe, and in top health, thanks to you all." Rebecca advised. "She again wanted me to pass on her thanks, and if there is anything she can do to help, then she will be happy to. That goes with the President too. I informed him of your success this morning."

"This is so surreal." Jayce laughed. "Four weeks ago, we

were nobodies. Now we're known by world leaders."

"You never were 'nobodies' Jason," Harriet assured him. *"This has been prophesied for centuries. You were always meant to be a Custodian."*

The meeting continued to discuss the Hellion High Order, examining in detail tactical decisions we made, and the Peace Conference itself.

It continued as planned, with several delegates noticeably absent, Rebecca concocting up a cover of a flu virus that incapacitated them.

The cavern had been sealed off, and covertly dissected and analysed by one of her specialist teams. They concluded that the closet door was in fact a portal to the Hellion's underworld realm, the cavern being one of many ceremonial locations for human sacrifices.

Significant intelligence suggested that this was one of many, spread across the entire globe.

"Right, we have an early flight tomorrow and I want to get some exploration in. Is there anything else you want to talk to us about?" I asked, as the meeting drew to a close.

"No honey, I think we've covered everything. On behalf of the United States of America, I want to thank you for your service. I look forward to working with you all again in the future." Rebecca smiled, her joyful, southern accent filling the room with warmth. "You're all dismissed, darlin's."

We all stood, queuing for a friendly embrace from our American liaison, who had suddenly became a close friend within a matter of days.

I was sad to be parting ways with her.

"Marco." Brandon interrupted, nervously. "I need to speak with you."

"Sure mate." We moved to a discreet corner of the conference room, away from the others. "What's up?"

"It's Grayson. I think he might be a *Hellion*."

FIFTEEN

I sat in Vegas departures, fatigued at the unworldly time of two in the morning, still dwelling over Brandon's shock revelation, desperately attempting to put the conversation into the hidden depths of my mind.

I knew Grayson too well, and Brandon more than likely misinterpreted any feelings directed towards him.

Yeah. That was it.

Grayson wasn't particularly great with meeting new people, becoming extremely shy or distant, which some would construe as rude or arrogant.

I'd politely requested for him to keep his intuition to himself, assuring him I would consider what he said.

I did consider it.

I considered it to be *false*.

There were no ill thoughts towards Brandon, as he deemed he was doing the right thing, though it didn't prevent a wave of irritation from circulating through me.

I'd no suspicions of Grayson in the slightest, but then again, neither did Jayce about Jo.

Stop it Marco!

He's not a Hellion for goodness sake!

He can't be!

We landed back at Heathrow at around ten o'clock in the evening, UK time.

Brandon offered to be our transport home, so we didn't endure the five-hour journey back to Cornwall.

Once we cleared passport control and customs, Brandon led us to a large, decorative pond in a discreet area, outside the entrance to Terminal Five.

The pond formed part of an impressive, abstract display, which decorated the outside of the Terminal, alluring expectant passengers into a sense of affluence.

The body of water appeared large enough for Brandon to manifest a portal, the cyclone of waves magnetised by the motion of his hand.

When the turbulent whirlpool reached its peak, we all vaulted in one by one, with our luggage in tow.

The portal materialised into the familiar, discreet spot of Lust Glaze beach, propelling us from the vortex and scattering us across the beach, the sand creeping into every exposed crevice.

Our luggage ensued, being deposited in a heap mere feet away.

"You need to work on the landing!" Yi barked at Brandon, as she clutched hold of her left arm in slight pain.

"Nothing to do with me!" He protested. "I just open the portals up. It's up to you how you land the other side!"

Yi unimpressively rolled her eyes, before hoisting herself to her feet.

I gazed intriguingly up at the moon, as I dusted myself off, and admired how bright and brilliant it was.

The light accentuated the entire beauty of the coastline that I was accustomed to these passing years, which pulled me into a slight trance.

I quivered my head as I dragged myself back to the here and now.

"What do you say about getting a pint?" I suggested, my craving for a cold beer suddenly radiating through me.

"Ah mate!" An excitable Brandon, jogged towards me, throwing his arm around my shoulder. "I'm in."

"I'm much more of a gin girl," Yi reminded me.

"I know you are. There's plenty of Gin where I have in mind." I smiled, heading off across the beach, collecting my suitcase and struggling to remain upright as I ventured across a pebbled road that weaved into the sand.

I'd guided the team on a short five-minute walk, to a small, quaint little bar which overlooked the harbour.

We entered, impeding on the late evening bustle from both locals and holiday makers.

The ambience of an empty cosy corner, highlighted by a cluster of Victorian lamps, enticed us in further.

Being the leader, I offered to get everyone the first round. Brandon, Jayce, and I all settled for a local brewery beer, whilst Yi requested a Rose Gin with slimline tonic.

I requested our order, paid the bartender and steadily

balanced the tray of drinks towards our snug area of the pub, placing them down in front of an expectant group of Custodians.

Brandon's snatched his beer from the tray and gulped the entire contents within seconds.

"Steady on!" I exclaimed.

"Sorry Marc. I'm parched!" Brandon said, his breathing laboured from drinking too quickly.

"I wonder what will happen now?" Jayce asked, sipping on his pint. "Do you think that was it?"

"Rebecca and Harriet didn't seem to think so." said Yi, swirling her gin around in her hand; the ice chiming as it clinked against the glass.

"I think we bided a bit of time, but I have a bad feeling that something bigger is on its way." I disclosed.

"Ever the optimist mate!" Brandon said, playfully slapping me on the back. I winced in slight pain his brute strength, convinced he'd left a handprint.

"I'm being realistic. I highly doubt our ancestors were given these powers to fend off a dozen or so. When I first met Harriet, she showed me a timeline of what all our ancestors have been through. They fought catastrophic wars. This seemed more of a battle."

"So, the best is yet to come." Yi sarcastically smiled, before slurping a mouthful of her drink.

"I thought you weren't coming back until tomorrow?"

A familiar voice interrupted our flowing conversation.

It was *Grayson*.

"Hey you!" I beamed with excitement, instantly leaping into his arms.

He barely reciprocated.

His muscles were tensed tightly and could I sense a hint of anger.

"Sorry, the meeting ended up being cut short, so we came back slightly early. I wasn't going to be long - we were just having a quick drink."

Grayson's eyes glared malevolently at the group, which my naivety translated as him expecting an introduction.

"Oh, I'm sorry. Yi, Jayce, this is my partner Grayson. Grayson, this is Yi and Jayce." I gestured to each of them as I called out their name. "Brandon you've already met."

The three of them greeted him with a welcoming smile. Jayce extended his hand out, which Grayson rudely ignored.

Something wasn't right.

"It seems like you have a lot of excuses these days Marc." Grayson growled, his face turning a slight shade of red.

"Gray, what are you on about?" I asked, my cheeks turning red with turmoil.

"Oh, I don't know. Popping off here and there. Suddenly spending all your time with your new friends and colleagues who you've never mentioned before. What's going on?"

His voice raised, abruptly halting chattering from the patrons scattered around the bar. I grabbed his arm and pulled him to one side, away from the population of the pub's prying ears.

"What's gotten into you Gray?" I asked him, concerned. In our fifteen years together, he'd never taken a raised tone with me before.

We bickered like any couple, but never had a full-blown

dispute.

"You're having an affair, aren't you?" He uttered through gritted teeth, his tone, sinister.

I compacted my arms firmly into my chest and shook my head in disbelief, suppressing a sarcastic chuckle at the absurdity of what he accused me of.

"You have got to be kidding." I could feel the rage bubbling in my stomach. "After fifteen years, you're really going to play at this card?"

"So, you're not denying it!" He yelled.

This wasn't Grayson.

Something was off with him.

I discreetly exchanged a glance with Brandon, who nodded his head, a woeful expression apparent on his face.

My knees weakened.

My heart raced.

No.

It couldn't be.

This was Grayson.

No. No. No. NO!

Goosebumps sprouted over my entire body, every single strand of hair standing to attention as my heart sank.

"Have you ever been to Utreah?" I begrudgingly asked.

"Don't try to change the subject." He growled at me.

He began to manifest peculiar, stark twitches which seemed to worsen as time went on.

"I'm not. Answer the question." I sternly requested, the remainder of the team stood behind me, observing like a hawk.

Grayson clenched down on my bare arm like a vice, his

surprising superhuman strength painfully causing an instant bruise.

I lashed out at him, kicking and punching him as he violently dragged me towards the exit. I couldn't help but yell at him to release me.

Jayce launched to my rescue, brutishly stomping towards me and Grayson.

"Get the fuck off him!" He barked.

"Fuck off!" Grayson yelled back at him.

Being the lawyer, he was usually the peacekeeper one out of us, choosing to use his words over physical retaliation.

This man may have looked, smelled, and talked like Grayson; it wasn't him.

"I don't think you quite heard me right, mate." Jayce's brows crossed and the blood rushed to his face, his cheeks emanating a cherry red. "Get the fuck off him!!"

Jayce threw back a clench fist behind his head, directed it towards Grayson's face.

Grayson caught the fist with his free palm and tightly squeezed, a gruesome crunch sounding as Jayce's knuckles all collapsed into each other with his steel grip.

"Grayson stop!" I screeched at him, as Jayce let out a gut-wrenching cry from the intensity of his shattered fingers.

The earth began to agitate under our feet, my emotional tie to my powers sensing my peril and rising to the surface, like a defence mechanism.

Beer tankers shelved on the wall fell to the floor as the intensity of the quake increased, the patrons all squealing in terror as chunks of the ceiling loosened and fell at their feet.

They split into two groups, some scurried out the exit, abandoning their beverages, whereas others took immediate shelter underneath the solid, oak tables dotted around the main lounge.

Glasses and bottles shattered as they took a dive to the floor and cracks forked up the walls as my fervent anger fuelled my magic.

Grayson's grip loosened on my arm as he struggled to remain on balance, sprinting out of the door during a gap in the rumble.

I subdued my power, stalking him out into the street, which had been deserted by the locals from the unexpected quake.

I made my way out of the door and onto the cobbled road, Grayson's features barely noticeable as he stood under a poorly lit street lamp.

"I know you're not Grayson." I said, intently staring at him, my eyes drying up as I refused to blink.

"Well done, detective." He hissed, the tone and pitch of his voice menacing. "Looks like all those years in the Police have finally paid off." He gave an evil smile, before pacing towards me. "You know, I thought I'd done a good job trying to convince you I was him."

I struggled to observe the direction of his path as he meandered into the dark of the night, the tension between us brewing.

"Human emotion. Human affection. Oh, how I loathed every minute of it." He continued, his voice echoing in the abandoned street. "I've waited years for this moment. I can finally put an end to the Custodians."

"How long have you been posing as him?" My eyes welled up as I came to the grave realisation that the man I loved, more than anything, was more than likely dead. "Weeks? Years? Months?" My voice trembled with every word I spoke, increasing in volume.

"TELL ME!!" I screamed, the strain prickling the back of my throat.

The creature before me laughed in reply. It was an evil, calculated, taunting laugh which stabbed me like a dagger.

The rage of losing Grayson began to pulsate through my veins, like powerful elixir, energizing my ability to control the earth.

I threw my arm out, a wooden vine materialising from the cracks in the cobbles on the road. As they creeped towards him, a pair of glowing red eyes appeared – noticeably different from the standard Hellion green.

As we'd learnt from our Vegas encounter, members of the High Order could remain in their human forms indefinitely, and still possess the strength and power of the Hellion creature from within.

I strained at the imposter's silhouette, barely witnessing a wave of his hand obliterating my magical creation to dust.

"Do you really think your little magic tricks are going to work on me?" He repeated his sinister laugh.

The temperature in the atmosphere dropped, as a large gust of wind formed around him, accumulating in power, harvesting any loose debris in its path.

I turned to see Yi with both her arms extended, her hands swaying as she co-ordinated the path of the vortex.

The other two stood close behind her, Jayce cradling his

injured hand, which would be supernaturally rehabilitated within the next ten minutes or so.

Grayson's doppelganger slipped through the path of the tornado with ease, without an ounce of a scratch on him. This was the most powerful Hellion that we'd ever encountered.

Was he the leader?

Under our noses this whole time?

What if it's still Grayson, but under a spell?

What if killing him also kills Grayson?

A strident, sharp pain filled my head, as the internal questions overwhelmed me.

I needed to focus.

If this was Grayson under a spell, I'd no idea how to break it, either way, if killing him helped to save the world, I didn't really have a choice.

The *real* Grayson would have agreed.

"Let's do what we did in Vegas." I directed the others. "Combine our powers together and end him."

"Are you sure?" Jayce asked.

"We haven't a choice." I uttered, my eyes heavy.

I thrust my hand at the ground, willed with all my might for Grayson to be encased in a cage of weeds, twigs and thorns - anything to stop him from closing on us.

As the foliage protruded from beneath the cobbles, a trail of fire, thanks to Jayce, began to engulf the vines and surround Grayson in a prison.

Yi and Brandon stood next to each other, motioning towards the demon in a synchronised manner, combining their powers and magically generating a waterspout.

It passed through the cage, the flame invigorated, as opposed to extinguished, as the water made contact.

The demonic Grayson screeched as the ember began to burn his skin, producing a foul stench which disagreed with my nose.

We unanimously willed for our magical creations to close in on them, burning, drowning, encasing and exposing him to high velocity.

I dropped to my knees as my power slightly weakened, my emotive state fluctuating at the sight of my fiancée being burned alive. I compared the sights of him and Golubev, which were identical.

They were also both imposters – I needed to remember that.

I culminated my anger, upset, confusion and hurt and refocused them towards igniting the spark in my magic.

We can do this!

"I know we can." Yi replied.

"You heard that?" I asked, amazed.

"Didn't you say it?"

"No, I *thought* it. Since when have you become a telepath?"

I instantly recalled memories of me as a child in Hong-Kong, with my grandfather. Wait… no, me as a child in Sydney, riding on a surfboard with my mother's new boyf…. No, wait…. Me playing with my sister… Jo?

They weren't my memories.

They were memories of the *others*.

I couldn't tell if I was Brandon, Yi, Jayce, or Marco. I was everyone, but no one, simultaneously.

CUSTODIANS: THE PROPHECY

We were connected, in a way I'd never experienced, all part of each other, our magic, strong; our will, mighty.

As with Golubev, we radiated a colourful glow, however, this time, all four colours danced around us in a display of mystical pirouettes.

Grayson's ear-piercing scream resonated throughout the Newquay streets, as our hold over him intensified. The fire burned brighter, the water flowed fiercer, the wind bellowed harder, and the vines wrapped tighter.

A group of local residents gathered around us, a bidding audience to the supernatural Custodian prophecy, their terrified murmurs nothing but white noise.

This couldn't distract us from defeating this creature.

I briefly recalled the unforgettable times I spent with Grayson; our first date, moving in together, relocating to the Westcountry and him proposing to me, the rest of the team sharing in my despair.

When the time comes, you must do what must be done.

My father's voice broke through my trip down memory lane. This was the moment he was referring to.

When the time comes, you must do what must be done.

When the time comes, you must do what must be done.

The phrase remained on a loop in my head, bestowing us with the strength to end this.

I clasped my saturated palms together, orchestrating the cage of vines to constrict, the evil Grayson letting out a long, drawn-out horrifying screech.

I shut my eyes, and pushed my hands harder into one another, turning white from the sudden draining of blood, causing the prison to crush even tighter.

The sound of Grayson's bones cracking made me instantly nauseous, which I shared with my temporary symbiotic quadruplets.

A final scream erupted before a catastrophic blast discharged from Grayson's core, which rippled through the streets.

The entirety of the street cowered, expectantly awaiting the cloud to disperse.

There it was.

A pile of ash.

He'd gone.

My knees crumbled from beneath me, collapsing to the floor in a heap, as my vision blurred with tears of agony.

"GRAY!" I screamed, as I crawled over to the residue of the demon, scooping up handfuls of the dust and letting it gently fall through the gaps between my fingers.

Yi was the first to comfort me, wrapping her arms around my shoulder and planting a kiss on the top of my head.

A strong hand gingerly caressed my right shoulder, I immediately knew it belonged to Jayce. I rested my cheek on his hand as I succumbed to my grief.

"You had no choice, Marco." Yi whispered softly in my ear.

My anguish was so intense, that I hadn't noticed the sudden onset of onlookers encircling us.

Some appeared to share in my grief, others stood unsympathetically videoing us with their phones – no doubt instantly uploading to various social media platforms.

"What was that?!" A woman yelled.

"The Police are on their way." Another man said.

"They saved us!" Someone else yelled.

"We've got to go!" Brandon fiercely muttered to us, gesturing over to the crowd.

I rubbed the stream of tears away from my swollen eyes and was helped to my feet by Yi and Jayce.

We purposefully walked through a gap in the crowd, the lights from mobile phones stalking us as we started to sprint away, heading onto Towan beach.

Sirens wailed in the distance, which filled my stomach with a prominent sense of doom, adding to the cocktail of emotions that my body was enduring.

Brandon gestured us towards the shore, scanning for any pursuers, motioning his palm towards the sea mid sprint.

A swirling vortex materialised, the four of us diving in without any hesitation.

We materialised in the decorative pond at the reception entrance of Operation Myst, deep within MI6 headquarters. We stepped out of the water onto the glistening marble floor.

"What now?" Jayce asked.

"I have no idea." Yi replied.

"We need to tell Harriet." I said, softly, through a blanket of tears. "Hopefully she can sort all this shit out."

"You okay?" Jayce asked, squeezing my left arm caringly.

"Well obviously not." I harshly replied, with a stale expression.

I felt empty.

I was none the wiser whether the last fifteen years were truly real, or if Grayson had been a Hellion all along.

No, he couldn't have been.

Grayson had a family in Chelmondiston in Suffolk, where he grew up. I'd met his parents, his sisters. Even their pet budgie, Pablo. They were all real.

No. It wasn't all a lie, I'm certain of it.

"Marco, he was just asking." Yi sharply commented at my dismissal of Jayce.

"I know." I uttered, turning to Jayce, and embracing him. I'd briefly overlooked that he'd lost a sister in the same way. "I'm sorry."

"It's okay mate." Jayce pulled me in tight. The soothing warmth from his body somehow made my grief a little easier to bare. "I understand what you're going through."

"I can't believe it. How did I not know? He had me fooled!" The fury simmered within me.

"I should never have said anything to you in Vegas." Brandon timidly hung his head, noticeably placing all the blame on himself.

"It's not your fault, mate." I released my grip from Jayce and sauntered over to my sorrowful friend. "It's these fucking Hellions. They're the ones to blame. I tell you what, I'm not going to rest until I've hunted every single one of these bastards down."

A vibration in my pocket interrupted our conversation, and noticed Harriet was calling me.

"Hello H." I answered, with a very sombre expression.

"Marco. Are you all alright? I've heard about what happened in Newquay."

"Word travels fast I see."

"One of our undercover operatives was in the crowd and advised

me what had happened. I've got my team trying to keep this all quiet." she explained.

"We're at your office." I said. "We didn't really have anywhere to go."

"I'm at home, but I can be there in about forty minutes. Wait for me. In the meantime, speak to my Deputy, Evan, he will see to your needs until I get there." p

"Thanks H. See you soon."

Harriet arrived in less time than she'd anticipated, bursting into the conference room, where Evan set us up with an unlimited amount of tea and coffee.

A plate of pastries also sat on the table of refreshments, which Jayce instantly devoured upon sight.

I couldn't even think about eating anything.

I sat in silence, replaying the previous few minutes before I killed my 'fiancé.' My mind was still in pieces, fragmented from all the lies and deceit that I'd been exposed to over these previous weeks.

I didn't want to continue being a Custodian.

Before I found the amulet on St Mary, my life was the best it'd ever been. There was Grayson, a decent job, and a positive outlook on life.

All that amulet brought me was pain, death and suffering, as well as the knowledge that this entire world was threatened by an evil demonic plot.

No. I wanted that amulet gone. I wanted Harriet to rid me of my pain and suffering.

"Marco." She kindly greeted me, whilst I remained still in my chair, my arms tightly weaved together. I looked away, refusing to meet her gaze.

"I don't want to hear it, Harriet." I barked, desperately holding back a wave of tears. "I don't want to do this anymore. These powers have brought me nothing but misery."

"Marco. I understand how you are feeling, but this is your destiny."

"Says who?!" I bolted up from my chair, almost knocking over a full mug of tea. "You?! I should have walked away from all of this in the beginning. At least Grayson would still be alive."

"Mate. That wasn't Grayson." Jayce pleaded with me, attempting to rest his hand on my shoulder, which I promptly batted away.

"No! Leave me alone!" I yelled, the ground surging as it mirrored my anger. "I didn't know that it wasn't Grayson. If I'd've never found that amulet, I would have been none the wiser, and he would still be here!"

"Marco!" Yi raced up to me, abruptly grabbing hold of my arms, vigorously shaking me. "Now you listen to me. You have been telling me these past few weeks to look at the bigger picture and stop being selfish. I'm going to tell you to do the same. If it weren't for you finding that Amulet, I would never have met the rest of you." Yi's eyes glistened in the light as a well of tears erupted from her ducts. "You three are the best thing that has ever happened to me. You are the only friends I've ever had. I know it's shit that Grayson is gone, but you have to deal with it!"

Yi was right.

Wait, did I actually just say that?

Well, she was.

She *was* right.

I stood, lost in the magnetism of her deep brown eyes, before fervently embracing her.

We didn't speak.

We held each other.

This was the first time I experienced any real emotion from Yi.

I briefly recalled our symbiotic connection during the battle.

They felt every ounce of my soul. They all understood. We were closer to one another.

"I will sort this, Marco." Harriet said, with a surprising air of compassion. "I've already informed the Prime Minister, and she is enacting all her powers to keep all of this from the media. As far as the rest of the world is concerned, Grayson died of natural causes."

I nodded in agreement, too overcome with emotion to speak.

"Now go home. Grieve. Do everything you need to. Leave everything else to me."

"Thank you H." I managed to say.

"Come on Marco. We'll help you with whatever you need." Brandon said. "We'll be here for as long as you need us. We're family now."

I managed to force a smile, Brandon always seeming to have that effect on me.

He was right though, no matter how much I wanted to distance myself from our destiny, we *were* family.

SIXTEEN

I woke up in Grayson's childhood bedroom, which hadn't been renovated since he'd left for university.

I admired the 'Matrix' and 'Die Hard' movie posters adorning the walls, Grayson being much more of a film buff than me – my catalogue being anything with 'Marvel' in the title.

The birds sang outside the window, as I lay in solitude, patting the empty space beside me. This was the first time I'd visited his parents alone.

Twenty minutes passed for me to gather the momentum to prise myself out of bed.

In all honesty, I wanted the duvet covers to swallow me whole and transport me to another realm.

A realm where he remained alive.

I shuffled downstairs into the living room, where Grayson's mother, Wendy, sat at the dining table, her eyes red and puffy.

She was such a kind and caring woman.

I lost my own mother ten years ago from cancer, she perfectly slotted into the maternal role absent from my life, treating me as one of her own children.

His father, Paul was sat stiffly on the sofa, staring blankly at an episode of 'Only Fools and Horses' playing on the television. I could tell he wasn't really watching it.

"Morning Marc." Wendy forced a smile, her pain obviously still apparent. "Did you sleep well?"

"Not really." I replied, planting a kiss on her cheek, and comforting her with an embrace. We both needed each other today. "How are you this morning?"

"Still trying to come to terms with it all, love." She said. "Did you want a cup of tea?" she asked, trying to keep occupied.

"I'd love one, thank you." I shot her a small smile.

"Erica and Rachel will be here in a bit." She informed me, hoisting herself up from her seat and heading into the kitchen.

Erica and Rachel were Grayson's sisters; older and younger, respectively.

Rachel had been estranged for the last three years.

She didn't really appeal to me, as I knew how much she'd hurt Grayson and his family.

For some inept reason, she took an instant dislike to me. During our early years, she told Grayson to leave me for her best friend, as she preferred him better – Grayson obviously refusing and disclosing a few of his opinions of her, which ultimately caused them to fall out.

Over the past four months, she attempted to reach out

to her brother, desperately trying to make amends, but still remained significantly hostile towards me.

It was a shame that they didn't fully put things behind them before he died.

Erica his older sister, he was very close with.

They spoke every other day, planning halfway meets between Cornwall and Suffolk, when their diaries allowed.

That was probably one of the hardest phone calls I'd ever made; telling her he'd died.

I sat at the dining table, looking over at Paul, his expression still vacant, grieving for his son.

An enormous pang of guilt overwhelmed me, as I began to hold myself responsible for Grayson's death. It was difficult to not divulge the truth to his parents.

"What time is Lucie coming over?" Wendy asked me from the kitchen.

Lucie was my sister, who'd flown over from America, leaving behind my brother-in-law Scott and my nephews, Dylan, and Cain.

She'd stayed in a hotel in the nearby town of Ipswich, much to the protest of Wendy, who offered her to stay at the family home.

"In about an hour." I replied to Wendy, who appeared from the kitchen, clutching a tray of three mugs, containing freshly poured tea.

"I wish you'd've told her she could have stayed here." She said, her brow crossed.

"I did." I insisted. "She didn't want to put you and Paul out. You know how stubborn she is."

"Like her brother." Wendy let out a slight chuckle.

"That's true." I smiled back.

She distributed the beverages, and took a set at the table, opposite me. We stared at each other silent, tentatively sipping at our tea.

"I'm dreading today." Wendy muttered, clearing her throat.

"Me too, Wendy." I replied, a crushing sense of dread overpowering me.

"I don't understand it, Marco. How could this have happened? A heart attack at his age?"

Harriet wove her abilities into the coroner's investigation, the death certificate detailing that Grayson died of a heart attack.

"You never know these things." I said, trying to alleviate Wendy's concerns, reaching for her hand from across the table, in solace.

I spent the majority of the next hour, laid on Grayson's bed in tranquillity, changing into a brightly coloured pink shirt and smart, grey trousers at the last moment possible.

Grayson always hinted at a vibrant, joyful funeral – a celebration of his life, as opposed to a more traditional, sombre occasion. I wanted to honour that.

His family were ignorant of the details, especially the casket being absent of any physical body, which added to my ever-expanding guilt.

Their Chelmondiston home was a beautiful country, thatch-roofed cottage, with Tudor beams accentuating the walls and ceilings, slotting in perfectly with the character of the quaint village.

I lumbered back down to the living area, where I laid my bulbous, tired eyes on Lucie, my sister.

Lucie was over six foot, like me, with a slim build and olive skin that we inherited from our father. Her dark, silk hair draped over her shoulders, which contrasted with the bright yellow dress she sported.

"Marco!" she cried out, her tears streaming as our eyes met. Her heels clicked on the stone floor as she teetered to me, squeezing me in a loving hold. "I am so sorry."

"Thank you for coming, it means the world to me and Grayson's parents." I mumbled into her shoulder, drops of my grief trailing down her back.

"Scott and the boys send their love." Lucie said, as she wiped her eyes dry. "They wanted to come, but the boys start school next week."

"I understand." I nodded, forcing a half smile.

"You know how much they love their Guncles." she laughed.

I smiled a bit harder this time, thinking about my two nephews Dylan and Cain. Dylan the oldest at ten years old and Cain being a year younger.

Grayson always treated them as if they were our own, purchasing the newest console games whenever they were released, no matter if it was a special occasion or not.

In true Grayson style, he would always gift it from the both of us, when in reality, he was the thought behind it.

I suspected they favoured him over me, which I couldn't blame them for - he is.. *was* an amazing man.

"The cars picking us up in about ten minutes." I

informed her, trying to keep it all together.

I sauntered into the kitchen, Paul and Wendy sitting at the table, staring into space.

Grayson's sisters arrived, sat on the patio furniture in the bright, scenic, immaculate rear garden, courtesy of Paul's green fingers.

I ventured outside, approaching Grayson's older sister, Erica, first. Rachel was sat on a patio chair, oversized sunglasses mounting her face as she puffed away at a cigarette.

Erica immediately rose to her feet and embraced me.

"Marco." She quivered, as Rachel nodded at me in acknowledgment.

"How are you?" I asked, which I immediately realised was a thoughtless question.

"As well as I can be. It's not every day you bury your younger brother. How are you, should be the bigger question? I mean you're burying your fiancé."

"I'm trying to hold it together for your Mum and Dad. I think they're taking this the hardest."

"Well, they've lost their blue-eyed boy, haven't they?" Rachel interjected, her tone sharp and slightly venomous.

"Rach! Enough!" Erica scolded.

Rachel, a prima-donna and extremely materialistic, never seemed to be able to adapt herself to her surroundings, often using sarcasm as a defence mechanism.

"Sorry." She apologised, taking a long drag of her cigarette, before blowing out a sequence of smoke.

"Thank you for coming Rachel. I know you and Grayson had your differences, but he would have appreciated you being here." I batted away any rage that fizzed to the surface, deciding to extend an olive branch instead.

"He's my brother." She sternly replied, before hurling her cigarette on the floor, stomping it out with her Jimmy Choo before strutting off inside the house.

"Just ignore her Marc," Erica shook her head. "She's grieving, but in her own way. She feels guilty."

"She has a funny way of showing it." I commented, as my eyes stalked her in the kitchen, pouring a glass of red wine and gulping it in one go.

"The car's here." Lucie announced, her voice echoing throughout the cottage.

We all meandered out to the front, three black, saloon vehicles all parked in a row, the polished paintwork like gloss as it reflected the sunlight.

I couldn't bring myself to witness the lead carriage, which contained a pine casket, a display of rainbow shaded flowers spelling out 'GRAYSON.'

We took a scenic route to the crematorium, travelling parallel of the Orwell River along the strand, the view of the titanic bridge giving me a sense of inferiority.

Being one of Grayson's beloved scenes, it was only apt that we took this route for his final send off, albeit him only being present in spirit.

I'd succumbed to the fact that I'd never see him again, starting the process of letting him go, even if it did seem very final.

I glanced out to the picturesque scenes, my chaotic emotions struggling to fight to the surface.

The entourage of cars entered the long driveway of the crematorium; no less than a hundred people greeted us, gathered along the route, which only exasperated my sorrow.

I spotted Yi, Brandon, Jayce and Harriet, all stood within the crowd, wearing a multitude of vibrant shades, causing me to weep into my hands.

The car came to a halt, the usher opening the door, as I hesitantly stepped out, the visitors remaining respectful and keeping their distance from the family.

I noticed Carole perched on the end of the mass of mourners, huddled with a group of my close work friends.

When our gaze met, she hurried towards me, launched her arms around my neck, as I crouched down to her height.

She planted a firm kiss on my cheek, leaving remnants of her bold, pink lipstick.

"Thanks for coming, Carole." I muttered.

"It's the least I could do darlin'."

"I'll speak to you at the wake." I nodded, as I walked over to my fellow Custodians.

Yi was the first to hug me, shortly followed by the boys. Harriet, being a more dignified person, gently took hold of my hands and mournfully bowed her head.

"I really appreciate you all being here." I said, starting to tremble with grief as the service drew nearer. "I couldn't have done this without you all."

I joined the rest of Grayson's family as we lingered outside watching the remainder of the congregation heading inside to take their seat.

As we followed the casket, Lucie took hold of my arm

in comfort, as I struggled keep back the tears.

I didn't want to do this.

Entering the service hall, the piece of music I chose, Christina Perri's version of A Thousand Years, resonated in the acoustics. It was the song we'd planned to walk down the aisle to.

I tried every ounce of my being to hold it together, but as soon as I heard the lyrics, I broke down, Lucie managing to guide me to the front pew where I collapsed in a pile of raw emotion.

My grief echoed throughout the hall, a virus of sniffs and tears rippling across the assembly.

The service, however, was beautiful.

I pulled myself together once the entrance music ceased, intently listening to the words that the celebrant relayed about him, including the comedic time when Grayson's patio chair collapsed at a family barbecue, sending the guests into roaring fits of laughter.

She was a woman in her fifties, with curly grey hair and half rim glasses perched on the end of her nose. She took the time to meet with the family prior to the funeral, asking for memorable moments of Grayson's life.

She'd captured them perfectly.

I authored a poem, which I couldn't face reading out myself, Carole offering to perform it in my place.

"I would now like to read out a poem, written by Grayson's partner, Marco. I think you will all agree with me that no-one has seen love quite like what they had, which is why it is an honour to be able to see Grayson off with these touching words.

CUSTODIANS: THE PROPHECY

When we met, our hearts were young,
As time went on, our love grew strong.
The kindest man, the purest soul,
Like two halves together, you made me whole,
And as your burning light fades away,
In my heart, you will always stay."

There wasn't a dry eye in the room.

The service though short, was extremely colourful and vibrant, closed off by Erica singing one of Grayson's favourite songs in her angelic voice.

The final moment hit me.

As the curtains sluggishly closed around the casket, it symbolised the end.

The end of us.

Once the service concluded, we made our way to a small, charming pub within Chelmondiston, an exquisite buffet, full all of Grayson's favourite foods, welcomed us.

I briefly smiled as I pictured him sitting next to the buffet table, picking at the cucumber sticks and baby tomatoes and dipping them into copious amounts of onion and garlic dip.

I'd spent most of the wake catching up with old friends, family and work colleagues of both mine and Grayson's, their conversation diverting my attention from my mourning.

After some gruelling hours of an emotionally difficult meet and greet, I took a break, venturing outside for some fresh air and to bask in the glorious sunshine that bestowed the day. I perched on the table of a picnic bench, far away from the chaos of the wake, to have a moment of solitude.

Carole appeared, grasping a large glass of her favourite red wine, taking momentary sips as she ambled over to me.

"Mind if I sit next to you babe?" She asked.

I shook my head, gesturing to the empty spot next to me. Carole hoisted herself up as elegantly as she could, draping her red and black floral dress over her legs, all whilst still clutching her wine.

"Thank you for reading my poem out." I half-smiled, focusing on a herd of horses playfully galloping in a farmer's field in the distance.

"Don't be silly!" she scolded me, scrunching her face. "You don't have to thank me!"

"What am I going to do now, Carole?" I asked, vacantly. "He's been my life for the last fifteen years, and now he's gone."

"Well, don't worry about work. I can get Lou to step up for you. Have as much time off as you need."

"Thanks." I said, taking a sip of beer, I rested on my knee.

"Marco." Carole's tone changed. It was the tone she used in meetings when she was about to drop one of her bombshells. "There's something I need to talk to you about."

"It's not bad, is it? I can't manage much more sad news right now."

"No. It's just I haven't been entirely honest with you these past few months."

My neck pulsated as my heart raced with anxiety.

"Go on,"

Carole paused, eyeing the floor.

"I know about everything."

My throat constricted and my breathing laboured.

"I know about you, your friends, the Hellions, Agatha. All of it."

My defences immediately raised, and I vaulted up from my seat, releasing the full glass of beer, which smashed on the patio beneath me.

"You're one of them aren't you!" I yelled. "You can't help yourself can you! Especially today of all days!"

"Marc, wait!" Carole brought her hands up in protest. "I'm not a Hellion!"

"I don't believe you!" I screeched, as the ground beneath shook.

Carole pulled out an intricately decorated, gold stopwatch from underneath her bosom, the chain flaccid around her neck.

It instantly reminded me of Agatha's amulet, as the calligraphic style of the inscriptions were comparable.

She clicked one of the dials with her thumb, a flash of bright, brilliant white light filled our surroundings. As the radiance cleared, I immediately ended up back next to her, with my beer resting on my knee.

"I'm not a Hellion." she explained. "I'm a Time Custodian."

My eyes widened in shock.

"A what?"

"Time Custodian. A magically enhanced human with the power to bend time."

"Was that you that sent us to the future?" I asked, the

absent pieces of the supernatural puzzle starting to neatly fall into place.

"Yes. I only involve myself when I need to. You had to be shown the future to see how dyer the threat was. I sent Yi with you as she needed the most convincing."

"Gruffydd? That was you?" I asked.

"Yes. I erased that moment from time, to help protect you." she explained.

"Why didn't you tell me?"

"I shouldn't even be having this conversation with you, but with everything you've been through I thought you should know. My abilities allow me to see different future possibilities, I never know which one of them comes true."

Carole's persona changed completely. Her broad London accent still dominated, but her serene and profound tone felt alien.

"I sent you and Yi to one of the possible futures. The outcome will depend on these next coming months."

"Can you bring Grayson back?" I desperately asked, already suspicious of the disappointing answer.

"Oh, darlin' I would if I could. There are some things not even I can do."

She held me once more, our tepid cheeks sparking as they met, before leaping off the table, her wine glass still in hand.

"Don't say anything to the others." She whispered, as Yi, Brandon, Jayce, and Harriet strolled over. "It's our secret."

"I won't." I smiled, her revelation dampening my anguish.

"Hey Marc, how are you holding up?" Yi asked, resting

herself on the bench where Carole sat.

"Not bad actually, it was a beautiful service. Grayson would have been pleased with his send off." The corner of my mouth raised.

"He may still be out there, you never know." Jayce commented. "I still have hope that Jo is out there somewhere."

I tried hard not to get myself too caught up in Jayce's theory. I'd decided to let Grayson go. I'd concluded that I'd never see him again.

"It's great you think that Jayce, but I need to let him go. For my own sanity."

I swirled the half empty pint glass of Bira Moretti around in my hand, creating a small vortex within the glass, reminding me of Brandon's portals.

"I know mate," He replied. "I guess we all deal with things differently."

"If you don't mind." Harriet interrupted, "I'd like to speak with Marco alone."

The remainder of the team nodded in unison, rambling through the rear garden of the pub, so they were out of ear shot.

"Everything okay H?" I asked, wondering why I was suddenly so popular.

She pleated her arms firmly to her chest, her colourful blue and silver summer dress tickling the tips of her toes. Her jet-black hair was set free over her shoulders, in tight silky ringlets.

I preferred her hair down like that.

"There's something I need to talk to you about if you

don't mind. I know you've got a lot going on."

"It's fine H, you can speak to me about anything."

Harriet remained fixated on a patch of gravel beneath our feet.

"I hear from Jayce that you know about my past." she started.

"Sorry, I don't understand?" I crossed my brow.

"His mother, Michelle told you that Agatha fostered a girl and a boy; Danielle and Harvey, and that she'd no knowledge of a 'Harriet'."

I'd an idea of where the conversation headed, not having the heart to tell her I already knew what she was about to disclose.

I let her have her moment, it was obviously something she wished to unveil to me herself.

"Oh?" I asked, playing dumb, but remembering she was a telepath, and more than likely knew every intimate thought I was processing.

"I *was* that little boy. I *was* Harvey." she said exhaling deeply, a metaphorical weight being lifted from her shoulders.

"Harriet, it's fine." I shot her a sincere smile. "I mean, thank you for confiding in me and telling me, but honestly you didn't need to. You're Harriet, and that will never change."

"Thank you, Marco." she bashfully smiled back. "I didn't want you to think I was keeping anything from you."

"H. It's none of my business what you do. It only matters to you."

"If only everyone else had the same opinion as you." she

said. "My colleagues all know and have been incredibly supportive. My family on the other hand, hasn't."

"Then they're not worth it H." I commented. "Chose your own family. I've had gay friends who have taken their own lives because they weren't accepted by their own flesh and blood. We're your family - don't ever forget that."

Harriet discreetly rubbed her eye from underneath her glasses, believing I'd not noticed she'd shed a tear.

I placed down my beer glass and took hold of her hand that sat gingerly in her lap, rudely interrupted by a vibration in the breast pocket of my jacket.

I reached in, and pulled out the amulet, forgetting I'd deposited it there, always keeping it close to ensure it didn't cascade into evil hands.

I lay it out in my palm as it exuded a glow of a colourful aura.

"What's happening?" I asked, intrigued.

"I think it's chosen the next overseer." Harriet whispered in awe.

"Me?" I asked in bewilderment.

"I don't think so." She said, mesmerised by the amulet, gently taking it from my palm as the light intensified with her touch.

Harriet sealed her eyes, letting out an invigorating sigh as it seemed to energise her. The glowing immediately ceased, and she met my gaze.

"Well, in my opinion it's chosen the best person for the job." I smiled at her.

Harriet sat, stunned in silence at the honour the amulet bestowed upon her, even though she'd already carried out the Overseer's responsibilities without the official title.

"Come on," I said, gesturing her to follow me. "Grayson's Mum's made his favourite cake; a triple chocolate brownie stack. We'd best get first dibs before it all goes."

I exchanged a glance to my teammates, who remained close by, for them head inside with us. Harriet, Jayce and Brandon strolled briskly ahead, whilst Yi held back to accompany me.

"What did she say?" She queried.

"She was letting me know who she really is." I replied, a small grin of content painting my mouth.

"And who is she?"

"Harriet, of course."

SEVENTEEN

I'd spent the following days after the funeral in Suffolk, spending some much-needed time with Grayson's family.

The farewells this time were extremely emotional, Wendy propelling her arms around my waist, and refusing to release me.

Despite our turbulent relationship, I'd suppressed any hostility towards Rachel, and made a point of burying the hatchet, which I knew Grayson would have approved of.

I received a surprising invitation from Buckingham Palace, to attend a luncheon and private ceremony with the Queen, in honour of our Service to the United Kingdom.

Harriet assured us that this would be a discreet and private ceremony, considering that the details of our achievement could not be disclosed to the wider population.

I couldn't get enthusiastic about it, my grief piercing through my internal shield, rising to the surface, with vengeance.

I caught the ten twenty train from Manningtree station to London Liverpool Street, being waved off by an entourage of Grayson's family.

The others headed back to Cornwall the day after the funeral, giving me some alone time to be with family, time that I really did appreciate, especially as the month was somewhat of a blur.

As I sipped the much-needed coffee that I purchased from the quaint station café, I was immersed into the beautiful scenery of Essex countryside that occupied the majority of my journey.

The rhythmic rocking of the train threw me into a brief siesta, the conductor gently shaking me awake before requesting my ticket, pulling into London Liverpool Street station ten minutes later.

The tube journey was surprisingly stress-free, the morning commuters already snug in their collection of office buildings that rose high above the London skyline.

I greeted my teammates, huddled expectantly outside Green Park tube station, a striking fragrance of opulent perfume and aftershaves hitting me as I admired their elegant attire.

Jayce wore an open collared shirt which accentuated the grooves of his burly torso, finished off with a blazer, chino trousers, and the glossiest of brown boots.

Brandon sported a simpler black tie, his usual mop of hair moulded into a sleek and suave style, whereas Yi dressed in a sophisticated shimmering number, similar to what she donned in Vegas.

"Good to see you buddy." Jayce smiled. "How was your

time with Grayson's family.

"It was nice. I wish I'd've still been with them to be honest, rather than being here." I said, the excitement still absent in my soul.

"I know mate, I understand how you feel, but when will you ever, in your lifetime get to have lunch with the Queen?" Jayce said, his volume descending to a whisper when he mentioned our monarch.

"Will this lunch bring Grayson back? Or your sister for that matter?" I snapped.

"Marc!" Yi exclaimed. "We get how you're feeling, but we didn't want to do this without you. Don't take it out on Jayce."

I held my hands up apologetically, something I was repeating on a regular basis.

"Sorry," I said. "That wasn't fair. I'll try to be a bit more positive, but don't expect miracles."

"We won't buddy." Brandon interjected. "We'll only do this if you want to."

"Well, we're here now."

As we strolled through the park towards the palace, I surrendered to the sound of the wild birds; their tuneful melodies performing high up in the towering plane and lime trees that lined our path.

The impressive view of Buckingham Palace appeared through the sunlit tree line, as we ventured towards it, the depths of my stomach simmering with nerves at the realisation I was about to meet Queen Elizabeth II.

I pictured my father, dressed head to toe in his Police tunic, his breast decorated with an assortment of medals, a proud smile beaming from his face as he observed me shaking hands with the royal.

I yearned he was here. I yearned Grayson was here.

"Harriet!" Brandon chirped as he spotted our mentor lingering at the side entrance to the Palace, dressed in her usual two-piece business suit.

"Hello, Mr Turner." She gently nodded, flashing her identity card to the eagle-eyed, armed officer stood on the gate. "I hope your trip wasn't too strenuous."

"I think we've climatised to Brandon's portals by now." Jayce laughed, but Harriet refused to break into a smile.

The armed guard waved us all through into the main concourse, where we assembled in front of a Royal butler, a tall, slender man with a balding head, his formal attire suited to his surroundings.

He provided us with a brief to the strict etiquette we were required to follow to when meeting the Queen, overwhelming my already frayed anxiety.

We were lead inside, the stunning interior breath taking, as I studied the assembly of Royal portraits decorating the lengthy, gold accented corridors.

The stiff butler permanently pointed his nose to the sky, and escorted us to an elaborate dining area, the pristine bone china and polished cutlery laid perfectly symmetrical upon an elongated cherry wood table.

"Please wait here, where Her Majesty will receive you and invite you to sit with her for luncheon." He instructed; his lips tightly pursed as if he'd sucked on a lemon.

He parked himself in the corner, stood to attention, staring blankly into space, as if awaiting further instructions from his commander.

Another man entered, seeming far less uptight than the stiff-lipped butler. He was in his early sixties, with white hair, and rounded glasses which flattered his charming, navy blue suit and striped tie.

"Good afternoon, Martin Edwards, Private Secretary to the Queen." He extended his hand out to each one of us, applying a firm shake. "Her Majesty will be shortly joining us, but I would like to confirm some details so I can introduce you all."

We provided our names and occupations, being cautious not to expose our supernatural persona - the genuine reason the sovereign asked to meet with us.

Martin hurried back out into the corridor, and we all exchanged terrified glances.

Then, she entered.

Her Majesty, Queen Elizabeth II.

She dressed in a light purple, plain dress, accessorised with a set of pearls and a silver broach which glistened as it hit the light from the extravagant, hanging fixtures.

Despite her small, delicate stature, her presence was colossal, but her warm smile put everyone at ease.

I suppressed a chuckle as group of tan coloured corgis stalked her feet, almost toppling her over as she ambled towards Harriet, who was first in our line-up.

The Queen extended her hand, as Martin introduced her.

"Hello." The Queen smiled, as Harriet performed her best curtsey.

The monarch made her way down the line, my heart

racing as she loomed on me, the final guest in the parade.

"This is Detective Inspector Marco Ramirez of Cornwall Police your Majesty." Martin introduced me, the Queen's hand warm and cosy as I accepted it.

"Hello, Inspector." She smiled. "You must have a busy job."

"Yes.... Er... Ma'am, you..... could say.. that." I chuckled, my voice quivering as I spoke.

"Don't worry, Inspector, I won't bite." She laughed, easing the noticeable tension I held. "Despite what they may tell you."

The Head of State turned her attention to our collective group, welcoming us to the palace and offering for us to join her at the dining table, our names embossed on ornately detailed, ivory place cards.

We parked at our designated seats; my puzzled expression apparent as I analysed the assorted cutlery.

"Start from the outside and work your way in." Yi whispered, leaning in as she rescued me from my torment. "I learnt that from *Titanic*."

I playfully rolled my eyes at her, replaying the famous scene from the James Cameron blockbuster.

The Queen dismissed Martin and her prune mouthed butler, granting us a private audience.

"Now prying ears are out of the way." She began, "I invited you all here today to thank you. The Prime Minister has informed me of your heroics. The country owes you a great debt. I understand there were some tragic sacrifices, which I can only extend my condolences."

"Thank you Ma'am." I uttered. "We really appreciate it."

"You're quite welcome. Now I think it's time to eat, don't you think? I am rather famished."

She tinkled a bell positioned next to her place setting, and a river of servants, dressed in vibrant red and gold jackets, burst through the doors and presented our lunch.

We were treated to a wonderful three course meal of onion and stilton soup, braised beef and salted caramel cheesecake.

The only thing that was missing for me, was Grayson.

I kept sombre throughout the dinner conversation, noticed by everyone, including the Queen.

"Is everything okay Inspector?" She quizzed, tucking into the final mouth full of her dessert. "You seem very distant."

"I'm fine, thank you Ma'am." I forced a smile her way.

She looked at me curiously, her expression clear that I hadn't convinced her.

"Marco," Yi nudged me. "I'm sure she wouldn't mind you telling her."

"Telling me what Ms. Chang?"

"Please don't worry Ma'am. I don't want to bring a downer on the afternoon." I said, lightly patting around my mouth with the silk napkin we were all individually issued.

"I insist, Mr Ramirez." The monarch said.

"Well, we only had my partner's funeral three days ago, so I apologise if I've not been very talkative." I announced.

The Queen remained silent for a brief minute, resting her cutlery down and taking a large gulp of her gin and tonic, from a crystal beaker.

"I was going to save this for after lunch, however, I

believe this is perfect timing." She smiled.

We all paused our dessert, as she collected her polished, black handbag laid beside her feet, the 'snap' resonating throughout the dining room as she unclasped the gold lock mounted on the rim.

She deposited her hand inside, rummaging through and withdrawing her famous oversized reading glasses, and a neatly folded piece of paper.

As she rose to her feet, we followed suit, ensuring we obliged by the instructions set by her butler.

She perched her glasses on the end of her nose, her dark eyes magnified as she perused the room, unfolding the piece of paper containing her beautiful calligraphic handwriting.

Clearing her throat, she poised herself upright, tightening her posture and gazed down at the letter and took in a long breath.

"When incidents such as these happen," She began, "We tend to focus on the heroes, and those that were valiant in battle. However, we sometimes glance over those we have lost. In my opinion these people are as important and should be remembered in the same way."

My eyes pooled with tears as the Queen continued her heart-felt speech, full of dignity and refinement.

"Therefore, as Sovereign, I provide honours for Josephine Anna Stevens, and Grayson John Blackford for their sacrifice towards the good of this country. May their memories forever live on, in the heart of the nation."

"Thank you, your Majesty." I sniffed. "That was very thoughtful."

"You are very welcome. The Prime Minister did brief me

on the loss of your loved ones to this god-awful demonic plague. It is the least I could do to honour their memories. I'm glad this was done privately though, as having me to oneself is a rare occasion." She radiated her smile, ridding me of some of the returning grief.

After dinner drinks ensued, insisted on by the nonagenarian, but I barely touched any of my beer, not trusting my untethered inhibitions.

We were ushered into a ceremony room, adjacent to the dining hall, kitted out especially for us, with a small, intimate audience, containing only members of Harriet's team.

No one else from Buckingham Palace sat in on the ceremony, as the Queen was the only member of the household that knew of our true nature.

She devised another speech, similar to the one she'd delivered at lunch, with more of an emphasis on us, rather than those that had fallen.

Her Majesty called us up, one by one, officially presenting us with the 'British Medal of Honour,' a gold crest with red, blue, and white lapel, which she pinned effortlessly to the left side of our chests.

Harriet took to the front of the hall, her anxiety fully apparent as she visibly trembled.

"Good evening everyone. Your Majesty." She said, glancing down at a selection of cue cards she rigidly clutched. "I will keep this very brief, as most of you know, I am not one for lengthy conversation." The intimate crowed rumbled a titter. "I wanted to say, how immensely proud I am of these four incredible humans. A month ago, they were ordinary, unsuspecting citizens, shielded off from the world of the supernatural. Overnight, they have had to contemplate a notable change in their lives and became a team of extraordinary people. They have risked their lives on numerous occasions and prevented a significant global threat. Please join me in showing our appreciation for the Custodians."

The room erupted in a sea of applause, resulting in a standing ovation, the four of us visibly touched by Harriet's unexpected sermon.

The ceremony concluded, and it was time for us to bid our farewells to our Royal host, who appeared significantly more earnest and heartfelt than I expected, secretly confessing her detest over the official protocols, referring to them as 'old-fashioned.'

Even with her lack of visible emotion, she genuinely seemed to care, her wisdom from seventy years on the throne prominently apparent.

Harriet also departed, bestowing us all with an uncharacteristic embrace, before proceeding back towards MI6.

We unanimously elected to journey back home, via public transport, Brandon being too fatigued and slightly intoxicated to portal us back.

"We are relying on that a little bit too much." I commented. "Maybe we should use that in extreme circumstances from now on."

The team nodded in agreement.

Jayce perched himself next to me on the train, his bulging

thighs barely fitting in the seat. If I hadn't been so emotionally exhausted, I would have more than likely mentioned it to him in a playful anecdote.

Yi and Brandon made themselves comfortable directly opposite us, spreading a pack of cards and a library of books on the table lodged in the centre.

"What are your plans tomorrow?" Jayce asked, the carriage agitating as we sped along the tracks.

"I need to bite the bullet and start sorting out the apartment. I've not been in there since the whole incident." I muttered.

"I can come with you?" Jayce suggested.

"I couldn't expect you to do that."

"We'll all come with you." Yi said, glancing up from a game of patience she'd immersed herself in. "We can't expect you to do this on your own, Marco."

"Yi's right mate. We'll come with you buddy." Brandon chimed in.

The willing volunteers caused a flock of raw emotions to fluctuate within me, unsure of which to select and deal with first.

"A month ago, I didn't even know your names. Now I couldn't imagine my life without any of you."

I couldn't prevent the involuntary tear from racing down my cheek.

Jayce squeezed my hand, comforting me.

"I know." Yi said. "To think I hated you all when I first met you." She playfully laughed.

"I won't even tell you what I thought of you." I forced a chuckle through another stray drop. "Thank you, guys. I really appreciate it."

Two train changes and four hours later, we eventually arrived in Newquay.

EIGHTEEN

I stood, staring at the front door of our…. My, apartment.

I was numb.

I didn't want to go in.

My heart ached, longing to be back in Grayson's arms once again. I still held a glimmer of hope that he would re-appear, but as time passed by, that became a distant reality.

The others gathered with me for moral support, which I initially protested against, overwhelmingly outvoted by three to one.

"You don't have to do this." Jayce reminded me, resting his palm on my shoulder.

"I know." I said, my eyes swollen and bloodshot from my constant flow of sorrowful crying. "But I need to."

I was so appreciative of their company.

My sister needed to travel back to New York to organise my nephews for their new school semester. She was comforted in the fact that I'd a group of friends to accompany me.

Lucie was younger, but her robust streak of confidence portrayed the illusion that she was the older sibling, a fiery trait she inherited from our mother.

I slid my apartment key into the lock and slowly turned it, the click of the mechanism piercing through me.

I gingerly opened the door into my vacant home.

Even from the communal stairwell, it seemed empty.

As I walked through into the hallway, I picked up a sepia photograph of us both from the side table, entwined in each other's arms, succumbed to the effects of the free bar at my friend Annie's fortieth.

I couldn't help but smile back, focusing on Grayson's cheesy grin.

I no longer held back my tears, embracing the full effect of my grief, the river of sorrow streaming down my cheeks and dripping onto the glass frame.

"Come on Marc," Yi said softly, removing the picture out of my hand and tenderly placing it back on the sideboard. "I'll make you a cup of coffee."

Yi came the furthest out of us all, her glacial personality slowly defrosting over the course of the last month. She'd still slight remnants of her irritable character, but nothing as severe as our first encounter on St Mary's Island.

The three Custodians escorted me into the living area, Grayson's case papers still covering the kitchen table.

Brandon joined me on the sofa, whilst Jayce and Yi beavered away in the kitchen.

"I'm sorry," Brandon said, lowing his head. "This is all my fault."

He cried into his hands.

"How exactly is this your fault?" I asked.

"If I hadn't have told you how I felt about him, you wouldn't have found out he was a Hellion. He wouldn't have died."

Oh Brandon.

"Then he would have killed us. Then they would have won." I said, trying to impart him with a sense of logic.

I draped my arm around him, pulling him in closer where he rested his mop of hair on my shoulder. "You should be the one comforting me." I chuckled slightly.

I didn't blame him at all.

I blamed the evil demonic creatures that infiltrated my life and posed as my beloved fiancé, tarnishing our cherished memories.

Yi waltzed from the kitchen and sited a mug of steaming coffee down in front of me on the coffee table. She and Jayce positioned themselves on the adjacent sofa.

"This view is beautiful." She commented, staring intently out of the windows, admiring Fistral Beach in all its picturesque glory.

"I know." I muttered, taking a sip of my drink, my asbestos mouth shielding me from the burn. "This was always Grayson's favourite place to come on holiday, which is why we chose here to live."

"Do you think you'll stay here?" She asked.

"I don't know. Maybe."

"Jesus Yi! give him a chance!" Jayce scolded her. "He's barely even got his foot through the door and you're already asking him that?"

"I was just wondering!" she remonstrated in return.

I didn't take offence by her question - I would have asked the same if the tables were turned.

Jayce was being extremely overly protective of me, which seemed to have amplified since Grayson's death.

"It's fine!" I held my hand up. "Please don't argue." I was like a parent trying to diffuse squabbling children.

They both apologised in unison.

"Thanks." I realigned the conversation. "I don't think I could have done this without you."

We spent the next coming hours sitting and chatting, watching television and drinking copious amounts of tea and coffee, helping me to take my mind of Grayson.

I'd offered for the three of them to stay over, preferring not to spend my first night back in the apartment in solitude.

When it got to about seven o'clock, we ordered Pizza.

I shared a meat feast with Jayce, whereas Brandon, a vegetarian, devoured his own colourful miniature pizza with spinach and tomato.

Yi had a low-calorie option, giving the excuse that she needed to maintain her svelte figure.

"Are you sure you don't want some of this Yi?" Jayce asked.

"Why?" Yi queried. "Have you poisoned it?"

They quibbled again, causing me to berate them like a parent.

"You two are worse than me and Lucie!" I remarked.

"I was only joking!" Yi protested, her palms overturned.

After pizza and some restitution of friendships, I

surrendered a collection of white wine I'd cooling in the fridge, dispensing out the glasses between my friends.

As the booze flowed, my pain was temporarily suppressed, allowing me to enjoy the evening and suggest a game of charades.

Yi and Jayce surprisingly grumbled at the proposal, but Brandon, as expected, bounced in excitement.

I chose Jayce as my teammate.

Brandon, being from Australia, wasn't up to speed with the most current British popular culture, frustrating an extremely competitive Yi.

I wasn't fussed about winning, I bathed in the enjoyment of watching my newfound family enjoying much needed down time from our supernatural duties.

Jayce selected a miniature strip of scrap paper I found amongst Grayson's files, each of us writing down our choice of genre before the game commenced.

He hastily examined it, letting out a huge sigh, signalling the difficulty he had.

Over the next five minutes, I'd managed to establish that it was a Film and TV Series with two words, but his gestures and actions couldn't bring me any closer to solving it.

For the first word he was pointing up to the sky, I shouted out an array of answers; 'Sky,' 'Space', 'Blue', 'Clouds', 'Air', but none of them were correct.

Frustrated, he held out his palm and magically materialised tiny twinkling balls of fire, all interweaving in a series of stellar constellations.

It was a clever and exceptional display.

"Star!" I shouted, excitable.

Jayce gestured enthusiastically towards me, signalling my success.

The second word was easy, as he meandered around the room clutching an imaginary backpack.

"Trek!" I yelled, even louder than before, jumping up from my seat.

He'd chosen my favourite television program – although *Voyager* was my favoured incarnation, having a childhood fascination of the fictional Captain Kathryn Janeway.

I briefly recalled me and my sister rushing around our childhood garden, re-enacting scenes of the show; me playing the famed principal character, and Lucie cast as the Borg-Human hybrid Seven of Nine.

Jayce clapped his hands in relief that I'd finally managed to solve the riddle.

"I give up." Yi threw her hands up in defeat. "You two win."

I shot up and wrapped Jayce a celebratory hug, which felt different.

He'd squeezed me a little harder than usual, a spark forming between us. It was rhetorical, rather than physical.

I was confused.

It'd been barely a week since Grayson died.

I shouldn't be having these thoughts.

I pulled away.

"I think it's time for bed." I said, looking down at my watch – half one in the morning.

I'd attempted to co-ordinate sleeping arrangements.

Yi immediately set up camp in the spare room, as Brandon made himself comfortable on the pull-out sofa bed.

Jayce peculiarly offered to stay in my bed with me. I was slightly reluctant, agreeing after much contemplation. He was straight, and I was an emotional grieving wreck, so nothing would happen.

I was secretly relieved he'd offered, as I didn't want to be alone.

I tended to Yi and Brandon's needs before retiring to bed with Jayce.

He stripped down to his extremely figure-hugging briefs, which didn't leave much for the imagination.

This was the first time I'd seen him with hardly any clothes on; his thighs were bigger than his head, and his chest and abdominal muscles weren't chiselled, but toned, with a slight dusting of body hair.

I tried to refrain from staring at him, swiftly tucking into my side of the bed, my Marvel themed pyjama's cosy on my skin.

Jayce stood still at Grayson's side, hesitating.

"Are you sure this is okay? I can sleep on the other sofa?" he said.

"No, It's fine. To be honest, I'd appreciate the company."

Jayce leaped into Grayson's side of the bed, the warmth of his body distributing under the covers, keeping a friendly distance.

I lay flat on my back, looking up at the ceiling, before plunging the room into darkness.

"How are you feeling Marc?" Jayce whispered.

"There is so much going on in my head at the minute, I

don't know how to answer that."

"I know. I felt the same way about Jo." He sighed. "Look. If you ever needed to talk to anyone about all of this, you know where I am."

"You've all done enough already." I said, bravely turning over and facing him, barely making out his handsome features in the pitch black. "Just all of you being here is helping me."

"I know Marc. But you're special to me."

What?

I'm special to him?

"I am?"

"Yeah."

"In what way?"

"You just are."

Jayce slowly reached out to me and softly grabbed my hand, the magnetism igniting a jolt of electric that ran through me.

Something didn't feel right.

What would Grayson say?

Then it hit me again. Grayson wasn't here.

I wasn't sure if it was my need for familiar comfort, or the three glasses of wine circulating through my veins, but I squeezed his hand in return.

His strong leg brushed against mine, as we closed our lips together, interlocking in a kiss.

It was passionate, lasting for what seemed like minutes, but in reality was mere seconds.

I sharply pulled away.

"What?" Jayce asked, an ounce of concern apparent in

his tone.

"But…. I…. You're…. You're straight?" I stuttered.

"You of all people should know not to stereotype someone." He rightfully reminded me. "Besides, I never told you I was straight."

"Oh… right." I mumbled.

"I want you to feel you're not alone." He said, brushing a hand gingerly over my forehead. "I don't want to take advantage of you though. We can stop if you like."

"No. I'm fine. You're not taking advantage of me." I assured him. I wanted this as much as he did – even if the guilt overwhelmed me.

We entangled ourselves together and kissed again, his muscular body rubbing against mine.

It turned into raw, instinctual passion.

We went as far as it could go.

Jayce fell into a deep sleep in my arms, which felt strange, yet familiar. The pangs of guilt continued, but I heard Grayson's voice, telling me to move on.

Although, this did feel too soon.

I eventually drifted off, as Jayce's rhythmic heavy breathing functioned as a sleep-aid.

My dream that night was strange.

I was a visitor in a dark cavern, a distinct smell of sulphur overpowering my nostrils. I was sweating profusely at the intense heat that surrounded me. Distant groans of tortured people emanated throughout the cavern.

I followed the lurid screams, my aim to come to the aid of those terrified people in need. A familiar growling sound erupted from behind me, causing confusion on which way to turn.

Do I head towards the growling or to the screaming?

I chose the screaming.

The heat intensified as I ventured deeper, a stinging soreness erupting over my entire body of skin. I struggled through the pain, the determination of saving innocents rescinding the need for self-care.

The growling stalked me as I stepped closer to the innocents, reaching the end of the cave.

I observed a fiery pit, similar to the one I encountered in the depths of the Venetian Hotel. The shrieking derived from an assembly of humans, hung around the walls on chains, their lifeforce projected into the ember.

Then I saw him.

Grayson.

He was one of the innocents. He moaned in pain as his energy sapped.

"Grayson!" I yelled, my voice echoing through the cavern, attracting the monstrous roaring, like a hunter to prey.

I witnessed a Hellion emerge from the route I took, bearing their spiked teeth, rushing towards me.

I thrust out my palm to activate my power, but it was fruitless.

I attempted to escape, hitting a dead end, with nowhere else to go.

I was trapped.

The Hellion gained on me and thrust out it's spear like talon, piercing my chest.

I awoke with a start, a sigh of relief expelling from my lungs when I realised it was a dream.

I looked down at Jayce, his arm still wrapped firmly around me, fast asleep.

"Marco."

A ghostly song reverberated throughout the room.

"Hello?" I whispered, conscious of not stirring Jayce.

"Marco."

There it was again.

Although dismembered, there was a familiarity to it.

"Marco. Help me!"

The voice increased in volume but still performed as a whisper in the wind.

My heart pumped heavily in my chest as I finally recognised it.

It was *Grayson.*

DAN ALEXANDER

To be continued in….

CUSTODIANS:
THE DARK REALM

COMING
AUTUMN 2023

DAN ALEXANDER

ABOUT THE AUTHOR

Dan is a newly self-published author who has always had a
passion for storytelling from an early age.
Born in Peterborough, Dan now lives in the beautiful
Suffolk countryside, where he enjoys venturing out in
nature on lengthy rural walks.
A huge fan of Marvel, Dan is an avid lover of fantasy and
the supernatural, which inspires his writing themes.
He would like to thank all his readers for supporting him
on his writing journey.

Ingram Content Group UK Ltd.
Milton Keynes UK
UKHW020655240723
425668UK00013B/486

9 781399 942270